An ATLAS, <(o)> ATLANTIS .

A Novel
By Kai Lelion

A Sun In Night Book
Independently Published
Copyright © 2025 by Kai Lelion
Cover design copyright © 2025 by Kai Lelion
All rights reserved.

ISBN: 9798242094000

First printing Edition 2025

Kailelion.com

"By the mere fact that you are here, we have succeeded."
-Mol

Preface

Samuel Clemens, under a fictitious name denoting a depth of two fathoms, has been purported to have said, "Never let the truth get in the way of a good story." Where Clemens demonstrated himself as a trustworthy narrator, I hold no such expectation of myself. While Clemens' concern was not to let the truth stand in the way of a good story, I might offer that there is also value in never letting the truth get in the way of a true story. For, as Clemens also noted in his exploration of a mysterious stranger, "Nothing exists save empty space—and you! And you are but a thought." So too, might this true story of Boy be nothing more than the thoughts you have about him.

1

On his eighteenth birthday, Boy was anxious. Despite how easy much of the day had been, he couldn't help fearing an interruption to his peace. No one so far had centered Boy as something in need of celebration, nor even mentioned his eighteen solar circumambulations, yet the relief Boy felt from this was tenuous at best. Maybe it was because graduation was only a few weeks away, but Boy doubted it. If there had been at least a little acknowledgment of his transition to legal adulthood, he might believe it, but the complete lack left him suspicious of intent. He longed for his relative anonymity to be true. He'd never liked birthdays and the obligations they brought. He disdained inauthenticity. He preferred people celebrate whenever they felt inspired, not out of a pressure to do so because of something as arbitrary as completing a lap around the sun.

Boy looked up at the golden hue beaming from the tops of the skyscrapers surrounding him, a reminder of the earth's rotation, of the night to come. He walked home through Lower Manhattan after band practice. He'd expected Will to say something about his birthday at least. Suspicious.

It wasn't dark yet, but it was no longer day. He left Mulberry to cross Columbus Park. Only a few people straggled around the benches outside the playground. Even though New York had become safer than when he was younger, his anxiety grew, remembering eight years earlier, and the man that had followed him from this very park into the alley he was about to enter, ironically between the New York Superior and the US District Court buildings.

Crossing Worth St. into the alley he could picture the strange man's face, stubble, lines of rage, dark hair surprisingly well kempt. The man grabbed his arm, jamming a gun into his side and demanding his watch and wallet. Boy was ten at the time, his wallet was more for show than anything, but his watch was a Rolex, which was probably why he'd been targeted. He hadn't worn a watch since. Luckily, the man hadn't noticed the necklace Boy wore. Boy could still hear the patter echo of footsteps from his run home, face wet from fear.

He'd always felt followed, even before his mugging. He wondered if this was from growing up in Manhattan. Exiting the alley, he saw his building looming in front of him. He breathed easier. He was glad to see home, One Center Street.

The monolithic building embarrassed him, a complexity he had often struggled with. He was glad for the safety of home, yet didn't want anyone to know that he and his mom lived on the top floor, slightly sunken into the building when viewed from the street, the windows framed in ornate weathered brass. It was a stately building, hard to place in time. It could have been built hundreds of years ago, or a decade, and Boy realized that he didn't know either way. The lower level was ringed with strange shields. One crest portrayed a beaver-like creature, another a windmill propeller, and his favorite a depiction of a smiling sun, shining over a distant landscape. The building even had its own Metro entrance, scaled with white, rectangular tiles. There was something reptilian about the walls and ceiling. Everything about it was embarrassingly ostentatious.

The main entry was on the east side of the building, facing a small square. A receptionist greeted him as he entered.

"Hey Boy," said the bolder of the two excessively done-up women sitting behind the welcoming desk. His mother required everyone who worked for her to be similarly 'fashionable'. He nodded politely to the woman. As the elevator doors closed behind him, he thought he heard one start to say "Happy birthday", and the other shush her. He hoped this was just his paranoid mind, and not an actual conspiracy. Music played in his headphones: I'm walking on sunshine, woe, oh, oh…

The elevator stopped at the bottom of the two stories he and his mother occupied. The elevator opened onto the first level, the business office of his mother's empire. There were beautiful women and men rushing around, engaged in office work. Not unlike the women at reception, all these workers were cartoonishly attractive (by dominant paradigm perspectives on beauty).

Almost everyone noticed his arrival. This was standard, but especially pronounced today. He noticed himself tense, as if unconsciously bracing for an attack. He walked down the hall, nodding at the few bold enough to say 'hi'. He was polite but disinterested, all of this rote. He ignored the chatter. He didn't care if it was his birthday, and he didn't want to think of what it might mean to this lecherous crowd that he was now eighteen.

As he arrived at his room, his phone buzzed in his pocket, too coincidental. He looked down to see who had written as he opened the door. Before he read the text, he was interrupted by a cacophony of voices all hollering "Surprise!" or "Happy birthday!" It was a swarm of gorgeous, scantly clad beauties, all smiling, cheering at him, and beckoning him to join them in his bed. He pulled his headphones down and around his neck.

"Thanks everyone," he said, offering a half-hearted smile before looking back down to his phone. "I just got this text I gotta respond to, so if you don't mind..." There were hems and haws. Boy never looked up from his phone but merely said, "Out."

"Come on, Boy, have some fun. It's your birthday," one complained. He was unfazed. Rote.

Boy was as disinterested as he had been by the hoard outside. Still without looking up from his phone, he offered in a firm but gentle tone, "Out everyone. Back to work."

Murmurs of disappointment, hands brushing his chest or rustling his hair as they passed him and left his room.

Closing the door, he pressed the call button, putting the phone on speaker. A phone rang in his room. He turned in confusion. Sophie, his best friend, was sitting on his otherwise vacant bed.

"I'm already here, dipshit," Sophie said as she answered her phone. Her black, thick-rimmed glasses slightly distorted the shape of her face, making her eyes appear awkwardly large. Her hair, half blonde, half pink, a shoulder-length mess, parted down the middle, was partially over her eyes.

As he looked at her, she snapped a photo with the Leica she always had on a strap around her neck.

"Stop it, Soph. Jesus, you scared the shit out of me." He wanted to be annoyed, but was glad to see her, a beacon of authenticity amongst the façade of his mother's world.

"Oh, whatever." She snapped another picture. "Happy birthday, asshole."

"Thanks, Soph. I'm glad you're here." He walked over to her, gave her a hug and sat down next to her on the bed.

"How was practice?" she asked, reviewing the pictures. "About to hit the big time?" She grinned, zooming in and showing him an awkward part of his upset and distorted face in the photo.

"Obviously," he replied, looking around his room. Clothes cluttered the floor. Magazines spread across his desk, intermingled with schoolbooks, partially completed assignments, and his laptop. His blankets were crumpled in a pile at the end of his bed. He was messy, an eighteen-year-old. He had never needed to care about being tidy. Every day, one of his mom's 'many' would organize his life for him. His room never looked this bad.

"Can you believe all those girls?" Sophie asked.

He figured his mom would have at least had someone clean up a bit before he got home, and before sending in the ladies. "Why didn't they pick this place up?" He wondered aloud.

Sophie laughed, punching his arm. "You are such an over-privileged little twerp. A dozen drop-dead, mostly naked models waiting for you in your room when you get home, dying to 'be the first to bed the prince', and all you say is, 'I can't believe my mommy didn't clean up after me,'" she mocked in a whiny high-pitched voice.

She took another picture of him before he started to defend himself. Boy's mom burst into the room. Despite being intimidating, she was elegant. Her long black hair didn't move as she entered. The extreme angles of her face were complimented by her thin glasses, which she leered over. She didn't look happy or angry, perhaps stern, darkly neutral.

"Why'd you send the models out? You didn't like any of them?" she asked.

Boy watched the oval of blood-red lipstick that was her mouth move.

"Hello to you too, mom," he replied, ignoring her question, looking back down at his phone. He was glad to have an excuse to look away.

"Hi," squeaked Sophie, barely audible.

"Hello, Sophia, darling," she said, keeping her gaze on her son. "Well, I tried. I had no idea what to get you." She was cold. He had never seen her exhibit anything resembling emotion, even when he was very little, and she would sing him to sleep: You are my sunshine, my only sunshine... The same cold, stern demeanor was unflinching even when he had come home crying, after being mugged. He remembered her asking him who had hurt him, how nonchalantly she had thrown down the paper the following week with a picture of his assailant dead.

"How 'bout my own apartment in Soho," he muttered, still caught in memory. He pictured his mom asking him, 'Was that the man?' And when he confirmed with a nod, 'You won't have to worry about him ever again.'

"You can leave whenever you'd like," she said, pulling him back into the present. "But I'm not ready to see you go, so I won't make it easy for you. And, I'm terribly sorry, but I won't be able to take you to dinner tonight. I'm too busy. I know you understand. Tell me where you'd like to go and I'll put you and Sophia on the list..." she turned her gaze to Sophie momentarily, "...on me, of course, dear." She turned and left the room.

"Thanks, mom..." he said, his eyes still on the blank screen of his phone.

"Your mom hates me," Sophie said. "But, you heard what she said, where should we go for dinner?"

"I think we should just order some sushi and have it delivered. I don't really feel like going out."

"As long as you get some sake, sounds good to me." She was being playful, hoping to pull him out of his mood, but she knew the best thing to do was to let him work through it on his own.

"Sure. I wish Masa delivered." He pulled up Kuruma Zushi in his contact list. "Glad you're here, Soph," he said as the phone rang.

"Me too. Happy eighteenth, dipshit."

2

To his knowledge, Boy had never met his father. He had only broached the topic once with his mother. Her reaction was so sharp he never brought it up again. You need not concern yourself with that matter, she had said, looking at him with so fixed a gaze as to render him frozen.

Accordingly, his mother and her minions had raised Boy. Not an average upbringing. His mother was no run-of-the-mill single mom. Behind her back, people called her empress. Behind her back people cowered in awe. Behind her back (and to her face) people were inspired by fear, yet longed to be near her. This was much the same for Boy. Though, for Boy, there was also sadness, longing, and a solitude, a feeling of being a side-project. His mother could have been in the Fortune 500 lineup, shaking hands with big names you'd recognize, and many unfamiliar, but equally significant people. She was the kind of wealthy that's hard to imagine. Yet she never appeared in a headline, never flaunted her status or wealth, never allowed a write-up in any print, never exposed Boy to the pressures of infamy.

Her industry was beauty. She was perhaps the primary shaper of what 'sexy' meant for the mainstream. Her most forward-facing edge of her empire was the modeling industry. Yet, she'd always been the type of person who runs the show, points the beam, but never stands in the limelight. Boy's mother was someone you think you've heard of, but you can't quite picture. A 'puppet master'.

Despite her severity and constant orientation towards work and away from him, Boy loved his mother. He had vague memories of her sitting next to him in bed at night when he was young, stories of space travel and aliens, lulled into dreams...you are my sunshine...always cold, and still somehow kind. He grew to find comfort in her cool directness, solace in her piercing eyes, the only part of her he ever felt he could fully trust. He remembered her placing the amulet he still wore now around his neck, a gesture of a love he knew she had despite her lack of warmth and affection. When he needed a hug he'd grip the amulet, a curved serpent, half a moon protruding from its mouth and tail, completing a circle. The moon only touched the snake on the tail side, leaving a small gap near the reptile's open mouth, leaving the space inside the half circle of the snake's body empty. The amulet was a black metal Boy had never seen elsewhere.

Being saturated in his mother's world, Boy had always been surrounded by 'exceptionally attractive people'. He figured his mom took lovers, but no one ever lasted long enough to start a paternal relationship with him. He'd never trusted anyone's romantic advances; wary others' desires for him were really veiled striving towards his mother. He also suspected that she would ask her favorite models to try to sleep with him. The idea of a pity-fuck organized by his mother he found repulsive. Not unlike his eighteenth birthday, Boy always turned sexual offers down.

Sophie was Boy's only female friend. They went to the same private school. Sophie was there on a full ride. Her family, whom Boy had never actually met, was of a distinctly different echelon. She'd share tales of being raised poor with him. He often attributed this lack of privilege as key to making her such an amazing person. Her honesty endeared him to her instantly. Where so many were falsely kind, the first thing she'd said to him was, get over yourself. He couldn't even remember what it had been in regard to, but he loved that she didn't put him on a pedestal. They'd been nearly inseparable since.

Despite Boy bitterness towards the world, he was always polite. It wasn't that he disliked people, he just didn't trust anyone, a result of the mendacity he had grown up surrounded by. He learned early, and quickly: most of the time, people were nice because they were hoping to get something. Sophie was his exception, her persistent rebukes relieving.

He'd always struggled with privilege. When people asked what he'd do with all the opportunity life had handed him, he'd avoid responding. He knew it was privilege that made him hate his privilege; the very thing that oppressed him was the thing everyone else coveted. He didn't really care what he did, so long as he did it on his own merit. He hated the idea of succeeding merely because his mother had paid someone off, or pulled some strings, the way she had his whole life. He yearned to live outside the nepotism he felt trapped within. He was almost desperate to prove himself to himself, fuck the world.

    He secretly started a band. He even gave one of his friends the money to rent a practice space and buy sound equipment and instruments, so that it wouldn't be under his name. They'd been playing since they were freshmen. His plan was to release the first album without his mother's knowledge. 'Fit To Burst' was 90s retro-pop-rock meets Euro-future-disco. His goal was to see how far he could take it on his own. He wouldn't have guessed how successful FTB was about to become.

3

Boy's band was a five-piece, modeled after Doug Martsch's, consisting of himself (songwriter, singer, and front man); two guitarists, Clark and Stanley; a bassist, Nico; a drummer, Kevin; and a keyboardist, Walter James (whom everyone called WJ, and who arguably knew very little about piano). Clark's dad was the editor of an international magazine, specializing in paparazzi and propaganda. Stanley's parents were national best-selling self-help book writers. Nico's mom was a board member of their school, and the heiress to a large German fortune, which no one ever talked about. Kevin's dad was a professor of economics at NYU. WJ was the only one of the five who was not a self-proclaimed music nerd. WJ's parents were 'artists', who never reached a level of notoriety to be considered famous but had done well enough that they could live in Park Slope and send WJ to private school.

WJ was the oddball of the group, as his parents weren't of the same aristocratic breed as the rest of the band. WJ's parents were the rare exception to those of the hippie generation. They called themselves psychobiologists, and following a psychedelically induced hunch, had made huge discoveries concerning the effects of community on the brain physiology of primates, which they published about with corresponding poetry and dance pieces. WJ's parents saw him as 'artistic research'. WJ was, accordingly, very self-possessed, if not also somewhat dissociated as a consequence of understanding life as one big experiment.

WJ was the unofficial supplier for the band, a talent everyone appreciated, but no one openly acknowledged. Despite his own enjoyment of alteratives, WJ had an uncanny ability to remember and retain large amounts of the most entertaining and improbable information, such as the origin of his favorite punctuation, the interrobang, which he claimed was the perfect existential expression. He was also the band's token conspiracy theorist. WJ was convinced the amulet around Boy's neck was carved out of a stone from the Pleiades, a silly idea Boy had always secretly held onto, but never openly embraced. Outside his near trust for Sophie, Boy came the closest to trusting WJ.

While WJ was by far the most laid back, Nico was the most high-strung and serious, unofficially playing the role of day-to-day band manager. With the exception of WJ, the band, including Boy, had the hyper-entitlement of extreme privilege. While there were downsides to this entitlement, it also bestowed a high level of agency through which they had become particularly talented.

Boy arrived at the practice room, surprised to see someone he didn't immediately recognize waiting with the rest of the band. The unfamiliar face belonged to Jimmy "The Gun" Sezousky, a world-famous producer. The Gun smiled at Boy as he walked through the door. Boy's band members looked excited and nervous.
 "Hey, Boy," he reached out to shake Boy's hand, "Jimmy."
 "Yeah, I know." Boy's voice betrayed him, showing confusion, with an edge of annoyance. He tentatively shook the man's hand.
 "Dude," Nico said under his breath. Nico was standing next to the door Boy had just entered through.
 "It's alright Nick, let the kid speak," replied The Gun, amused by Boy's indignance.
 "Sorry, I don't mean to be rude." Boy fought frustration, sure The Gun's presence was at the behest of his mother. "Did my mom send you?"
 "Your mom?" Jimmy cracked a smile.
 "She's trying to 'help me along' again. But I don't want her help, man. I want to do this on my own. I know I can. I need to." Boy's voice shook as he spoke.
 "Dude," repeated Nico, getting pissed. The other band mates looked at Boy the same way, except for WJ, too busy watching the wall breath.
 "Does your mom even know you're doing this,"

asked The Gun, "Nick was telling me..."

"It's Nico," said Boy.

"Right, sorry. Nico was telling me he had to put the studio in his name so your mom wouldn't find out." The Gun maintained a smirk, but was bored, wondering how long he was going to have to put up with Boy's antics.

"Why'd he tell you that?" asked Boy, turning to Nico.

"Because The Gun asked us why we hadn't had your mom get someone to produce for us, you being so well-connected and all. I just told him you didn't even want your mom to know we were doing this," Nico rushed through his words, hoping to resolve the awkward situation quickly.

"So how did you find out about us then?" Boy said, scrupulous.

"Your good buddy, Kevin, sent in a demo," and with this The Gun produced a thumb-drive and dropped it onto an amp next to him. "It's good. You have potential."

Kevin sheepishly avoided Boy ire.

"I didn't even realize we had a demo. What did you send him, Kevin?" Boy's questions were calm, but everyone knew he was upset.

"I just sent him a couple of recordings from practice. I guess I didn't really think he would even listen to it, let alone show up like this." Kevin maintained eye contact with the floor. "We just keep talking about the next step, but you keep holding us back, saying 'we aren't good enough'." He looked up at Boy, "Why aren't you stoked? I mean, look, Boy, its Jimmy 'The Fucking Gun'!" Realizing what he'd said, Kevin started stammering, "Sorry, The Gun, I mean Jimmy, I mean..."

"Don't worry about it kid," Jimmy chortled, "I

kinda like it, 'The Fuckin' Gun'." He turned back to Boy, "Look. I would love to stick around and chat longer about who did what and all, but I gotta boogie. You fellas can sort everything after I'm out. If you don't mind?" He looked at Boy for agreement. Boy nodded and The Gun continued. "I came to see if you fellas will come into the studio this summer."

Everyone but Boy and WJ shouted out excited affirmations. WJ laughed, and Boy stared at the ground, pensive.

"What do you think, Boy?" asked The Gun, smiling big at the general enthusiasm, and Boy's ridiculous resistance.

"We'll think about it," said Boy.

The rest of the band stopped cheering and glared at him.

"What?" screeched Nico. "No we won't mister, uh...The Gun. We'd love to. Shut the fuck up, Boy."

The Gun didn't look flustered at all. "Let the kid think about it." He walked over to Boy and handed him his card. " Give me a call whenever you're ready to talk. No pressure. No rush. I dig your style. You'll do well for yourself." Each statement The Gun made was followed by a cool pause. He gave a final small laugh before Jimmy 'The Gun' left.

4

Boy expressed his concerns to the band, his fear that getting into contract might end up making them have to compromise their artistic integrity. After what felt like an eternity of discussion for Boy he ended up relenting to the excitement and desire to sign. He promised to call Jimmy the following day. They would go into the studio. Boy was reticent to admit his own excitement and kept it veiled behind a facade of resignation that he himself was convinced by.

They decided to celebrate instead of practice. They went to The Boom Boom Room. Two of his mom's ex-models ran the door. Both were bitter, wishing they were still modeling. Still, they appreciated such a high-profile job, and knew their positions had only come by the grace of Boy's mom. It was mostly because of this they let him and all of his friends in whenever he came around. Despite their resentments towards his mom, neither could help but like Boy.

Despite the venue's snobbiness, Boy had always enjoyed the vaulted ceilings, and the way the central bar almost looked like a mushroom born of the large, gently sweeping wooden beams surrounding it. The interior design was pseudo-art-deco, regaled with old-fashioned light bulbs, suggestive of the prohibition era. The furniture and walls were monochromatic, shades of brown, skin-tone highlights, flowing, crisp edges. The main bar was circular, a great arched pillar at its center. The pillar curved out, into the ceiling, a stem of the huge mushroom whose under-cap was the elaborate ceiling. The panoramic view of the city from this top floor also gave Boy something to lose himself in while his friends chased dopamine.

WJ believed this to be the bar at the center of the Pleiadian underground, which he insisted was led by the mushrooms, hence the mushroom-shaped bar and room. Boy loved listening to WJ's conspiracy theories, finding them more entertaining than most sci-fi.

Boy and his friends took their usual table, just inside the door, down a small set of stairs. A large window offered views of the Hudson, and it's constant murky flow, a churning that reminded Boy of times ceaselessness, and the Jersey shoreline, a flickering mess of lights, and somehow a world away. Boy marveled at how many people he realized he would never know.

Boy was caught in a maze of skeptical feedback loops, having a hard time not believing his mom had something to do with The Gun's sudden appearance. He wished he could be confident he was accomplishing this on his own. Something felt off, which was usual for him.

He never really liked clubs, and sat at the table for most of the night, watching his friends get wasted and dance. He didn't like social scenes because he didn't trust that the people he interacted with were there because they genuinely liked him, and not because of whom his mom was. He mostly trusted his band mates, especially WJ, who spent the whole night dancing like a Muppet, hands flailing, mouth in an unabashed grin. He wished he could have such an uninhibited approach to life, and was glad for the example WJ made of joy.

He would try to avoid telling people his name, as 'Boy' was so uncommon. He also disdained lying, so people usually found out. He would see people's faces light up with the excitement of meeting a celebrity, and he could almost hear the gears in their heads start to turn, wondering how they could become close with him. Not all of them wanted something material, they were just moths to the light of his fame, his connection to the celebrity of his mom and her empire.

They would offer drinks, drugs, their bodies,

whatever was at their disposal, and things that weren't even really theirs to offer. He was happiest when people didn't know who he was, because then he felt he could trust the interaction more. He wondered why he wanted recognition in the music scene if he already disliked how people treated him based merely off his mom's infamy. Why did he want to 'make it', if he already wished for more anonymity? He couldn't answer these questions, so he drank.

Tonight was Russian vodka with a twist of lime, on the rocks. Before long, he was lost in inebriation.

He gazed up at the TV above the bar and noticed Saturday Night Dancers was the feature of the moment. Boy had always felt a strange affinity for the film's leading man, Johnny T. He never felt like Johnny T. was a particularly amazing actor, but he had always enjoyed watching his work, particularly his early work. It was an interest that felt like déjà vu.

In his drunken state, Boy started wondering about what had brought the actor to his cult-like religious beliefs. He thought about how awkward 'Warstar Planet' had been. He turned to WJ and mumbled something like, "What a fuckin' trippy dude, huh?"

"What's that, Boy?" WJ hollered over the loud music.

"Johnny T. Strange fuckin' dude, right?" Boy's eyes had locked into trying to focus on the liquid in his glass. He was on the brink of incoherence.

"Yup," said WJ, who'd had at least as much as Boy to drink, but never appeared affected. "Not quite as trippy as his guru Hubbs though."

"That's just, I was just thinking about," Boy replied, swiveling his head up awkwardly, trying to focus on WJ's face. "Didn't he start Scientology as a bet with some of his sci-fi contemporaries, 'r something?" His eyes were having a hard time focusing; a sign Boy's night would end soon.

"That's the story I heard. He did say one thing I liked in Dialetics, though." How the fuck is WJ so sober? Wondered Boy. WJ continued, "To paraphrase, something like...'all of life is one process, one single thing aiming at a single goal, and that goal is survival.' I always thought that was pretty insightful. Your phone's beeping at you, Boy." WJ noticed Boy had probably not taken in anything he'd said, but he didn't mind. Instead, he merely pointed at the pocket, making noise.

Boy found his phone, with the help of WJ, and saw a text from Sophie. He had forgotten they were going to hang out after practice. He was ready to go home, but wasn't sure he was sober enough to sit in a car. He was barely conscious of texting her back, and instantly had no recollection of what he had written. The blackout that had been approaching took over.

5

Boy woke up, head throbbing, no idea how he'd gotten home. He could feel someone in the bed behind him. There was a rat's nest of hair leading to a purple sweater. This wasn't the first time Sophie had come to his rescue, returning him home at the end of a bender. The veins in his forehead throbbed with hangover. He went back to sleep.

Quickly he was in a dream. He was young. His mother was next to his bed telling a story. She talked about distant stars called The Seven Sisters.

She told him the stars were young now, but some day they would become very important. Without the future of those stars, neither of them would ever have come into being. She was proud of him. Nothing previous had felt strange, as she always told stories when he was a kid, but her pride was so unexpected it startled him awake.

His mind quickly returned to everything that had happened the night before, replaying the interactions with Jimmy over and over again in rapid succession. He started spinning trying to evaluate The Gun's authenticity.

The Gun was known to be terse. Why had he been so patient with Boy? Why would he have even listened to a random demo in the first place? Let alone a demo from someone he didn't know, and hadn't ever heard of? How could a recording of one of their practices been good enough to get him interested?

There were just too many things that didn't add up. So, after a forever of 20 minutes of mental treadmill, Boy hopped out of bed and donned a bathrobe. Just before opening the door out into the hallway he paused. He realized his head was still throbbing, and he was in no mood to deal with all of his mom's minions. He contemplated returning to bed.

Sophie grumbled, "Where are you going? We didn't get back 'til 5:00." Looking at her cell phone, "It's not even 8:00." Her head dropped heavy back onto the pillow. She was still mostly asleep.

Not even 8:00? Awesome! Thought Boy. "I gotta talk to my mom."

Boy figured it was so early there wouldn't be many people yet. He hurried down the hall, into his mom's office. Though it was early, he knew she would already be working. She was often there when he woke, or returned home early in the morning after big nights out.

She looked up. Her hand at the base of her skull, her hair the closest to disheveled Boy had ever seen it. He was so determined none of this registered.

Her office was art-deco-meets-mid-century-modern. A large wooden desk faced the door. Papers were neatly filed in a two-tiered metal holder on her right; a thin, brass lamp, off-white, slight patina from age, sat on her left. The walls had dark oak panels, which were knotted with undertones of deep red. Behind her loomed a large, lifelike mural of a man he had never met, wearing a distinguished three-piece suit, sanguine tie, and light-blue shirt. The background of the painting was angular and grey, a faded image of a corner office buried somewhere deep below the surface of the earth. The painting hung between two overbearing bookshelves. Both were filled with leather-bound first editions of interesting-sounding books: A Genealogy of Morality, On the Order of Nature, Phenomenology of Spirit, Beelzebub's Tales to His Grandson, amongst many others. Boy was pretty sure his mom had read every one of them.

She looked at him as though it were the most natural thing for him to be there. In a cool, emotionless tone she noted, "Seems like you had a good night last night."

Boy hoped to emulate her coolness, "Don't bullshit me. You know why I'm here." He played it like he had already figured everything out. "The Gun told me you'd hired him." His upper lip curled under with anger.

Her look didn't falter, save an almost imperceptible grin in the corner of her mouth.

"Jimmy?"

"You know exactly who I mean. Stop playing dumb. It's offensive." He looked straight at her, trying to read her, something he hated that he could never do. No one was able to read her. She was always so collected, as though the blood running through her veins was ice.

"I haven't thought about Jimmy in a long time. Did you see him at Boom Boom? What would I have hired him for?" She gave a small guffaw, but seemed honest. "I have work to do, so only keep bothering me if there is something you actually need."

"You're lying." Unable to hold back his emotions, his tone escalated quickly. "You're doing it again. Just let me do one thing on my own!"

"What in heaven's name are you talking about, Sunshine? What did Jimmy tell you that upset you so much?" She looked him right in the eye, unflinching.

He wished he could tell if she was lying, and knew if she was, she had called his bluff. He knew there was no way to win.

"Never mind," he said, turning, defeated, towards the door.

"Okay." She never pushed. He wished she would. "Let me know if you need me to call Jimmy and chew him out. Okay, Boy?"

"It's fine. I'm fine. Don't call him." It took all his self-control not to slam the door. He sulked back to his room. He collapsed back into bed, not caring if he woke Sophie. She pretended not to notice. She could tell he was frustrated. They both fell back asleep.

His dreams were much more abstract. *A warm field, a strange sense of floating, a deep and unexpected sense of trust.*

6

Boy awoke on top of his covers, Sophie still asleep next to him. He glanced at the clock, 11:23. He rubbed his eyes into focus, got up and staggered over to his crumpled pants in the corner of the room. Finding his phone, and The Gun's business card, he dialed the number.

"Boy." Jimmy didn't bother with the standard, obligatory greetings.

He's probably a great liar, too, Boy thought. "If you really want to get us into the studio, I have some terms. Send the papers over to my mom's lawyers and they will take a look at 'em. I'm no idiot, Jimmy. I know what the music industry does, hell, what the whole entertainment industry can do to artists, and I won't fall for it. I can afford good lawyers, so don't send a bullshit contract, 'k? If it all looks good we can start as soon as you're ready."

Boy realized some of his venom was anger at not feeling sure of the situation, but he didn't know how to back down at this point, so he continued.

"You're a trip kid, but you got it. I'll send the papers over this afternoon. Let's talk again tomorrow. And, don't worry kid, everyone's way too afraid of your mom to try and pull anything over on you. Honestly, I just dig your tunes, and think we could make a bunch of money working together, that's all." Jimmy was amused by Boy's cockiness, but not surprised, given Boy's upbringing.

"It's not about money, Gun. It's about the art. Got it?" Boy's voice got quieter as he became more serious. "Play it that way or I'm out."

"You got it, kid." Jimmy suppressed a chuckle. "Talk to you tomorrow."

Boy could hear Jimmy's amused tone as he hung up the phone. He didn't care. He had made his decision. The band would give it a go and see what could happen.

"What was that all about?" He had been so determined in his conversation with The Gun he had forgotten Sophie was still sleeping next to him.

"We're going to record with The Gun," he said more nonchalantly than he actually felt.

"What?!" asked Sophie, perking up. "Really? That's awesome. Congratulations, Boy. You're really doin' it. I knew you would." Even though her eyes stayed closed, Sophie's face lit up.

Boy felt proud, despite himself. "Don't congratulate me yet," he responded. "Wait until I produce something worth listening to first."

And somehow, producing a camera from nowhere, even in those early stages of waking, even though she had barely slept, even though she could barely open her eyes, Sophie took a picture of him before dropping her head back on the pillow and pretending to fall back asleep.

Boy stared at the ceiling, not moving. His mind was trying to find a crack in the story, proof this was all a set up, something provided by his mom and not something he had earned on his own. Finally, he couldn't take it any more. He went to the kitchen and made himself a cup of coffee. After his first cup he called the band and made plans to meet later that afternoon.

He was waiting for anyone to say something they shouldn't know. In the past it was easy to find out what his mom had lined up for him because one of her model minions would inevitably drop a preemptive hint.

He kept expecting everyone to say, "Congratulations on the recording contract, Boy." He was almost disappointed when no one did. He realized he was even a little unnerved by the lack of preemptive response, as he thought it indicated everything might actually be real.

He was surprised at how hard it was for him to believe this could happen without his mom. This is how other people made it, right? He asked himself. He thought maybe he was just afraid he wasn't really ready yet, or he would try and fail, or worst of all, he wasn't really cut out to be the rock star he dreamed of becoming. None of these thoughts felt right. He knew he was ready musically. His songs were at least as good as anything popular. He knew he could do anything he set his mind to, if he was committed. And he especially knew he could handle fame, he'd been famous his whole life.

Sophie joined him in the kitchen and he compulsively asked, "Do you think this is the right thing to do?"

"Well good morning to you too, and yes, I would love a cup of coffee. Thanks for asking." She smiled, but also looked like she might punch him. Her hair was a mess, her eyes puffy.

He poured her a cup and passed the cream before saying, "Seriously, I want your opinion."

"Just go with it, Boy. You're always trying to struggle. You have so much luxury in your life you don't know how to be happy. One of the best producers in the business wants to produce you and you're acting like someone is asking you to choose between killing your mom or your best friend." She jokingly pointed at herself before taking a sip of coffee.

It was too hot and she nearly spit it out. "Fuck, ouch." She set down the cup and looked up at Boy. "Look, you might as well go for it. There's nothing wrong with trying and seeing if it feels right, is there?"

"No. Yeah, I know. You're always right. Can I keep you around forever?" he said, pretending to be joking, but knowing they both realized he wasn't.

"Sure, but managers ain't free," She chortled. "Now can we have normal, pleasant, hung-over conversation for the rest of the morning? This is far too serious for me right now."

"Eat an ass." He sipped his scolding coffee and tried to relax. This is happening.

"You wish," Sophie smirked.

7

When Boy entered the practice space he could feel the fellows trying to not look too excited, save WJ, who bending some awkward sounding sine waves on the Moog. Boy was doing his best to present unaffected, but the anticipation was palpable.

"Did you call The Gun?" Nico finally burst.

"Yup," Boy's response was intentionally understated.

"And?" Even WJ was looking at Boy now, a single drawn out oscillation from the synthesizer lingering in the bated air for a desperately long feeling 5 seconds.

"We got a record contract if we want it," Boy finally replied, swiftly adding, "But...we gotta make some agreements, fellas." He looked around the room. The boys were fit to burst from excitement. "We can't do this half assed. If we do this, we gotta do it right. Practice harder, and make sure it sounds as good as it can. Okay? This is not just a game."

"I gotta bottle of whiskey to celebrate." WJ unzipped his backpack, producing a handle of Glenfiddich 15. Boy was resistant to releasing into revelry, and could still feel last night's chemicals churning, but decided everyone deserved a celebration. He tried to let himself bask in the excitement they were all sharing. He took a big swig when the bottle got to him, internally citing solidarity. The tension of his apprehension and excitement made it hard to be fully present, and he noticed himself observing the room more than participating.

He didn't know what was building. He wondered if everyone felt this way when they found their destiny unfolding in front of them. He wondered if it was destiny, or if it was intention. He felt proud. He felt nervous. He had no real idea of what he was doing, but felt compelled. He had been riding on his mom's coattails his entire life, but assured himself this was going to be different, this was going to be his. He was determined be seen for himself, Boy, no longer merely his mother's son.

When the bottle came back around, he drank with more vigor. "Get it Boy! Hit that shit. Let's fucking celebrate," rang the chorus of band mates. And celebrate they did.

After the bottle was done they played a couple of sloppy songs, just for fun. They kept getting lost in melody, and forgetting breaks. No one cared, not even Boy. The spirit of Bacchus had joined the group, and debauchery was underway.

Even quicker than the night before Boy found himself awaking. Once again, he had very little memory of the end of the night. Again he was in his bed, a puddle of drool connecting his cheek to the pillow. Again Sophie, tornado of hair, was next to him.

He had a vague memory of Greasers playing on a large screen at a club. How strange is that, he thought to himself, Johnny T., two nights in a row. He also had hints of getting into another silly conversation with WJ about Johnny T.'s strange acting career and spiritual life, and something about reptiles running the deep state.

He smirked, remembering discussions of how Johnny T., pre-Who Started Talking, seemed almost a completely different person from the Johnny T. in all the movies since; how it was really Quincy Turpintino who brought Johnny T.'s career back to life, with his role in Fictitious Fluff; and even Johnny T.'s soap commercial, from before SND. He was amused by the conversations he'd gotten into about this funny actor on two consecutive nights. He was surprised by how much WJ knew about the man.

He thought back through his childhood and wondered if his mom had ever dated the actor. She had dated anyone who had caught her attention. From Boy's experience his mother was powerful and beautiful enough to get anything she wanted.

Sophie shifted. As always, she was still dressed. Fuck, he thought to himself, his head pulsing with post-party-pain. He rolled to his side and watched her sleep. She hadn't even taken off her glasses. Her lips were puffy with sleep and he felt a sudden urge to kiss her. Remembering who he was looking at he chuckled. Sophie is like a sister, he assured himself. She was family, not a romantic interest. Right? He certainly felt safer with her then his mom, the one person he was related to.

The few times Boy had asked about his dad his mom made it clear it was a subject she would never talk about. He knew she loved him, but he never felt safe enough to fully receive it. He imagined his pendant was a lost artifact his father had left him. At times it became his primary source of comfort, a symbol of the love he believed his mom felt but was too callus to show, and a reminder that somewhere in his past was a father. He knew this might all be a fantasy, a coping mechanism to protect him from the grief he felt at not knowing his father, but he clutched tight to story, and a hope he might some day meet the other half of his biological origin.

He knew Sophie loved him, and he loved her back. He trusted that she would always be there for him. He loved knowing he could go on a bender and, at some point in the night, she would inevitably come save him from whatever craziness he had gotten into. He loved that she loved him for who he was, and not just what his mom might be able to do for her. He whispered, "Thank you," under his breath, wondering if she almost smiled when he did so. He closed his eyes and drifted back to sleep.

He was running away from something. It was chasing him through back alleys, until he ran down into the subway, hoping to escape. But he knew it was still behind him. Suddenly he was running through his home, but all the doors led into rooms he didn't remember. He heard snarling. He was in his mom's office, she was sitting behind her desk, and he realized the snarling was coming from her. She looked up at him and her smile was inhumanly large, alligator teeth clattering together as she snarled. He turned and ran to the door of the office. A voice both his mom's and somehow inhuman called his name. He snapped awake.

8

Boy's mom was gazing down at him. "Up," she announced.

He took a deep breath, struggling to not superimpose the dream over his mom's face. He grumbled, barely lucid, and a bit shaken from an uncomfortable feeling the dream had left his with. "What?" He finally managed.

"It's nearly 1:30, pm. I am politely reminding you the world keeps running while you are asleep, and it's now time to enter the world of the living?" Her tone was matter-of-fact.

"Seriously? Mom, I..."

She stopped him. She wasn't explicitly forceful; yet her strength was unyielding. "I'm waking you because it became clear to me you had no intentions of waking yourself, and your girlfriend would only try to keep you in bed longer." She gazed incredulous, though without malice, at Sophie, who was as still as possible, in hopes of avoiding wrath.

"She's not my..."

"It is also apparent you have forgotten we have a party this afternoon. A party you promised you would attend. I therefore took it upon myself to conjure you from your spell in dreamland, with enough time that you could get yourself ready before we left."

Trying to respond she interrupted again. "Save your breath, Boy. I don't ask much of you, and it is the least you can do to follow through on the little bit I do ask. This is the Zarachov Gala. Because they are a family-inclined association, it looks good in their eyes to have you with me when I attend.

You know this, and you know you will be getting up presently to get yourself washed and dressed. See you in the kitchen in 30 minutes."

He started to protest, but she left the room saying, "Good morning, Sophie." Boy couldn't tell if she meant it positively or as a threat. She closed the door firmly.

Boy waited a moment before saying, "God, I'm glad it's you here."

Sophie squinted her eyes curiously at him, implying she thought he was flirting with her.

"Not in that way. I mean I'm glad...well...if anyone besides me had to be subjected to my mother first thing, at least it was you."

Sophie smirked, "Thou dost protest to much."

Boy suddenly felt like he was trapped and scrambling. "No. God. Look." He pivoted, "You know you can't get upset with me for being a blubbering idiot right when I wake up, especially after last night." He would have been embarrassed if it wasn't Sophie.

She smiled, "It's ok. You don't have to apologize, Boy. I actually thought it was kind of nice she said good morning to me." She sounded vaguely nervous. Boy figured it was a reaction to his mom.

"See. That's what I was trying to say. It's so nice I don't have to apologize for her with you." He looked at her, squinted his eyes, brow furrowed.

"What? No!" She turned away, wrapping herself in blankets. .

"What are you doing now?" His tone was escalating.

"I'm laying here, trying to wake up slowly. And the answer is no, emphatically." She looked at him with conviction.

"Aw, come on, Soph. It would be so much more fun if you came along. Please?" He drew out his please making a silly smile until she smiled back.

"You are such an asshole," she said, burring her head beneath a pillow.

"I know. So you'll come then?"

"Stop Boy, you know how much I hate them, because you hate them just as much."

"I know, that's why it's better if you come along, because then we can at least hate them together, commiserate."

"Yeah, but these parties are even worse for me because they all look at me like I'm some kind of…disgusting thing the cat dragged in. Everyone stares me down like I'm the blemish on your otherwise immaculate honor. You, at least, are your mother's son."

She flinched, realizing what she'd said. She knew how much he hated the privilege being his mom's son brought, and even more the way people treated him because of it.

He looked at her, lips pursed, jaw clenched.

"That's not what I meant," she added.

His nostrils flared.

She fumbled, trying to make it better, "I know, shit, I'm sorry…ok…I'll fucking go?"

He glared at her, but she knew he was just playing now.

Seeing her recognize his façade, he said, "Great! Let's get ready."

He hopped out of bed and started rummaging through his closet.

"I have one condition," Sophie said.

"What?" he asked.

"I'll only go with you if you take these mushrooms with me." She pulled out a small bag of liberty caps.

He looked at her as though she were joking.

"I mean it," she said, responding to his disapproving look. "Here's how I see it. If you're really want to become the rock star you dream of being, you'd better start acting like one."

She took a pinch out of the bag, awkwardly placed it in her mouth, grimacing at the pungent flavor. Having difficulty swallowing, she threw the bag at Boy.

Picturing all the uncomfortable and stuffy people he expected to see at this party, he paused in consideration. He thought about what his mom would do if she found out. After a moment Sophie's plan seemed brilliant. He had done mushrooms a few times before, and figured he could handle himself. Likewise, it would add an exciting edge to what would otherwise be incredibly dull experience. He tipped the bag up to his face and dumped the contents into his mouth.

Sophie was staring at the ceiling brushing her tongue against the roof of her mouth in an attempt to cleanse her pallet.

"Yuck!" she burst, turning to see Boy swallowed, the bag empty. "Oh shi…!" she said, trying to stop herself.

"What?"

"Nothing. You just took the amount I would have normally split between three people."

"What!?"

"Don't worry about it. It'll be fun. You gotta remember what WJ always says, 'Taking a safe amount isn't taking enough,'" she laughed.

"I can fucking handle it," he said, hoping it was true. It was probably psychosomatic, but he could already feel his body tingle, the mushrooms integrated into his system.

They continued getting ready, engaged in idle chatter. It was the kind of awkward conversation that avoided the elephant in the room, specifically when the elephant is a substance that hasn't kicked in yet, and even more especially when someone has taken more of the elephant than they meant to.

After a few minutes their conversation became fluid. Comfortable with each other they quickly stopped focusing on their imminent trip.

Dressed a little early they went to find Boy's mom. As usual, she was in her imposing office, meticulously dressed, pushing papers around, undisturbed by their entrance.

"How can you stand it in here?" Boy asked as they walked in. "It's so dark."

"I like it," said Sophie, euphoria setting in.

"You look delightful, Boy. You as well, Sophia. Were you going to ask if you could bring a friend?" she addressed her son typically stern.

He knew she didn't mind. "Yeah. Sophie's coming with us." He stifled the giggles.

"Of course." She looked back down at her papers, picked up her mug, took a long drink, stood, and announced, "Let's be on our way, then."

Boy's eyes followed the mug down, noticing how beautifully it had been glazed. He wondered why he'd never noticed its beauty before. His mom always drank out of it, yet he'd never really noticed it.

He looked to Sophie, who poorly subdued a smile, staring at the ground, body swaying subtly.

His mother somehow was already at the door. She opened it, looked at Boy with what he interpreted as curiosity or knowing, and asked, "Well?"

Sophie looked up. They smiled at each other as they turned to follow. His mom slightly raised an eyebrow as they walked by. Did her gaze hold an accusation towards Sophie? Boy assumed this was just a figment of his imagination. He knew how his mind got when he was high, so he tried to compensate by assuming anything even remotely smacking of paranoia was simply paranoia.

"Just because you're paranoid..." he mumbled to himself.

"What's that?" his mother asked.

"It doesn't mean they're not after you." Sophie giggled at him.

His mom ignored them, and again suddenly she was gracefully ducking into the limo. They clambered in behind her, grins wide. Is time broken?

The drive was inexplicably enjoyable. This is different. He and Sophie gazed out of the windows, taken by the beauty of the city as they moved through it like a twisting current in a manufactured stream. Twilight hung anticipation over the city.

They arrived at the party. It was a routine Boy was so accustomed to that mounting intoxication didn't affect the procedure at all. They paused near the entrance for photos, shook the obligatory hands on their way in, offered polite nothings with veiled smiles.

He and Sophie wandered around the party, faking conversation with the people that came over to kiss his mom's ass. He repeatedly assured that Sophie was just his best friend, noticing something shift in her each time he did so. He decided this was a symptom of drug-induced paranoia, along with the awkward looks he felt everyone was giving him. He started to lose capacity for small talk. He excused himself, grabbed Sophie, and headed to the balcony, hoping fresh air would help.

"Man, it's stuffy in there," he said when they got outside. "Ohhh, it feels so good out here." He gulped down the night air.

Sophie closed the door. It was somehow just the two of them on the balcony.

"I was having a hard time bullshitting. I think I'm getting pretty high," he said, looking at the stars.

"Me too."

There was something strange in her voice. Where he expected the same kind of exuberance he was feeling, she sounded down.

"What's up, Soph?" he asked.

"Nothing," she said producing a sudden smile, "I'm great."

"Stop it. There's no one else out here. Let's talk for reals." Looking towards Sophie, and through the window behind her into the party, he saw a human-sized reptile, on its hind legs, dressed like everyone else, standing against the far wall. But as quickly as he saw it, the reptilian disappeared through a door, vanishing into the wall. Boy hoped it was just a compelling hallucination.

"Holy fucking shit!" he mumbled, his eyes wide with confusion and excitement.

"It's not that big of a deal," said Sophie, not realizing what Boy had seen, thinking his fear was about her.

"You saw it?" He was trying not to freak out. Was he just high? How could Sophie have seen it, she was facing him? Was there another one behind him? He spun around. The night sky gazed back at him, empty.

"What?" Sophie replied, confused. She turned back towards the window looking into the party.

Everything looked normal.

"The reptile?" he said, turning back.

"What the fuck, Boy? I'm not that high."

She turned and scanned the room to see if she could figure out what he was talking about. She saw the same uptight oligarchs milling around, pretending to like each other, engaged in unspoken power dynamics, just as they had been for time immemorial. She noticed concern arise. Boy had taken a significantly larger amount of mushrooms than her, but he was usually able to handle his highs better than this. She was definitely not so high. She was happy, however, that the distraction had taken his focus off her. She wasn't ready to tell him, not while they were on mushrooms, and especially not in such an uncomfortable social setting. She knew it was probably just such a circumstance that was going to end up bringing the truth out of her, but at least it wouldn't be now. To make sure she added, "What exactly did you see?"

"It was huge. Bigger than a human. But it was definitely a reptile. Something out of 70s Star Trek, or something. It was over against that far wall." He motioned with his head as his eyes scanned the rest of the walls.

"Did anyone else noticed?" She couldn't tell if he was being genuine. This was the kind of joke he loved making, but he looked serious. "Where'd it go?"

"Through the wall. I don't get why no one else reacted." He arrived at his mom's face looking directly at him from across the room. Her gaze was locked, hard, and yet tranquil. Had she's seen? He felt as though she had, but he knew he couldn't ask her, knew all this was probably a result of the mycelial influences in his brain.

"If no one else is freaking out, then it must have been a hallucination Boy?" She had also noticed Boy's mom gazing at them, and wanted to calm him so she wouldn't come to see what was happening. "It went through the wall? What wall?" She worried he was getting too high to function in 'normal' human interaction.

"Let's check it out. If there's a secret door we'll probably be able to find it." His face sardonically playful. "But first we have to make it look like we are having a normal, good time, so my mom doesn't interfere." He turned to her awkwardly grining, "Smile."

"You're crazy," Sophie chuckled. But she smiled and playfully pushed his shoulder. Getting his mom off their track was a good idea.

"She still looking?" he asked, pretending he was saying something funny, and punctuating his statement with a guffaw.

Pretending she was turning in laughter, Sophie scanned to see if they were still being watched. Boy did the same. His mom had returned to her conversation. His smiled dropped, replaced by determination. He clutched Sophie's hand, dragging her back inside, swiftly through the party and over to the wall. It was seamless. If there had been a door, it was incredibly well hidden, eluding the two of them.

"Am I just tripping?" Boy asked.

Sophie was staring intently at the trim board.

"Well, I don't know about 'just', but you're definitely tripping."

Boy's mom's voice came from behind them. "Tripping?" she inquired, her tone even. Was she upset or merely curious?

Boy could feel his cheeks flush as he turned

towards her. His mind scrambled for a plausible way out. "Figure of speech, mom." He nudged Sophie.

"Uh, yeah," Sophie said. "Why? Are you high?" she blurted, uncharacteristically bold, towards the looming figure in front of them.

"Of course not, dear." Boy's mom had an amazing knack for being unfazed by things. "But by the looks and sounds of it, the two of you are."

Is she fucking psychic? Boy thought to himself. "What are you talking about, mom?"

"Look, Boy, I was around for the sixties. First, you started saying slightly socially awkward things as we were doing our rounds. Then you suddenly excused yourself. When you got to the balcony you weren't so much breathing as drinking the night air in, a very psychedelic experience if you ask me. Then the two of you rush in here and start staring at the wall, and rubbing your hands along the wainscoting."

Boy was still trying to find some way out of this, but he knew he couldn't deceive her.

"I think it is great to experiment, to opening your minds."

Boy couldn't believe his ears. Was she condoning this?

"The most important thing for me is that you are honest with me about it, and I would prefer you get your substances from me, so I can know they're clean."

Boy and Sophie just stood there, stunned. Their long silence would have given them away if their dilated pupils hadn't.

"So which is it?"

Boy looked at his mom and wondered if this was a ploy to get them to admit something she would punish them for. He remembered a friend saying to always deny everything if you are ever being interrogated by a police officer, no matter what they tell you, even if they offer immunity for the truth. But before he could deny anything, Sophie spoke, again uncharacteristically bold.

"It was me, ma'am."

Ma'am? Boy thought.

"I convinced Boy."

Boy turned white, completely forgetting the huge reptile he had been trying to find.

His mother was still a moment. Then in the same calm manner that scared the shit out of him, the manner in which she always spoke, she asked, "Cubensis or cyanescens?"

"Huh?" inserted Boy.

"Psilocybin, I think?" Sophie replied.

"What the hell are you guys talking about?" Am I having aural hallucinations now, or are they speaking a different language? Boy wondered.

"Liberty caps?" Sophie asked.

"Psilocybe, but not cubensis. Semilanceata, then, if memory serves." His Mom looked half impressed at Sophie. As impressed as she ever looked, slightly less stern for a brief moment, the corners of her mouth faintly considering curving up, though they never actually did.

Does my mom do mushrooms? Boy wondered.

"That sounds right," Sophie offered, her confidence boosted. Noticing Boy's confusion she added, "types of mushroom, Boy, don't worry about it."

He couldn't believe Sophie and his mom were having a conversation about the type of 'shrooms they were on, at a stuffy party, and his mom wasn't only not pissed, she even seemed pleased.

Why does my mom know so much about mushrooms? Boy thought, squinting, gazing up at her.

"Do be careful, and next time I highly recommend going upstate and in to the woods. Kaaterskill Falls used to be one of my favorite places to go." She's returned to blasé. "As for now, I'll have to pretend like I am oblivious, obviously. And Sophie, since you gave them to him, and since you know more about what you're doing, make sure the two of you keep it together until we leave, understand." She turned and reentered the stuck-up overdressed crowd.

"Of course," Sophie offered as his mom wandered away.

After his mother was a few paces away, Boy asked, "What the fuck just happened?"

"I know, right? Your mom's even cooler..." She realized what she was about to say and caught herself. Complimenting Boy's mom usually only pissed him off.

"Right?" he said, taking a relieved breath. "I can't believe how cool she was. I hope she's still that cool in the morning."

Sophie noticed Boy was swaying.

He looked around the room. Things normally solid now fluctuated to some subtle pulse he didn't usually see. People's faces were not their standard stagnant pallor, but were a constantly shifting slightly more pink here, more undertones of green there, a pulsing of distant blue. Nothing unrealistic, just nothing consistent either. It was like watching a TV having a hard time auto adjusting the color settings, cyclically oscillating.

There was also a pulse to the sound in the room, a type of beehive-like interdependence in the volumes of conversations. He sensed when the communal volume was going to increase and when it would dissipate again. In a low-volume moment, he let out a short, loud, laugh, which echoed through the room. Many turned to look at him as he stared blankly out into the crowd of people he could tell would rather be at home, unencumbered by the obligation of sociality.

"What the fuck is this?" he asked Sophie. She had been watching him the whole time, not sure how high he was until then. She was hoping he was just processing the interaction, but it was apparent he was, indeed, considerably more inebriated. She was high enough that she merely laughed at such a ridiculous question.

Boy looked at her, and they both fell into hysterics. She had the presence of mind to control herself a bit, but Boy just let it roll out of him. Wishing moments a driver was escorting them to the elevator and down to the car. They were driven around for a small eternity in unrelenting giggles, reveling in the bright, blurring, running lights they passed, as the congested island of Manhattan laughed and smiled right back. Their night ended in a heap on his kitchen floor, eating whipped cream out of the container, talking about how strange it was they were in a building, hundreds of feet off the ground. Boy opined that such dislocation from the earth, in a literal manner, might be the reason urban people were so disconnected from the rest of the natural world. In his intoxicated state, he could feel this disconnection, longing to dig his feet and hands into the dirt, to remember his place among the mycelial networks of the forests.

Boy mind would return periodically to the reptile, but every time something more entertaining happened, and his focus would wonder back to the immediate.

Their conversation meandered, briefly touching on psychobiology and mycology. Sophie shared ideas WJ must have told her, all more significant now than when she was sober. WJ's parents attributed at least part of early human mental development to the consumption of mushrooms. His parents also, unofficially, believed mushrooms might have been responsible for the origins of art, and language, and that this co-origination was necessary, as art allowed us to record our language. She couldn't remember if it was his parents, or WJ himself who had told her mushrooms spores could float out of our atmosphere, into space, survive, float back through our atmosphere, land, and still grow. Boy was particularly impressed by this. He decided mushrooms must be messengers from the aliens.

"Which was why," he thought aloud, "Mushrooms changed our perception so much."

He had a vague recollection that his mom had told him a similar story when he was a kid, but all he could remember was that most of his mom's stories had been about a 'very special boy' the aliens had brought to the planet.

"Mushroom spores must have floated here from far-away planets with all kinds of genetic information, influencing terrestrial evolution."

Sophie loved this. She remembered from biology class that many of the Earth's ecosystems were connected through mycelial networks; these root systems acted like the subterranean brain for the ecosystem, interconnecting all the plants. She wondered about the way we cut the ground up by tilling it, and by putting roads through it, compacting topsoil.

"Could this damage to the topsoil actually be damaging the mycelial-neuro-network, damaging each ecosystem's ability to communicate with itself, and potentially others?" she asked Boy.

"Maybe that's the message these mushrooms were supposed to give us," Boy suggested.

"Yeah," Sophie responded, "and we are receiving the message so we can tell others. Are we the mushrooms messiahs? Or are the mushrooms our messiahs?" She looked at Boy, serious for a moment before realizing the absurdity. Seeing the silliness, and even more significantly, how seriously they had taken it, they were overtaken by a fit of laughter. In hysterics, enjoying the chaotic comfort of Boy's disheveled bed, they expressed gratitude for having each other. The warm glow of their evening eased into slumber, hints of dawn above the buildings outside Boy's window.

9

As summer approach the band started in the studio. Jimmy explained they had two weeks before the summer touring season. Though this was a push, they had the material, and The Gun on the boards, a dream Boy was still skeptical of.

The first day was fun, but Boy could tell Jimmy wasn't impressed. Jimmy told Boy not to worry about it, and to enjoy getting acquainted to the studio. At the end of the day, before they left, The Gun pulled everyone together and gave a little speech.

"So here's the deal fellas. I know today was kind of like getting used to everything, but I gotta be clear about how this is gonna work. This is a job. A capital 'j', job. It's ok to have fun when you're working, but, like any other job, it requires work! We're going to be spending most of our waking life for the next weeks in here. To hold this studio costs more per day than I care to think about. Not to mentions some value projects got pushed so that we can be in here right now. I'm not trying to stress you out, but I am trying to impress the significance of this time. No joke. So, tomorrow, we get to work." His tone wasn't harsh, but it was the honesty that can sting. Everyone except Boy and WJ looked down, like reprimanded children. WJ grinned mildly, while Boy glared with determination at Jimmy.

"Is that going to work for you fellas?" Jimmy said looking at Boy.

"We take this really seriously," Boy replied. Boy kept trying to read Jimmy, and was frustrated that there didn't seem to be anything hidden in his comments.

"We appreciate the opportunity," chimed Nico.

"Great. See you all bright and early tomorrow morning then." Jimmy started marking levels and cleaning up the board.

The band left, but Boy stuck around. "This is what they need to get in gear," he finally said.

"Oh, shit, I thought you left with everyone else," Jimmy said, startled.

"Yeah, I'm going now. I guess I just wanted you to know, I do take this seriously."

"I know Boy. That's why it's gonna work." Jimmy smiled at Boy.

10

The next two weeks were grueling. Many nights they never left the studio. Jimmy's perfectionism impressed Boy. The Gun often stayed working after everyone else left, editing, adding texture and dynamism to the day's recordings.

Things sounded clean. The songs were somehow better on playback than they were live in the studio. Boy had done some recording before, so this wasn't such a surprise, but the music was becoming something even more than he originally imagined. It was like seeing a piece of art take a life of its own. He was getting excited.

The last three days were the toughest and strangest days of the entire session. On the third to the last night the Gun had them all take what he called 'microdots', a synthesized mescaline. He put on the soundtrack to the movie Hair, and made the band listen as they came up. As the final song was playing, '…Let the sun shine, just let the sun shine in…', Jimmy told everyone to shut their eyes until the song was over. Before the song ended he turned off all the lights.

Jimmy had set up the studio so all the phantom lights on the equipment would also turn off. Without any lights, and no windows, the studio became pitch black. After the song was over The Gun let everyone sit there, in darkness, in the silence.

Boy was high, watching the darkness unfold. He thought he opened his eyes, but nothing came into view. He could hear everyone else breathing. He kept blinking, thinking his eyes must still be closed. It was the same for all of them, and the only one who knew what was going on was Jimmy, and the only one who wasn't nervous was WJ.

Before anyone spoke, The Gun pressed play. Their songs started playing through the studio monitors. No one really understood what was going on. They instinctively stayed quiet. They listened, their minds dilated from the mescaline, their attention focused. They had nothing but their own thoughts to distract them.

In their hallucinogenic states the music was more than amazing, it was beautiful, dynamic, inspirational; it was a pilgrimage. It was raw, and vulnerable to hear themselves played back, to hear their effort, their desires translated into sound. They all knew this was a cumulative moment in their lives. They listened, taken on a odyssey, more profound because it was a journey they had created.

Boy was consumed by the fractal patterns blossoming in his mind's eye. He was in awe of the way the geometric shapes interlocked, ever changing. It was what the projected artwork at raves were always attempting to emulate, only purer, simpler, more ornate, and vastly more beautiful. He remembered the end from Mobius' movie, Renegade (Blueberry). He was seeing the patterns of the music, the unfolding sound waves, going on forever now that they had been expressed, ever diminishing, ever present.

He thought of Sophie, of how much she would enjoy this. He wished she was there.

The music ended and the phantom lights came on, then the board lights, then the room lights. Everyone remained silent, still high. They blinked back into the room, WJ keeping his eyes closed, a broad smile across his face.

"What'd you hear?" Jimmy asked.

They slowly eased into a long discussion, dissecting the songs into atomic parts. Jimmy had already backed up the recordings. He handed over the controls and encouraged them to try anything they felt moved to with the songs. They went for it, adding intricacies, psychedelic subtleties to the music. Creativity was pouring out of them. They didn't even noticed at dawn passed outside.

After a late breakfast they decided to end the session. Jimmy encouraged them to go home and get at least a few hours of good rest. They agreed to meet back up that evening to engaged the arduous task of siphoning through everything they'd done, to see if any of it was worth keeping.

When they came back together Jimmy explained, "Last night was so you fellows could get fresh perspective on the music. It worked, but the work isn't over."

They spent that next night, and all of the following, honing, refining, and detailing the songs. It was mostly Boy and The Gun detailing automation and perfecting the sound. Everyone else waited until they were asked to replay a line, try something new, or add something different to a track. They were all exhausted and getting grumpy. Boy and the Gun sent them home so that they could keep at it, uninterrupted.

The time was coming to an end and Boy turned to Jimmy, "How do we know when it's done?"

"When does the sunset up?"

Boy was confused, thinking at first the clear answer was when the sun has passed the horizon, but then he got it. The colors keep changing, the night begins, but the end of the sunset is when ever you deem it done.

Boy took a deep breath, anxious.

He nodded to Jimmy. They'd finished.

Instead of feeling relieved, Boy felt sick. The Gun assured him this was normal. Jimmy assured him, in the 23 years he'd been working as a producer and studio engineer, music of this caliber was exceedingly rare to be a part of.

They gave it one last listen, agreed it was time to put it down, and sent it off for mastering.

It was one of the most exhilarating, frustrating, and frightening moments of Boy's life. It was exhilarating because it was a dream coming true; frustrating, because he knew it could be better; and frightening, because there was no way to know how it would be received.

The Gun smiled, seeing, knowing, the complexity of what Boy was going through. "You did good, kid." It was the best thing anyone could have said.

11

The mastered version came a week later, a demonstration of what someone with Jimmy's cloud can get done. The Gun called them into his listening suite, decked out in the cleanest sound gear that had been made, along with a replica of a crappie car stereo that Jimmy insisted everything be tested on, 'in order to know what most people would hear'.

They were proud, even Boy. The album was fun, more pop than Boy originally imagined, but even Boy acknowledged that this made it more listenable. Boy resisted his excitement.

Sophie had come along to the listening party, and was notably stunned. She admitted to Boy that it was way better than she had expected, something he shouldn't take offense to, as she'd expected a lot from him.

Jimmy explained that the next step was promotion, and suggested touring. He'd already sent copies of the single out to the European summer festival circuit, and booked them a release show at Webster Hall. Their debut performance, only two weeks.

They were exuberant, except for Boy, who couldn't help but feel there was something off about how quickly everything was happening.

Sophie saw his trepidation. "What's your deal, Boy?" she asked, confused. "Isn't this your dream?"

"Yeah, I guess. I just have this feeling my mom still has something to do with it, that's all." Anxiety was pushing in on him.

"Are you fucking crazy," she replied, half laughing. "Did you hear the music? That was you, Boy. You made that, not your mom. Let it go." She playfully hit him in the arm.

"Okay," he said, trying to shake his mood.

12

The next day, as Boy walked the streets of lower Manhattan, hoping the size of the surrounding buildings would help temper his anxiety and excitement, Nico called him in hysterics.

"We're on the fucking radio!" Nico sounded like he might cry.

"What?" Boy asked in disbelief.

"Are you near a radio?"

Boy opened his radio app, which was tuned to 92.3, and there, through the tiny speakers on his phone, was his voice.

"I can't believe they're already playing us on

92.3," Boy said.

"92.3? I'm listening to 104.3. Wait."

Nico spun his dial. They were on both stations.

"Holy shit!" he exclaimed to Boy. "We're blowing up. Is this really happening?"

"I guess so," Boy responded incredulous.

They listened for a moment longer before Nico had to go. Boy was so dizzy he sat down. It was actually happening, and it didn't feel anything like Boy expected. He closed his eyes, took a deep breath, and continued his walk, gazing up at the sky scrapers, trying to remind himself he was tiny, trying to not let his idea that this was all his mom, or even more that maybe this was actually him, turned into an insurmountable anxiety. *What am I to the universe?* He reminded himself.

13

Before Boy knew it their single hit the charts. They were being aired, almost even over-played, everywhere. They got picked up for dates at 3 of the major European festivals, and would probably get more. The Gun wanted to set up a North American tour, stops in most major cities in the US, Canada, and Mexico.

It all happened at once. A sudden sunrise, a fade from the cold, dark, anonymity of a fameless night, to the bright, glimmering sunshine of the spotlight. They started playing TV shows, touring like crazy, being booked as far away as Moscow. There were interviews, red carpets, invitations to fancy parties and exclusive clubs—they'd joined the awkward elite that was the rich and famous.

For Boy it wasn't much different, but for the rest

of the band (save WJ), it was the honeymoon period of a dream-come-true. Boy laughed at how unfazed WJ seemed, always present and yet always somehow a million miles away. Boy watched the glitter and glitz reflect in the dilated pupils of his band mates, half wishing he could be as captivated, and glad he wasn't feeling as swept away. He was glad Sophie seemed mostly unchanged, now the official photographer for the band. Boy noticed that he was starting to believe it himself, noticed that he was now being seen as 'Boy', and not just his mother's son. Even so, he often found himself holding his breath.

14

At one of the high-class, fame-laden, elitist parties that came with the band's success, Boy ran into Johnny T. It was an awkward exchange. Boy was used to people recognizing him, but surprised when really famous people were shocked or even excited upon introduction.

Boy had been talking with some rich hipsters, all trying to out-do each other with who had been first to find Fit To Burst, when he felt a tap on his shoulder.

A strangely familiar voice asked, "Boy?"

He turned. Johnny T. stood before him, looking confused, even taken aback. Or was it excited?

"Hey Johnny T.," Boy said, unsure of how to interact. Boy didn't believe they'd ever met, and yet, obviously, he knew who Johnny T. was. Boy found this part of meeting other famous people confusing. Some pretended to not know each other until after meeting, but obviously, often, there was at least already a knowing of names.

Boy was trying to play it cool, trying to be funny so as to cut a strange tension he couldn't quite place. "How's it goin'?" he continued.

"Uh, good," Johnny T. said. The strange actor appeared irrationally pleased to be having this interaction. "Do you remember me?" he asked.

"No," Boy said. "Have we met before?"

Johnny T. appeared to be scanning Boy for some form of recognition. After apparently not finding what he was looking for Johnny T. Offered, "Yeah, at a party a couple of months back. You were with your mom and your, uh, friend, Sar, no…Sophia?"

Boy narrowed his eyes. Johnny T. knew his mother. Boy figured that must be why the old actor was so acting so awkward.

Boy loved to freak out guys who had been with his mom. "Look. It's not weird if you slept with my mom, okay? You realize you're not the only one right?" He tried to laugh, but realized he was being an asshole when Johnny T. T. looked disappointed.

"Your mom and I dated, but that was a long time ago. I hadn't expected to talking about that." Johnny T. cracked a charming smile, Boy was impressed with his charisma.

Johnny T. continued, "I just wanted to say, you made the party much more entertaining. Your mom told me you were 'shrooming." Boy was stunned, why had his mom shared that with this guy?

Seeming to notice Boy's discomfort Johnny T. quickly added, "Honestly, I was pretty jealous." Seeing this ease Boy Johnny T.'s smile broadened. "I used to do crazy shit like that too, you know."

Wait a minute. Is Johnny T. really talking about doing mushrooms?

"You added some needed spice. After you and your girlfriend started laughing uncontrollably, and then were escorted out, the whole part subtly opened up. We all had something to focus on to take the tension and boredom out of that stagnant cesspool of wealthy mediocrity. Anyways, look, I just wanted to say thank you, and congratulations. The album's great. I'm sure your mom's proud."

It was clear that Johnny T. had no idea that this was the last thing Boy wanted to hear. Boy had been enjoying that people were starting to think of him as his own being, not just a consequence of his mother.

"Thanks," Boy forced out.

What Boy didn't expect was that Johnny T. was a fairly sensitive guy, having gleaned a lot concerning how to read people's emotions from the self-reflective training his awkward religious experiences had offered him. Johnny T. proceeded to shock Boy.

"Yeah, hey look, I'm sorry."

"Uh…For what?" asked Boy.

"I didn't mean to bring your mom into my compliment. That must really piss you off."

Boy looked at him with a mixture of surprise and appreciation.

"It's cool." This guy may have been able to peg him, but Boy wasn't about to open up.

"Really, all I meant is you did a great job kid. Keep up the awesome work. Oh, and, if you're ever in L.A. give me a buzz." Johnny T. patted and squeezed Boy's shoulder, then reenter the tumult of the party.

"Thanks. Uh, it was nice to meet you," Boy called out as the man walk away. There was something about Johnny T. simultaneously familiar, yet robotic, even hollow, a distance Boy couldn't place.

15

In the maelstrom of their sudden rise to international acclaim almost everything became a blur of similar moments, despite the exotic nature of each location. Press junkets, festivals, and clubs, in what quickly became Sisyphusian repetition. Not that the ride wasn't exciting, just nothing much stood out, until Moscow.

Russia had always intrigued Boy, and its capital city in particular. Accordingly he had decided to arrive a day before their schedule show. After dropping his bags at the hotel, and dawning a thick parka that had been laid out on his bed for him, he headed out to see what he could find. Despite having been advised to not go out alone, he opted for a solo adventure, figuring the advice merely typical city phobia. Having grown up in Manhattan, he let his hubris lead.

His city had become safe, but Boy knew the craziness New York had been. Despite his own mugging, and his acute awareness that it's much easier to be in the wrong place at the right time in a big city, Boy figured his street smarts would keep him safe.

Moscow was just confusing enough. Not long into his meander he ended up wandering down a relatively deserted street. A shady looking fellow turned the corner ahead of him and started walking in Boy's direction, staring directly at him. Boy didn't want to seem intimidated, or weak. He nodded his head and didn't avert his gaze. The man continued his swift pace directly towards Boy, also maintaining eye contact.

Boy's mind flashed to when he was ten, and his childhood mugging. He tried to shake the thought from his mind and keep an un-intimidated demeanor. As the man continued to approach Boy started wondering what his next move would have to be, when the fellow averted his eyes, looked down, and abruptly crossed the street. Only mildly shaken, Boy smirked to himself, thinking his confident stride and unbroken eye contact had worked.

In the moments that followed, as Boy continued his walk, his mind rehearsed the sudden shift in the man's behavior. He heard footsteps echoing off the buildings, and felt like there were more than would account for him and the man. Boy turned to see if there was anyone else that might have cause the man to cross the street. He was startled to see another man, not far behind him. His heart raced a moment, but then, to his relief he recognized this new fellow was wearing a uniform.

Seeing it was a police officer Boy sighed in relief. This was one time when being followed by the cops actually felt like a blessing. Boy wondered if the officer had been assigned to follow him. Boy's mind raced through stories of Russia assigning tales on any Americans in the country, a perpetual paranoia that any American was likely a spy. Boy realized the cop was unabashedly looking right at him, so he smiled and nodded politely. The officer called something at him in Russian.

Boy didn't understand, so he stopped and said, "Sorry, I don't speak Russian." The man continued a swift approach. Just as he arrived next to him Boy asked, "Do you speak English?"

"No," replied the officer, swiftly slamming Boy against the wall with his forearm.

Startled Boy stammered, "What the fuck?"

"No," repeated the cop as he patted Boy down, forcefully removing Boy's wallet from his jeans, pocketing it, and staring angrily into Boy's eyes the entire time. He snarled, spit at the ground near Boy's feet, knocked Boy to the ground, and walked away briskly.

What the fuck just happened?

The most violated and vulnerable Boy had ever felt was when he was mugged as a kid. This was worse. He had no idea how to process what the lack of safety he was feeling in this moment. He wasn't so naïve as to believe that just because someone was a police officer that meant they were good. But to be so brazenly attacked in broad daylight, in the middle of a major city, was a starker reminder of his privileged bubble than Boy had perhaps ever had to grapple with. He was double shaken by his wish that his mom was there, recognizing that some part of him believed she would know what to do. His independence felt shaken.

His fear became anger. He tried to find relief in the knowledge that, at least in America the police aren't so blatantly corrupt. He sought cognitive solace, slumped on the ground. A minute or so later he heard a loud, horrifying yell from the direction the officer had gone. He bolted up and started running. He ran blindly back in the direction of the hotel until at last he found it.

Once he had entered the lobby he stopped to catch his breath, noting the confused looks of the hotel attendants. Despite his exhaustion, and despite being back at the hotel, he still didn't feel safe. He hoped the police of his hotel room might give him respite from his panic.

When he got to the room he found Nico and WJ, drunk. They watched him enter, and though inebriated, they noticed his breathless state, and the tears pressing under his eye. Nico asked, "What's going on Boy?"

"Fuck," Boy said, clenching his jaw and trying to hold back tears. He hated that he felt so fragile.

"What?" Nico asked.

"A cop just bashed me against a building and stole my wallet!" Hearing the absurdity of his words helped to ease Boy's anxiety.

"No way," WJ offered, amused. "That's awesome!" Despite how incongruent WJ's response felt, it helped Boy relax.

"What'd ya do?" Nico continued, punctuating the statement with a loud hiccup.

"Nothing. What do you mean? I didn't do anything!" Boy tried not get angry, recognizing Nico's intoxicated state as Nico shook his head in an attempt to focus his vision.

"No, I meant what do you do now?" It was hard to tell if Nico was tracking the conversation.

"There's nothing to do. It was a fucking cop." Boy wasn't sure if it was worth even trying to attempt a cogent conversation with his friends in this state.

"Why not?" Nico asked, pulling his head back and looking down at his hands, clearly not remembering what they were talking about.

"It was a fucking cop--who the hell would I report it to? The cops!?" Boy was talking mostly to himself, heart racing, blood rushing to his face. The distress from when he was ten flooded back into his body. He hated feeling vulnerable.

"It's all good," chirped WJ, who didn't seem

fazed by Boy's distress. "Did they take your passport?"

"Just my wallet." Boy wished he could be as unaffected as WJ.

"See, no big deal really. And now you have an awesome story to tell." WJ smiled, his ease was so genuine as to be contagious. "We've been in Moscow for hours, and you probably haven't even tried 'true Russki vodka' yet, have ya? Priorities my good man!" WJ held out a bottle with a paper label covered in Cyrillic.

Boy paused, but realizing the futility of the situation relented, grabbing the bottle from WJ's outstretched hand.

"Give me that shit," Boy said, hoping to escape into a swift dissociation.

The bottle was gone swiftly, a circumstance WJ was prepared for, producing another from his luggage. They drank and played cards in the hotel room. For fear of venturing back out, when the munchies from their otherwise empty stomachs arose they ordered room service: pelmeni, sirniki, and more vodka.

The distraction was invited, and after a while Boy's mind moved on to other, more drunken thoughts. He noticed that the wallpaper and trim in this room reminded him of that party with his mom and Sophie, the mushroom fiasco that Johnny T. had apparently be there to witness. This was the first time since meeting Johnny T. he'd thought about that strange psychedelic night. He pictured the reptilian looking creature he had seen, trying to parse if it was just a mushroom induced hallucination. He realized he'd never told anyone besides Sophie about it, and they hadn't discussed it since that time. In this uninhibited state he decided to tell his two similarly sloshed friends. They found the story quite entertaining, laughing at Boy's description of his antics amongst such a stuffy crowd. Boy enjoyed the humor of his reflection, feeling more convinced of it merely being an amusing psychedelic experience.

"Sounds like the Anunnaki to me," WJ offered after the laughter had died down.

"The what?" Nico asked.

"The secret society of reptiles that has controlled human society since at least as far back as the Sumerian empires," WJ answered, his broad smile never dampening. "You know, Ike's babies."

"Is this another of your conspiracy theories?" Nico asked.

"Not mine." WJ replied. "The conspiracy has been going on a lot longer than I've known about it."

Boy narrowed his eyes skeptically. He loved the way WJ discussed conspiracies. WJ was never heavy handed. In fact, he was never anything but jovial. Boy was curious about this reptilian conspiracy, but far too wasted for a serious engagement of the ideas. He started to form a question when WJ farted, disrupting the considered drunk silence. "Damn pelmenis," WJ announced, waving frantically to dissipate the unfortunate odor. They all fell to the ground laughing.

"Who cares about the evil reptiles ruling the world, your gas is going to kill us all," Nico blurted amongst the laughter.

The conversation refocused to whose turn it was in the card game, and if it was too dangerous to order more room service, the smell still lingering from WJ atomic explosion.

Boy's awareness decreased as the night wore

on, taking his anxiety with it. After some indiscernible amount of time the rest of the band showed arrived. They continued to drink, passing out watching some poorly dubbed American movies (*is that Johnny T.?*), endlessly comical in their inebriated states.

16

They were startled awake by loud banging on their door. When Boy peered though the peephole he saw two police detectives.

"It's the fucking cops," Boy hissed back at his groggy friends.

Everyone couldn't help but feel scared after Boy's mugging. The officers banged on the door again. Boy's anxiety started to rise.

WJ yawned and said, "Well, open it up and let's see what they're after."

Boy opened the door cautious, but trying to portray a sense of confidence. Something was different about this officer. They looked at Boy without malice.

"Are you Boy?" asked the taller of the two.

"Uh, yeah." The clear English caught Boy off guard. His confusion didn't help his mounting anxious. Mixed with his hangover, and his lack of sleep, it was enough to make him have to vomit. He turned and ran to the bathroom, and the cops barged in after him, as though they thought he was trying to make a run for it. He puked into the bathtub. The detective who had followed him chortled and turned in disgust.

"We will need you to come with us after you are done," said the officer, leaving the bathroom.

Boy didn't know what do. He was afraid to leave with the detectives, but didn't see any other choice. As he walked with the officer out of the bathroom and back towards to the door he glanced pleading towards his band-mates. With the exception of WJ, the fear on his friends' faces only exacerbated his anxiety. WJ merely smirked, shrugged, picked up an notepad and pen, and asking for the officer's names, which he wrote down.

Boy was grateful for WJ's capacity for clarity even in chaos. He hoped the officers would be more accountable knowing that there were other American's aware they were taking Boy.

They brought him into the hallway.

"We can do this the hard way, or you can just tell us what happened," the tall man said.

"What?" Boy asked.

"Is this your wallet?" He pulled Boy's wallet from his breast pocket.

"Yeah," Boy said, trying to evaluate the situation, confused. Did these cops want him to admit he'd been mugged? "The only reason I didn't report it is because I didn't know what to report, or to whom."

"So you're admitting you did it?" The men looked surprised.

Boy's forehead crinkled. "Did what? Got mugged? I don't see how that's something I did." Boy was starting to give attitude, and quickly realized it was probably not the best idea. He amended politely, careful not to level an accusation towards a police officer in case they'd take his side, "Where did you find my wallet?"

The men's faces relaxed. "In the breast pocket of a police officer's uniform?"

"The guy that mugged me?" Boy felt like he

was entering precarious territory.

"You claim he mugged you. What did you do to him in response during the altercation?" The officer asked.

"Do to him? After he left I ran back here as fast as I could." Boy was still trying to figure out where this conversation was going.

"After you killed him?" The other officer blurted angrily, the tall man looking irritably back at his compatriot.

"What!?" Boy felt sick again. "Kill the who? What the hell are you saying?"

Vertigo. Boy felt another wave of nausea crest.

"We found this wallet, which you admit is yours, on an officer who was brutally murdered yesterday. What we're asking is for you to tell us what you know about his death." The first officer offered, the second's anger sour with hatred as he glared at Boy. Boy was afraid the man might choke him.

The angry officer spoke in Russian, "I'm going to scare the hell out of this kid."

In English he growled, "We know it was you!"

"What was me?" Boy's face lost color, his eyes partially rolling back in his head from dizziness.

"You killed him, and your stupid country can't save you from what you have coming to you." The venom in the second officer's voice stung almost as much as the accusation. "You already admitted to it. This conversation is recorded. There's no way out. You might as well come clean." The first officer looked away, impatient with his partner.

"Admitted to what?" Boy's stomach dropped.

"We have the CTV footage. You resisted arrest and fell to the ground, which we saw. Then you both disappear from view of the camera and we find his body brutally disgorged. We get it. You were pissed. Hell I would be too if my wallet was taken. But why rip out his intestines?"

Boy lurched slightly. The detective realized Boy might puke.

"Why would I leave my wallet on someone I had just killed?" Boy asked, feeling completely lost.

"I don't pretend to understand the mind of a killer. You clearly did something to make him take your wallet in the first place?"

"That guy mugged me," Boy said, feeling indignant, but trying to control his tone. Boy's anger brought color back to his face.

The detective gave a quick, harsh laugh. "Now you're trying to tell us a Moscow police officer mugged you, and then, by chance, was murdered shortly after, and it wasn't you?"

"I don't know how long after he mugged he was murdered. I don't even know if he was murdered. All I know is, a police officer slammed me up against a wall yesterday, and took my wallet." Boy's hangover wasn't helping his ability to stay calm. He was loosing his patience.

"You're one of the real crazy ones aren't you. First you disembowel him, like angry reptile, then leave your wallet so you can flaunt your Americanness." He reached for his handcuffs. "Turn around and put your hands behind your back."

"Do you know who my mother is?" Boy blurted involuntarily, an automatic response to the insurmountable fear rising inside of him.

The detective looked at him sternly, then smiled. He tossed the wallet at Boy, laughing maliciously. "It was joke, kid. You should see your proud little American face." He pointed at Boy snickering. "Do you know who my mommy is?" He mocked to the taller officer, busting into roaring laughter.

The first officer forced a smile, un-amused by the antics of his partner. "An officer really was killed yesterday afternoon. If you do know anything let us know, but we figured you wouldn't. Check and make sure everything is still there in your wallet."

Boy was about to explode, and the taller could tell.

"Just a joke kid, let it go." The kinder officer gave a look that implied pushing it wouldn't take Boy anywhere he wanted to go.

"Can. I. Go. Now?" asked Boy in short punctuated syllables through his locked teeth.

"Aren't you going to check your wallet," taunted the second officer.

Boy's lip curled as he quickly opened and glanced through the contents of his wallet. "All there," he forced.

The first officer handed him a card. "If you think of anything else that might help us, you…"

"Or your mommy…" The second officer interjected, scoffing.

The first officer continued ignoring his partner's antics. "…can reach us at the number or email on this card."

Begrudging, Boy accepted the business card before turning to head back into the room.

Boy tried not to focus on the second cop's laughter as they sauntered away down the hall.

He reentered the room, the rest of the band huddled nervously around WJ, who seemed to be describing plans of some kind.

"What the hell was that about?" asked Nico.

"My wallet. The cop who mugged me was

found dead." Boy was exhausted. He fell backwards onto one of the beds.

His friends waited silently for more information. not wanting to push him.

Boy's mind flashed to the harsh scream he'd heard, sensing it would be smart to never going to tell anyone about it. He remembered a similar scream the day he had been mugged in New York when he was 10, forgotten, repressed until then. His mind spun. He calmed himself down, considered his compromised physiological state and recognized it would probably only take him to bad places.

"The guy who mugged you is dead? That's some crazy shit," said Kevin, finally breaking the silence.

"I'm never coming back to this fucking place," Boy exclaimed.

"Why would you?" Nico asked.

Boy couldn't imagine ever returning. He never wanted to feel this powerless ever again.

"I always wanted to do the Trans-Siberian Railway," WJ added as if nothing negative had just happened.

"Shut the fuck up WJ," Nico said, concerned for Boy's sensitive state.

"It's okay, Nico," Boy said, actually appreciating WJ's levity. "I had the same dream, WJ." Boy took a deep breath. "I need to just lay here a while guys," he ventured.

"Totally," Nico said looking around the room at the others to confirm that they too would be quiet. "Let's all just chill."

Boy wished he could get a little more sleep. He reeled internally at the embarrassment of having turned to his mom to try to get out of a bind. Was he still just the weak little kid he'd been when he was

10, unable to protect himself in the world? Despite the wild success of Fit to Burst, he wasn't enough on his own, he needed to invoke his mother when he perceived a threat. He wasn't autonomous, he was still just his mother's child, still a hidden figure lost in her shadow. He noticed his mind returning to the officer's description of the dead man's guts being pulled out as if by a reptile. *Who would do such a thing?* There were no reptiles in Moscow, at least not big enough to inflict that kind of damage, and not running wild in the streets. His flashed to the strange hallucination he'd had on shrooms at the party with his mom and Sophie. Thinking of Sophie brought tears to his eyes. *What the hell is going on?* Maybe this is just a hangover, Boy tried to convince himself. *Just breath.*

That evening's performance Boy gathered all the enthusiasm he could conjure, trying to bring himself present. He noticed, however, that something was changing. Despite his best attempts, he couldn't shake the experiences of the previous days. He started to fear that this was a turning point in his arch as a performer. He worried that the wave of enthusiasm he had been riding would never return. He worried that the luster of this illustrious career was showing itself a veneer on a poorly made particleboard of fantasy. He wasn't sure what he needed to realign, but he knew the something that was off would stick if he didn't address it quickly.

17

After getting home Boy was so glad to be off the road. He allowed himself to mostly sleep for the first couple of days, much of his waking time spent with Sophie. He was shocked at how little he shared with Sophie about what he was going through internally. He would usually open up, but something felt locked. He gave her the details, but tried to present as though nothing was that big of a deal. He told Sophie about meeting other musicians, what it was like playing to huge crowds, the parties, the receptions, the press junkets, the brightness of which now seemed overshadowed by the reminder of his fragility. He had a hard time focusing on all the positive details of the tour because of how ever-present Moscow was in his mind.

Upon returning to NYC he received an official letter of apology for any psychological or physical discomfort he may have experienced in Russia. It was on governmental letterhead, signed V.P., punctuated with the statement, "if there is any way we can make your next trip to Russia easier, please let us know." The note left Boy sure that either the officers that had messed with him had looked up his mom when they returned to the office, or his mother had found out about what had happened and reached out to Putin herself to demand this apology. Either way Boy felt the burn of shame.

Eventually Sophie asked, "You okay?" She was genuinely concerned.

Boy's first impulse was to keep up the front, to say he was fine. He paused, realizing if he didn't share what he was feeling with Sophie, he wouldn't share it with anyone, and it would become a hidden festering wound. He took a deep breath and recounted his experience.

She listened intently, with horror and compassion.

"That sounds so fucked Boy." The care in her

eyes lifted something in Boy.

After a moment she continued, "At least it sparked some realizations about vulnerability and need for control." She immediately worried this was too much.

Boy started to sink back into himself and sat quietly a minute. He knew she was right.

"I guess," he finally said.

Noticing his discomfort she tried to change the subject.

"How does it feel to have become the rock star you dreamed of being?" she asked, smiling.

Thinking she was trying to get him to see that his dreams were delusions he asked, "What? Being so out of control?"

"No silly. To have made it?"

"Oh. Right, that... Have I made it?" he knew he was being a bit of a jerk, but was struggling to pull himself out of self-loathing.

"No, I guess not. You're totally not a household name or anything. Have you been reading any of the articles about you? 'The Man, Boy'." She made a dramatic sweep with her hands, pretending to see it on a huge billboard or banner. "Some people are even calling you the next bright face of rock 'n' roll." She glanced, playfully mocking.

"Shut up Sophie. You're so full of shit." He pushed backed, noting a crack in the grumpiness.

"You're kind of a big deal." She pretended to be in awe of him.

"Who me? I'm just an artist pursuing his art," he mocked back, feigning arrogant modesty.

"You're so trite." She was glad to see color returning to his almost impenetrable ennui.

"Well you're hackneyed," he smirked, so glad she knew how to break him.

He felt how important Sophie was to him.

"You look super fucking tired," she offered returning to tender sincerity. "Take a nap, I'll go get us some grub."

"You're a rock star," Boy offered rolling back into his covers.

"I'm pretty sure you're the rock star now Boy." She got up to leave, laughing at this internationally acclaimed musician curled up in his blankets, cuddling his teddy bear.

18

When Sophie returned with food she suggested they watch, The Festival Express, as Boy had just finished his first big tour. She told him it was time to compare and contrast his experience with the work of the first real rock stars.

They watched enthralled by the beauty of those early rockers. They particularly fell in love with Janis, her long lyrical rants between songs, her perpetual smile, and her resilience in the face of perpetual partying. Boy took mental notes. They were in awe of the amazing train ride, how the bands engaged with each other, the incredible time that had been had (or was at least portrayed through the editing).

Boy had a harebrained scheme start to percolate, the kind of idea that was likely to only be born of deep privilege and youthful naivety. The card from 'V.P.' had said Russia owed him one. He imagined into what that 'one' might be. What if he got a group of the amazing bands together and they hired one of those Trans-Siberian trains? What if they made a modern 'Festival Express', but instead of

Canada, Siberia?

His trepidation about Russia flooded him. He knew it would be the trip of a lifetime, but his anxiety started flooding his mind with all the negative potentials it could muster. These thoughts cascaded, an avalanche. Finally he realized being afraid to go back was giving away the very control he was afraid of losing. It became something he had to do, something he had to prove to himself, and this time he would take precautions.

He proposed the preposterous idea to Sophie, asking her to be the official photographer. Sophie was surprisingly on board. Not only did she love the idea, she thought they ought to take it one step further. There were few places they could stop to perform in order to pay for the trip. To fund it they'd make it a whole show, with cameras in certain cars twenty-four hours a day. Why just a movie when they could make a mini-series?

Boy's excitement started to escalate. He imagined a star performance for each stop, each episode. He imagined a train car that would unfold into a stage, sound equipment pre-set, and even a light array, all plug and play. He imagined tying in local music from the areas they'd be going through, local guest appearances, who might give tours of the locations to juxtapose against the crazy, 'rock star' party life aboard the train.

Sophie suggested Boy call The Gun and get him involved, while the wave of Boy and Fit To Burst's fame was still on the up swell.

Jimmy thought it a decent idea, and told Boy to figure out funding and sponsorship, suggesting Boy's mom as a resource in this department. Clenching his jaw and biting his tongue, Boy thanked Jimmy and got off the phone.

Seeing his mood shift, Sophie asked, "What's up Boy?"

"Nothing."

"Did he shoot you down?" Sophie asked, amused by the pun, trying to lighten the mood.

"No. He thought it was a good enough idea."

"Well, then what's your trip?" asked Sophie.

"He said to recruit sponsorship, and suggested going to my mom." Saying this out loud highlighted how silly and petty he was being, which didn't help his mood.

She gave him a playfully disapproving look. "Seriously? You have to think about how much fun this would be, and let it go. Your mom could totally help us get the backing necessary to make this thing happen. In fact, if we added a fashion element it might even sell better."

"Goddamn it, No! The whole reason I chose music was to do something authentic. Being surrounded by the fashion world made everything seem fucking fake."

Sophie was hurt by his outburst. He backed off.

"Look, you're right in one way. My mom could help us with funding, but I don't want to bring the fake fashion shit into this project. Isn't that reasonable?" He knew he was being an over-privileged ass. He didn't know how to help it.

"You don't have to be a dick about it," Sophie responded.

He looked at her and smiled. "You're right Sophie, I'm a spoiled bitch."

"Don't denigrate bitches by claiming to be one." She hated how easily he won her over, but knew there was no reason to fight it. "And, yes. I will help you write a proposal and build a deck."

They spent the rest of the night outlining their

vision, making it as professional as possible. They had so much fun it subverted some of the pressure of needing it to happen. They decided to present it to his mom the following day. Sophie was glad to see Boy opening to experience something other than distain for his mom. Watching his excitement and softening toward the powerhouse his mother was gave Sophie a glimmer of hope that Boy might someday be able to hear the uncomfortable truth she tried her best to keep hidden.

19

The next morning Boy felt a mixture of excitement and apprehension. They'd been up until nearly four working on the proposal. Everything looked professional and in order, but Boy was never sure of anything with his mom.

Boy had gotten less than 2 hours sleep, his mind racing with possibility and concern. After the light woke him he watched Sophie sleep, wondering if he ought to wake her as well. He knew he wouldn't be able to milk anymore REM out of the morning. Sophie was still asleep when he finally, quietly left the room.

It was Sunday. Nevertheless, his mom would be in her office. As he wandered down the hall he wondered why he hadn't moved out yet. He tried to imagine when he'd leave, and where he'd go. He was rich enough to afford wherever he wanted. He imagined a villa in southern France; a cabin in the redwoods of northern California; a penthouse looking out over Central Park.

Suddenly he was at the door to his mother's office. He stalled. He wasn't surprised, but a little disappointed at his hesitation. He hated that he was flooded with doubt.

What's wrong with me? He thought. When am I going to learn how to be confident with my mom? And why do I care what she thinks anyway?

He never felt comfortable bringing her anything that wasn't the absolute best he could do, which meant he never brought her anything. This was the first idea he was going to pitch to her, and suddenly he felt certain she would think it was foolish. He had been there countless times when she had crushed other people's ideas, some of which he knew were good.

He heard a strange noise down the hall, the 'vvvpp' of a zipper being zipped.

"Boy?"

His mom was in a state he'd never seen her in. She was in a long, black, silk nightgown. The skin on her face sagged, though it tautened as she spoke. Yet her hair was perfect, even now, first thing the morning. He was trying to understand where the sound he'd heard had come from, as nothing in her attire requiring a zipper.

"Why are you standing, staring blankly at my door, at six o'clock in the morning?" Her voice as cool and collected as ever. She squinted as she looked at the proposal in his hands.

He thought to shove it into his pocket, but it was too late.

"What is that?"

"Uh," he said.

"Boy, I did not send you to elocution lessons for you to merely enunciate the inarticulate and unintelligent utterance, 'uh'." She shrugged, giving up on something. She walked towards him, asking, "What is in your hand?" She wasn't upset, in fact her demeanor hadn't change at all.

"It's an outline for a show," he said, faking a courage he hoped to portray, though he knew he wouldn't have entered her room to talk if she hadn't caught him in the hallway. But now, pitch deck in hand, he leaned into circumstance.

"That's better than, 'uh', but if this is a pitch… I'm sure you and your girlfriend didn't get to sleep before four." He felt her gaze scan him for dejection. He held his posture.

She continued, "I find it admirable you are outside my door so early in the morning." Despite himself, he could feel his chest swell at her compliment.

"I'm not going to treat you any different than anyone else making a pitch. You're going to have to do considerably better if you even want to make it into my office. Have more confidence, Boy. Convince me that if I don't buy your pitch my life will be a life of missed opportunities and regrets." She looked past him towards the door, "And hurry it up. I'm thirsty."

"Okay. Here's the deal. We've had a great idea for a mini series staring me, my band, a bunch of the other bands we met on tour, and a group of your models…" What did I just say? Shit, I'm already pandering to her.

"And?" She started to move passed him towards the door.

"Let me finish. Are you familiar with the music documentary called, 'Festival Express'?" He was gathering confidence. Her hard manner, and unabashed self-assuredness was rubbing off on him.

"Of course, darling. I was there when they shot it." She moved past, leaving the door open behind her. "You have my attention. Close the door."

Confused, he followed her. "You were there when they shot it?"

"I was on the train. The whole thing was my idea, but don't tell Janis that."

Boy couldn't believe his ears.

"You were there? On the Festival Express?" He tried to stay calm. "Why didn't you ever tell me?"

"Why would I? There are far more things I haven't told you about, than I have Boy. That's the nature of being older than someone. How am I supposed to know what would be interesting to you?"

She took a long pull from her ornate ceramic mug. Boy remembered looking at it as he and Sophie came up on mushrooms. It had never looked the same since.

"So…" She hadn't taken her eyes off his as she drank, hadn't even blinked. Why is she always so intimidating?

"Uh," he caught himself. "Uh-of course. So, since you are familiar with the 'Festival Express', our idea is a modern version. Crossing the Trans-Siberian, instead of Canada. A mini-series instead of a single movie. A cross over reality TV experience, music and travel documentary, art-film."

He pulled the proposal out of his pocket and handed it to her.

"Hmm," she said, "I don't see anything about my models here."

Damn, he thought. "Yeah, I said that, but--"

"Well, I'll get you backers if you take models," she cut him off. "Just add it and have this back to me by noon." She handed back the proposal, drank from her mug, picked up a paper from her desk, and started reading.

"Wait," he said, suddenly feeling this had all been too easy.

"Wait what? Look, Boy, if you weren't my son you wouldn't question me if I had just told you I would find you backing for your project. You'd be running away as fast as possible to make revisions, hoping to keep my support." She didn't raise her head. She exuded the energy of a snake coiled, anticipating a strike.

"But..." he stammered.

"I don't mean to be harsh, Boy. I just don't want to pamper you, so you can do things in the industry for yourself, without me, that's all."

He decided to heed her advice. Adding nothing more, he turned and promptly left, gently closing her door behind him, her eyes still fixed on the papers she'd picked up.

His thoughts raced as his scampered down the hall and back to his room. He entered quietly, Sophie still asleep. He wanted desperately to wake her, but decided to lie down for a few minutes instead, trying to digest what had just happened. He wished it was different, but his mom continued to intimidate the crap out of him. This is really going to happen! He imagined the train, the bands, the reaction of his band mates, the adventure that was about to ensue. He went over what had just happened, confused by his mom quick agreement. He wondered if it was because she was in a good mood first thing in the morning. He pictured her approaching him in the hall. *What the hell was that zipper sound?*

20

It was jolting when his mom woke him two hours later.

"I see you're working hard on that revision I asked you for," she boomed.

He squinted through reluctant eyelids at her, startled and confused.

"It'll have to wait. Wake up your girlfriend. You're both coming with me." She was matter-of-fact, as always, in a hurry.

"She's not my--"

"Shut up, Boy…" His mom and Sophie said at the same time, Sophie flustered, his mom simply stern. They looked at each other, and Boy saw an unspoken understanding exchanged that he didn't have time to process.

"Get dressed. We have to leave five minutes ago."

As he opened his mouth his mother preempted him, "You're coming to a party. People likely to back your film, and I wont do the work for you. If you're serious, get up. Let's go."

This was his mom's way of being supportive, and though she showed no signs, he thought she seemed excited about the project, excited he was getting behind something.

"Come Sophia. We'll find you something worth wearing. I trust you can manage yourself, Boy?" She gave him a slightly disapproving look as he stumbled around the end of his bed and through the mess of clothes cluttering his floor.

"Ok, mother," he said, surprised at the sharpness of his tone.

Sophie left with his mom and he donned a vintage, black. YSL suit, a thin tie, and put just enough product in his hair to make it look like he wasn't trying.

He hurried to the kitchen and made an espresso, which he slurped down too hot as his mom and Sophie arrived. Sophie's glasses were off, and she was wearing a dress he was guessing his mom had just been shooting with her models. He was so shocked by Sophie's beauty he didn't notice forgot about the burn from the scolding coffee in his mouth. When the burn finally registered he spit the freshly-pulled, smoldering liquid back into its tiny cup, spattering his white under shirt.

"What the hell was that all about?" asked Sophie, hoping to embarrass him.

"Too hot," Boy said, realizing the double truth and becoming sheepish.

"Go change your shirt, Boy, we have to leave," his mom requested.

He ran back to his room and swapped out his clothes.

Sophie had made him another coffee. Handing it to him she mocked, "Do you need me to put an ice cube in it so you don't burn yourself, little guy?"

"Shut up," he replied, "and thank you."

"Shall we?" his mom asked, moving towards the elevator.

Sophie gave him a coy look as they left the kitchen.

She knew she looked good, so he said, "What? I'm just not used to you letting yourself get all dolled up."

"You think I'm pretty," she said, smiling big. "Admit it."

"Whatever," he said, as immature as a middle-school student stealing someone's backpack and throwing it over the fence to flirt. "You're always pretty, dip shit."

Boy's mom ignored them, focused on her

phone, but Boy knew she was listening. They exited the elevator, and moved toward the car waiting for them.

"Can you two children stop fighting and get in the car?" his mom asked, entering the back seat, leaving the door open for them to follow.

Sophie maintained her smirk as she clambered in after him.

Once under way, his mom coached them in how the ought to pitch, and who to pitch to. It was crucial they mention that her and The Gun were already backers, and to act like it was being offered as a privilege, not a need.

"Talk about it as though it was already happening, and offer to let them in, but never act like the project depends on them. Rich people are like any other mammals. They want be part of things that are better than them, and loathe anything that needs them. Never mention money. Simply tell people to reach out to the project's accountant team if they are interested."

Sophie looked at Boy, asking with a gesture if he knew who the accountant was?

As if reading their minds, Boy's mom continued, "While the two of you were sleeping in, I arranged the accountant. If anyone asks how much you're looking for, simply say, 'If you want in, just call Tom to work out the details.' And give them one of his cards." She handed Boy and Sophie a stack of business cards.

Tom's full name was Thomas Mortin, one of Boy's mom's project accountants ever since he could remember. Tom was a little stuffy, but had always come across to Boy as a generally good guy. Boy remembered the way his skin had a green undertone. When he'd mentioned this to his mom, she'd guessed Tom to be anemic, and told Boy she'd recommend iron supplements. Boy decided not to question using Tom, trusting his mom.

He realized he was no longer drinking coffee, and somehow, a glass of champagne was in his hand. "Do we have any orange juice in the car?"

"Are you listening to me?" his mom asked.

"Of course. I just would rather be drinking a mimosa, as it is still kind of breakfast for me."

A harsh silence followed. Why don't people believe you're listening unless you repeat them, Boy wondered to himself. He regurgitated his mom's thoughts back to her to reassure her he'd heard, setting the mood at ease as they arrived.

They dove into the swarming hoard prepared. Sophie and Boy schmoozed a wide variety of very wealthy people, pitching with perfection. Boy quickly felt exhausted, steeling Sophie away to the drink table.

"I don't know if it's worth it, Sophie." He refilled his mimosa glass, his fourth.

"If what's worth it?" She handed him her glass to refill.

"All this bullshit. When I was growing up my life was full of these parties. From my earliest memories I had to pretend to be someone I wasn't. The whole reason why I wanted to do music was to get away from this, was to be something where being 'me' was good, and encouraged."

He took a long dram from his drink. He didn't notice Sophie's mounting concern.

"I guess I just want to do something with my life where I can be honest. This isn't that."

Sophie's eyes bulged. She was trying to warn him with her looks but it was too late.

"You're taking it too seriously," came a

strangely familiar voice.

Boy turned to find Johnny T.

"I hear you're doing a show," Johnny T. said with a smug, yet charming smile.

"Word spreads fast." Boy tried to stay calm.

Johnny T. was far more sensitive than Boy had given him credit for. "Don't worry about voicing your disillusionment in front of me, I completely understand." His face was warm, understanding. "Oh, and just so we are all on the same page, I took your advice, and it is working out great."

Boy was thoroughly confused. "What advice?"

"You know how boring these parties are? You two were having so much fun last time, I decided to give it a go. Now I'm a fun-guy at the party." A devious grin curled into the corner of his mouth. "I gotta say, I don't know if I can ever go back. Did you two eat anything before coming today?"

Johnny T. was verging on maniacal. Had he just admitted to being on mushrooms? Boy looked at Sophie, who was smiling, flabbergasted.

"If you want any..." He produced a bag from his pocket, discretely showing them in the palm of his hand.

"Oh, and more importantly, I'm in." He grabbed Boy's mimosa, took a drink, and handed it back. "There is only one condition." He trailed off, staring blankly at Boy, carried off in an internal experience.

When it became obvious Johnny T. wouldn't be ending the silence of his own accord, Boy asked, "What's that?"

"What?" Johnny T. said, snapping upright and back into the room. "Oh, shit, sorry. Did you ever notice how similar our eyes are?" He kept his gaze locked on Boy, who suddenly felt self-conscious.

"Is that a condition?" Boy asked.

"Oh… The condition," he pointed a finger at Boy, and the finger moved slowly around in a spiral. "The condition is, I come along for the ride."

Boy thought this a strangely wonderful idea. He looked to Sophie for confirmation. She was still lost in disbelief at the whole scenario. He decided to play it cool. "We'll see what we can do."

"Did you forget how we started this conversation, Boy? If you don't want to bullshit, don't do it. Especially not when you don't have to. It would do us both a world of good if I came on the trip, so just say yes." He took Boy's drink again, finishing it, setting the empty glass on the table beside them. "I already talked to your mom, that's how I knew. She's fine with me coming along with the three of you."

Boy froze. Though he was looking at Johnny T. he felt Sophie tensed as well.

The three of us? My mom thinks she's going to come?

Again Johnny T. was more perceptive than Boy expected. Perhaps it was the mushrooms. He spoke right to Boy's feeling, "Oh shit, your mom just invited herself didn't she. That's so her."

Out of the corner of his eye, Boy saw Sophie's jaw drop.

"I'll talk to her and you take these." Johnny T. shoved the bag of mushrooms into Boy's pocket and walked away.

"What the fuck was that?" Sophie asked in disbelief.

"Johnny T."

"I know who it was. I was asking what it was. Since when do you know Johnny T., and since when does he know your mom?" She was incredulous.

"They maybe dated in the late seventies or something. I don't really know." He was being evasive.

"How the hell do you know him?"

"We met last summer. He was there when we lost our shit at that party, and I had you chasing the dinosaur with me, remember?"

"Yeah," she disregarded him. "When were you going to tell me you were buddies with good ol' Johnny T.?"

"We're not buddies." Hoping to change the topic, which was strangely uncomfortable for Boy, he said, "Why don't we get out of here and take these shrooms."

"Whatever." She looked at him sideways, admiration on her face, and noting how similar his eyes actually were to Johnny T.'s. "You're done pitching?"

Boy glanced around the room, evaluating. They'd talked to everyone he though was necessary. "We're good, let's jet."

With new glasses of champagne they headed for the exit.

At the door Johnny T. stopped them asking, "Are you coming to Atlantis later?"

"Atlantis?" Boy asked.

Johnny T.'s face contorted, as though he had divulged secret information.

"The club." Johnny T. tapped the side of his nose and winked. He seemed confused that Boy didn't know what he was talking about.

Boy wondered if Johnny T. was getting too high to be in public.

"Oh," Boy said, playing it off, "right. Yeah, uh…we'll see."

"Hmm. Well, check your mail for the invite, it's

must be there. It would be great to talk more about the show." Johnny T. took Sophie's drink this time, drinking it all before adding, "You should bring your girlfriend too." Raising Sophie's empty glass to her, in a cheers, "She's nice."

"Ok Johnny," Boy said, amused by Johnny T.'s antics.

Boy realized this was the first time he hadn't tried to correct someone for assuming Sophie was his girlfriend. She hadn't said anything either. Boy felt blood rush to his cheeks, so he moved towards the door.

"Have fun, Johnny," Boy said, Johnny T. smiling after them as they left.

21

Boy and Sophie were surprised with how quickly the funding came through. Boy was sure this was his mom's doing, Sophie reminding him to get over himself.

"Just because you were born with privilege doesn't mean it's wrong to use it, Boy. How much did you enjoy watching The Festival Express? And how many people will enjoy watching our new version?" Sophie implored.

"I know. I just hate it." Boy struggled with his perpetual tendency towards despondency.

"Not to mention," Sophie interrupted, "this is an opportunity to get a good message out to the world about the importance of free self-expression. And, You'll be performing free shows for some of the world's poorest people. How great is that?"

Sophie was right, but Boy struggled to not try to create some ulterior motive from which Sophie was offering her pep talk. He caught himself looking for proof that something was off, noticed his own resistance to his dreams coming true. His mom also told him not to be surprised by backing coming quickly. She had taught him how to play his cards, and he had followed her directions. He was a celebrity now, of his own right, which helped considerably. As the old adage suggested, the more money you have, the easier it becomes to get more. He looked at Sophie's subtly pleading gaze and decided to try to take in the moment.

Boy looked past Sophie at a huge stack of mail that had been amassing quicker these days. Nestled among the mass a shiny envelope caught his eye. He moved to the stack and pulled it out. It was covered in gold leaf, a faint indentation reading: Atlantis. Surrounding the word were three subtle dots, an implied triangle.

"What's that?" Sophie asked.

"Atlantis."

"Atlantis?" Boy's answer was clearly not clarifying enough for Sophie.

Why was this feeling familiar? After a moment's consideration, Boy remembered the strange interaction with Johnny T. as they were leaving the party.

"You going to open it, of just admire the gaudy envelope? Who coat's a letter in gold leaf?"

"Remember what Johnny T. talking about the other night?" Boy asked as he opened the letter to find a finely crafted invitation inside, paper soft to the touch, yet firm, that might tear into multiple layers if folded. The only word on the face of the card:

•

Atlantis

·   ·

Boy flipped the card over, where he found:

·

VIP

·   ·

"What the hell does that mean?" He handed the card to Sophie.

"Johnny T. seemed pretty into it." Sophie offered, flipping the card back and forth.

Boy's anxiety increased as Sophie looked over the card. "This seems pretentious. I'm a VIP at some club I've never even been to? What a cheesy card. Why was Johnny T. was so into it?" Boy wasn't even keeping track of the words as they came out of his mouth. He didn't want to admit it, but her was excited.

"Ok Boy," Sophie said, recognizing his fear of being seen as being into anything smacking of elitism.

"So glitterati, right?" he asked.

"Are you kidding?" She wasn't going to collude with his denial. "It sounds like an awesome experience. We gotta go. You can probably get a plus one, right? Johnny T. seemed to think so." If he wasn't going to admit his excitement she would.

"But I hate that kind of thing Soph. So do you, usually. It's gonna be a bunch of rich famous people trying to prove why they're 'VIP'. Another vapid cesspool of insecurity and wealth, an unfortunate combination of elements most often leading to depravity and depression."

Sophie looked at him funny. He was even shocked by how overdramatic he was being. They both chuckled.

"That's why you have to take me. It would be fun. We could take 2CB, or something entertaining, before we go, and just laugh at all the bullshit. If I took my camera we could get funny pics of you pretending to care about all these lame asses." Sophie's enthusiasm was infectious.

"You just want to have more famous people in your portfolio," Boy said, struggling to try maintain his bitter edge.

Though Boy was mostly joking, a little part of him wondered. He caught himself. Sophie had tons of pictures of him, of all the famous people she had come in contact with over the years, and she had never tried to do anything with them. He was pretty sure he was the only person she even ever showed them to. H liked the idea that they would laugh together at how seriously everyone took themselves. He recognized he was worried he might start to take himself seriously.

Before Sophie could respond Boy got a text from The Gun, 'Start packing'. He held his breath. Holy shit, it's happening. When he returned his attention to Sophie, she looked hurt.

"Oh, stop it Sophie, you know I was kidding. I love your photos, and you know it." His anxiety amplified, but this time the excitement was more pronounced.

Sophie was pouting, clearly suppressing a smile.

Despite the facade, her pleading eyes broke him. "Maybe we'll check the place out after we're back from our trip."

"What? That could be a year from now."

"Not so long. We have the funding. The Gun's

been working on a crew, and just texted, 'start packing'. Looks like they've already pulled a team together. Bands have been contacted and everyone's excited at the idea. It's not really touring season, and most musicians are down for any good party. Like my mom says, don't fight the tsunami, ride it. We're green-lit, baby!" he exclaimed.

Boy was expecting a bigger reaction, but Sophie merely looked stunned. He became self-conscious. Was this the first time he'd ever called her 'baby'? He worried that had thrown her off.

Sophie looked serious. Just as she was about to speak, Boy interrupted, "Let's go?"

Sophie shook her head confused. "What? Where? Atlantis?"

"No stupid," Boy tried his usual tactic of taking away the awkward moment by playfully jabbing. "We gotta collect the fellas. It's time to celebrate."

There was something Sophie had wanted to say, something she was holding back. Boy purposefully ignored the tension, beckoning her to get ready. He was glad this distracted her. He too recognized things unspoken between them, but was afraid naming it might make things complicated. They both let it go, choosing instead to venture out into the mayhem of Manhattan, and, with the rest of the crew, swim to the bottom of a bottle.

22

As the trip approached Boy maintained a goal of doing as much of the producing as he could. Boy reached out to various people he knew in the entertainment industry, worked to get as many recognizable and talented people on the project as he could. Not everyone was available, but there was always someone else who was ready to jump on board. Boy was relieved at people's enthusiasm, and part of him struggled to not turn towards the bitterness he could feel around privilege.

His humility came uncomfortably. He had been trying to pull strings in order to get the permits for Russia via the 'one favor Russia owed him'. He had reached out to the contact information on his apology letter from V.P. to no avail. His anxiety started to mount as, after all this work, he was now fearing that he might not be able to get permits.

He was so attached to the project that he knew the discomfort he would have to endure. He asked his mom for help. He saw no other way. He had asked Jimmy, who had directed him to his mom. He didn't want to ask anyone else on the project for fear that they too would suggest his mom's help, which would be even more humiliating. Sophie had no better ideas either, and even suggested that she thought it would be good for Boy to have to ask for the help he honestly needed.

Eventually Boy slithered out of his skin and walked cautiously into his mother's office. Unconsciously trying to hold onto some sense of agency he opened the door without knocking, something almost no one else in the world would dare do, a privilege he was blind to. His mom looked up, somehow un-startled. She was taking a drink from her mug. He was amused noticing that she was always finishing a drink when he entered. Her eyes fixed on him. He wondered if she knew what he was there for. He guessed she did. She set her mug down, folded her hands in front of her, maintained her unblinking gaze.

"Mom," he said.

"Yes, Boy?" she asked, monotonous, dominant, chilling.

"Okay, look. You know this is hard for me, so can we cut the bullshit?"

"What bullshit are you talking about Boy?" She was clear, not sarcastic, which was even more confronting.

Is she fucking with me? He couldn't tell if it was his ego, or if she was reveling in his obvious discomfort.

"I need your help mom." He fired at her, almost relieved, having released the cumbersome words. "I don't know how to secure the permits from Russia for our trip, let alone organize the train." He wanted to stare at his feet, but knew better and maintained eye contact with her.

"You're getting better at this." This time her non-emotional tone didn't bother him, it made him feel stronger. "So let's maintain our composure. I've already contacted V.P., secured our permits and the train, and had an itinerary written up by our experts over there."

Boy was floored, simultaneously angry and elated, though the latter was actually harder for him to allow.

"Before getting upset, realize this is an investment for me, too, so I was merely securing my assets, that's all."

His lips curled under despite himself.

"In fact," she continued, "I will walk you through everything I have done if you would like to see. Part of your education into the career you have chosen. In order to get fully financed, the trip will start in Shanghai, stop in Beijing, and Ulaan Bataar before we get to the actual Trans-Siberian railroad. It's called 'The Trans Mongolian Railroad'.

Shanghai and Beijing open up to some very important Chinese funding. Ulaan Bataar, because of your idealism about, 'free music for the poor', or however it is you're spinning this project as philanthropic."

He was flushed with indignation, but knew she would be expecting that from him, preparing herself to have to 'teach him a lesson about how things work'. He decided to not let her get the better of him. He wanted to shock her. He kept her eye contact and replied, "Great. What a relief. Thank you for your efforts mother. You can give me a full rundown later, I have a meeting with the lawyers to go over the artist contracts." He turned and left her office without waiting for a response.

He regretted his haste later, wishing he could have seen any signs of astonishment at his unexpected behavior. It was better he hadn't stayed. If he had, he would have witnessed the subtle look of a conquering parent reveling in the defeat of a rebellious offspring, and he would have missed the pride hidden beneath.

23

"Is that all there is?" Boy asked Sophie, "Compromise?"

"Come on Boy. Don't look at it that way." She didn't know how to reassure him because she couldn't deny his claim.

"How am I supposed to look at it? This has been my problem the whole time." Boy could feel indignation bubbling up in a desire for self-destructive behavior.

"Think about the great music and fun you're

bringing to people's lives, people who wouldn't otherwise get access to it." She was flailing.

"I just don't want to add to the din of buzzing refrigerator noise that entertainment has become." He was sick of his own melodrama, these bogus 'self-pity' episodes, and yet he couldn't figure out how to stop himself. "All of this is starting to look like more of the trite circus made by the media elite to reinforce blind obedient consumerism. Another piece of garbage, reinforcing social stereotypes, not the free access to art we dreamed of at the beginning."

"Not true, Boy. You're being a bit simplistic and hysterical. This project is worthwhile and you know it." She was also fed up with his entitled outbursts, but at a loss for how to combat them. "Let's get you packed." She smiled at him, but knew he could tell it was forced. "Which costumes are you bringing?"

"Their not costumes," Boy retorted, "These are nice vintage suites."

"Keep telling yourself that, it's all costumes and you know it." Sophie pinched Boy playfully.

Boy appreciated Sophie's attempts at cheering him up. Even though he could tell she was trying, he still wished he had someone he could talk to who might understand what he was going through. But he'd never felt connected to the rich kids he'd grown up with. He saw them as a group of over privileged twits, unfortunate and irreparably bent from extreme entitlement. He knew Sophie was being supportive. There were simply some ways she would never be able to empathize with him. He felt his problems were privileged problems, only existing in his awkward world of wealth, which only served to make him feel worse, another whiny privileged twerp.

He looked at Sophie's forced smile, her deep kindness, and was grateful a scholarship had brought her to him. She'd always been such a breath of fresh air. She was proof there was some good in the world, even if she couldn't understand his every struggle.

"It's ok Sophie, I know I'm just being a baby, you don't have to pretend." He wanted to relieve her from the pressure of saving him.

"Thank god. You are being a little gremlin." As he turned a scowl towards her she snapped a photo. After the initial shock they both laughed at the uncomfortable picture. "The true you shining through."

24

Boy's witnessed the inconsistency of his experience of time. *Had they been planning this trip for a year, or had it been a week? Was it still 2012? How had so much happened in such a short amount of time, and why did it also seem an eternity?*

Boy, like so many musicians he knew, had studied The Beetles like the perfect test study of what to aim for. Boy thought about how The Beetles had created all of that music in less than a decade, and how they had gone from unknown to worldwide pop stars in the blink of an eye. Boy could feel that kind of momentum pushing him forward, and laughed at the grandiosity he recognized in comparing himself to arguably the most important pop band of all time.

Boy also watched as he lost any real agency over the project. At the last minute Tokyo was added to the itinerary, even though Japan was in no way connected to the train. Both The Gun and his mom assured Boy Tokyo would be an important addition because of its economic significance, a huge boost to the proceeds of both the tour and the film. This was no longer his project, it had stopped being so when he brought his mom and The Gun in. He stopped arguing, it was futile.

Boy was informed Johnny T. would be joining the trip, making an appearance or two in the film, and the major performances. Boy was told that Johnny T. had gotten significant funding from his cultish religious organization, a group The Gun suggested Boy be vigilant to never get on the bad side of, as they had enough power to sway projects should they decide to, for better and ill.

Johnny T.'s cult left Boy uneasy, yet he was surprised at how glad he was to have Johnny T. along for the ride. He had enjoyed the strange interactions he had had with the strange actor, and was curious what antics he might bring to the table.

In a reflective moment Boy realized how any disappointment he might have historically felt around loosing control over the project was overshadowed by an excitement at how everything was coming together. While some part of him struggling with the sense that he wasn't the one steering the ship, he also noticed how much more peaceful things felt when he was able to go with the flow. He wished he could capture this feeling and never loose it, and yet he knew it would disappear again.

25

The crew for the project, who were from all over the world, were to meet in Tokyo, in the upper lobby of the Park Hyatt. The logistics team had arranged everyone's flights to and transportation from the Haneda Airport. Boy, having arrived a day early, watched one anxiety subsided and another emerged as everyone arrived, on time, to the upper dinning room. The view out over Shinjuku Gyoen, and the densely packed central part of Tokyo, felt simultaneously eerily serine while also bustling to the brim. The dinning room had been exclusively reserved for an orientation of the film's core crew and talent.

Filming had started with Boy, Fit to Burst, and the NYC crew's journey, but this night was the official beginning of the project. It was the first time all the major players involved would be together. Boy hadn't thought about how this many strong personalities in the same space would effect the evening. He knew people would be more comfortable getting to know each other without cameras but recognized that the discomfort of being filmed was inevitable, and might as well start.

Boy was only mildly put off when he noticed the wait staff were a collection of his mom's models, delivering the food as though walking down a runway, very aware of the cameras while pretending not to be.

The staff at the Hyatt had set up a screen and a projector in the room, which was playing the original Festival Express. Boy hoped this would help everyone get in the mood for the adventure they were about to embark on. In this spirit he also decided to try The Gun's method, spiking the champagne with a small amount of LSD, to bring everyone more into the experience. As he was coming up Boy decided to make an impromptu speech.

He tapped his glass, half yelling, "Can I have everyone's attention for a minute?"

The chatter in the room stumbled into quiet, the crowd turning to look at him.

"First, I'd like to thank you all for hoping on board what I hope to be a wild ride. When Sophie and I came up with this idea it seemed harebrained. It still does, but here we are." A gentle and encouraging laugh rolled through the room. "It means the world to me, to us, that you're all here. So, thank you. Second, I would like to let you know, while this is work, this is also about having the best time of our lives, and making beautiful art while we do so. Lights please."

As though it were planned, as though someone were watching Boy's every move and anticipating what he might want, the room lights faded and the screen became the focal point. In his mounting psychedelic state Boy didn't question the ease with which this transition was happening.

"May I present the inspiration for this project, The Festival Express."

To Boy's delight, everyone became quickly engrossed in the film, watching it all the way through. Mostly sober when the film began, they were surprisingly high by the time it ended. Noticing his own level of intoxication Boy wondered at the actual amount of acid he had put in the punch. Boy was glad they had reserved the dining room for the entire night so that the meeting could to turn into the first of many parties, which is exactly what happened.

At first conversations seemed to orbit The Festival Express, and especially how moved many were by Janis in particular. The conversations branched, fractaling out into myriad related and unrelated subjects, demonstrating the non-linear yet interconnected nature of consciousness. Soon the party was a writhing mass of mostly exuberant, wide-eyed, inebriated people. Unfortunately, most of the footage was unusable because the camera crew became to influenced by the spiked punch and found maintaining technical engagement elusive, leaving brilliant shots of corner, the ceiling, and the floor, jumbled sounds collected on the mics left strewn around the room. It was one of those nights that never ends, a meandering exploration of reality where textures pull so deeply that the sun rise is a surprise, many still awake, in awe, and confused at how the night has passed.

The next day most people found themselves in someone else's room, or with extra people in their room, often in giggling piles, often with broad smiles spread across their faces.

It was a beginning to the trip far surpassing Boy's preconceived hopes and aspirations. He was exhilarated, excitement overtaking anxiety. Despite not having slept, he somehow felt reborn, rejuvenated by the uninhibited expression he had helped coalesce. He let himself release into hope, and it felt relieving.

26

The next day was to initiate the outward facing aspect of the project. Boy had forgotten how rigorous even the first performance of a tour could feel, and almost everyone else seemed equally out of training. He was grateful that the trip started in one of the most forgiving cities, a circumstance he was sure his mom had calculated. Japanese politeness would have forgiven even the worst performance. Boy found the way the audiences in Japan even seemed to respect each others space, never clustering into throbbing masses like they would in so much of the rest of the world. The small squished collective at the front of the stage seeming speckled with henna gaijin.

Boy remembered a musician he'd met on festival rounds in Europe telling him they would always start their tours off in a small town as a test run. If their tour started in L.A. or San Francisco, they might perform in Santa Cruz first, a dress rehearsal of sorts. Boy felt a deeper sense of what a good strategy this was. Starting a tour of Asia in Japan seemed a similarly wise technique. His awareness that his mom had probably considered this tickled resentment in him. He knew it was silly to resent her for her intelligence and help, he just wished she wasn't always right. He could hear Sophie's voice in his head telling him to let it go.

He watched most of the performances, shocked by how many bands had pre-recorded tracks they played along with, or even lip-synched over. One of the lip-synching singers explained to him later they always had their set pre-recorded, in case they were too hung-over to play. They claimed it wasn't as much about the music being performed live for the audience as it was about the show, about seeing the celebrity, and feeling a part of something. This musician suggested the audience was there for entertainment, not necessarily live music per se. Great lip-synching, he justified, was still great performance.

Boy hated this inauthenticity and resented the

folks who pre-recorded any part of their set. He was a purist. Some tried to persuade him to join the vanguard of pre-recorded performance, and he was disgusted that they would consider 'fake' performance a vanguard. How had he not noticed more of this in Europe? Maybe he hadn't paid much attention, as he was consumed with the excitement of his first tour. Maybe he was paying more attention now as his name was tied to the project. He also hated that he could tell the audiences didn't notice the difference, and the pre-recorded performances were often more consistent.

Seeing through his 'producer' eyes he could see the value of this, having a clean track to edit to later that wasn't corrupted by a bad PA system, or the foibles of raw live performance. But the canned aspect of these performances left him feeling hollow, and his appreciation felt like corruption. He kept a stiff upper lip about it all, realizing it would be unprofessional for him to try to do anything about something so apparently established and accepted. He tried to not to even complain about it to Sophie, wanting to let her have her own experience, but reinforcing a sense of hopeless solitude pushing its way up from inside him.

27

The last performance of the evening had ended, and the packing crew had started their breakdown. Despite it being some desperately late hour of the night (or early hour of the morning), Boy's mom took him to a secret Yakuza Sushi bar. She could see something was off and said it would cheer him up. He guessed it was also her way of trying to make sure he didn't party too hard so early in the trip.

They took a cab from Shibuya to the back streets in an area of greater Tokyo, called Kichijoji. No signs on the door, it would be easily missed because of the downplayed exterior. Inside were four small tables and an L-shaped bar, two seats on one side, four on the other. The bar was the display case, minimally stocked with elegant raw fish. The colors were vibrant. A slight hint of sea lingered in the air.

A small group of impeccably dressed Japanese men sat together at a table, rosy cheeked, frowning, an expression of comfort, though Boy didn't realize it at the time. The men had either been sitting in silence with each other, or had stopped the moment Boy and his mom entered.

"イラッシャイマセ (irasshaimase)," said an elderly man standing behind the display cases, bowing slightly, and never looking Boy or his mom in the face.

Boy was surprised when his mom started speaking to the man in impeccable Japanese. She ordered omakase. She explained to Boy that this was leaving their meal to the discretion of the chef, and was the only 'appropriate' thing to do. She told Boy that the man serving them was considered by many the number one sushi chef in Tokyo, and likely the world.

The man never looked at his hands, holding a diffuse meditative gaze forward as he cut perfect slices of hamachi, sake, aji, saba, o-toro, toro, and maguro, slapping the fish with precision onto perfectly shaped balls of rice he use two fingers to mold. The man's presentation was immaculate, and without effort, as though a dance, or a subtle martial art form.

As the man handed Boy his first bamboo block tray with a single piece of nigiri displayed like artwork, Boy noticed a tattoo of a reptile in a suit on the chef's arm. Boy was flooded with *presque vu*. He couldn't place what was so familiar about the tattoo, but he knew he'd seen it, or something like it before. He didn't spend long considering it, distracted by the amazing meal, and delicious, unfiltered, sake, served in a square bamboo box. The sake was subtle, mildly sweet with a kick for complexity.

After a few glasses Boy had completely forgotten the tattoo. He was lost in the unrelenting presentation of perfect sushi, and the silence of the meal. After what must have been 13 rounds of nigiri his mother instructed him to place his chopsticks over the bowl of rice that had accompanied their meal to signal they were satisfied. Boy was more than satisfied, he was elated, feeling the warm glow of a particularly enjoyable meal.

As they exited Boy noticed what appeared to be the same image of the reptile tattoo carved above the door, almost hidden in shadow. Why was it familiar? Was it some kind of Yakuza symbol? Boy mind started racing.

Dawn had broken as they ate, and the sky was light blue with morning. Normally they would have hired a car back to the Hyatt, but Boy decided he wanted to try the Tokyo subway instead. His mom wasn't interested, so he thanked her for the meal and left her to find the entrance to the train station.

He walked along Inokashira Park, which was beautiful, and reminded him of a Miyazaki film. He got to the Chuo Line, wandered to the inbound platform, and hopped a train heading back into

Shibuya, and central Tokyo.

He stood, crammed in the quiet early morning rush hour masses of the train. He was impressed to see a woman's purse hanging open, money exposed, and he was the only one who seemed to pay it any mind. He thought about how different New York trains were, how much safer he felt here, even with so many more people crowded around him.

His mind distracted by the swaying movements of the train, he suddenly realized why the tattoo and carving were so familiar. They reminded him of the reptile he had seen at that stuffy, aristocratic party, so long ago now. The train's wheels sparked and he would have sworn he caught a glimpse of the very same reptile in the shadows of the underground. His skin crawled. It had to have been a hallucination. Perhaps the fish hadn't been so fresh, or maybe the sake was stronger than he realized.

He thought back to the sushi bar and realized none of the other customers had said a single word the whole time he and his mom were there. None of them were served, and none of them had left. His paranoia grew and it felt like everyone on the train was looking at him out of the corner of their eyes.

Shit. I'm going crazy. Or am I feeling paranoid because I've been getting high too much? He felt his temperature rise and his heart rate increase, an anxiety attack mounting. Though he knew he was likely overreacting, he wasn't sure his delusions weren't real. This is the problem with paranoia, he thought, it could be real.

Some of the people around him were definitely stealing glances. It could be that he was the only westerner on the train, or that he was famous enough to be recognizable. Maybe he was more recognizable in Japan than he had been at home.

But was it just a coincidence that the sushi guy had a tattoo so closely resembling the reptile he had just seen again? Had anyone else seen it? What the hell is going on…? He tried to calm his breath.

He nearly missed his stop, and was nervous he'd catch the wrong connecting train. When he finally left the station nearest the hotel he walk feverishly back.

He was so relieved back in his room that he fell onto the bed face first without undressing. He was eager to tell Sophie everything that had happened, but so exhausted he fell asleep.

His dreams were restless. He ran through the unfamiliar tunnels of the Japanese subway, from reptiles in business suits always just around the corner behind him. Suddenly in the more familiar tunnels of the New York subway, he hoped the familiarity would help him escape the reptiles still after him. He became desperate to find his way home. He finally reached the scaled station beneath his building, but as he approached the entrance the woman behind the desk transformed into a reptile. He startled awake.

He didn't recognize where he was, confused about why he was lying on an unfamiliar bed fully dressed. Reality came back. He mustered enough energy to take off his shoes before rolling back over and falling again into sleep.

28

The next morning Boy woke with just enough time to get shuffled and shuttled to the airport with the rest of the crew, moving on to China. He had intended to find Sophie to talk about everything that had happened the night before, but there wasn't enough privacy. He unsurprisingly ended up being seated next to his mom, who he would never confide in.

Boy's mind spun trying to make sense of the tattoos, carvings, and the visions he had had on the subway. He started to worry his mind was making the kind of associations he had been warned could come from 'too much partying'. He tried to find a way to let it go, to chalk it up to creative free association of completely explainable observations that he was taking out of context. This worked for everything but the subway reptiles and their striking similarity to the ones he'd seen at the fancy party, that now felt so long ago.

Somehow Boy didn't get a chance to connect with Sophie until they were on the high-speed, 'maglev' train connecting the Pudong Airport to Shanghai. He found her in the car reserved for crew. He scurried over to her and plunked down into the seat beside her. She looked up, startled at first, then smiled seeing it was him.

He didn't know how to start. "Hey Soph. Where ya been?"

"What?" She gave him a sideways glance. "I saw you off after the concert last night." Then, chuckling, she added, "But don't worry, I didn't tell anyone you went to have sushi with your mommy, instead of partying with us."

"Shut the fuck up." Boy chuckled at Sophie's jab, but didn't want to get sidetracked, "Shit got weird last night..." He told her everything, even the dream, punctuating his tale hushed, "So...do you think the drugs are making me paranoid? Or, I mean, reptiles?"

Sophie didn't know how to respond. "Boy, there

is something I have been trying to say to you since that party way back when." She paused, conjuring the courage to say something difficult. "Just because you're paranoid doesn't mean there not after you." She became exaggeratedly serious as she tried not to laugh.

Boy was taken aback that she had used the words he himself had thought the night before. Then he realized she was teasing him and blurted, "Goddammit, Sophie! This isn't funny."

Sophie's kind cadence hidden behind her mocking tone broke Boy's distress as she smiled sideways before contorting her face to demonstrate her care and incredulity. "But it is funny, Boy. You keep seeing reptiles, so what? You know how the human mind works, the more you look for something, the more likely you are to see it. If you want to see reptiles you will. If you want to see conspiracy, you will. If you want to recognize that life is amazing, you will. It really can be that easy. You really ought to be talking to WJ about this stuff. He knows way more than I do, and he'd probably convince you it was all real."

Her lighthearted manner won him over. "Life is one big, awesome joke if you want it to be. Remember?"

Suddenly the train felt as if it were knocked, a loud thud. The train pulled slightly to the right as something rushed passed. Then it was gone. Someone in the car exclaimed, "That's what happens when two trains going 500 klicks an hour pass each other!"

"Holy shit! That was crazy," Boy said. He took a deep breath and continued, "Thanks for the reminder, Soph. I wish I'd found you earlier, I was starting to spin a bit. Even if it's not real, the coincidences are pretty interesting don't you think?"

Boy's smile increased Sophie's interest in continuing the conversation. She was also disappointed she'd yet again gotten so close, but had ended up avoiding the uncomfortable honesty she knew she needed to share with him at some point. She refocused. She knew denying the experiences he'd had would likely only inspire him to take them more seriously. She chose another tactic. "It is interesting. I bet you they're part of WJ's Ananaku." She subdued laughter.

"The Anunnaki? Stop it Soph." He was serious again.

"No, I bet it is. I bet you the Yakuza work with them, which is why your sushi guy had that tattoo, and would explain the carving above the door. Didn't your mom tell you it was a Yakuza joint?" Sophie pretended to be pondering thoughtfully. "I also bet you accidentally saw some of the high-order, reptilian henchmen. They've been scoping you out to recruit you, now that you're famous and all. Or better yet, maybe you're one of them. We should totally ask WJ, he'll know what to do." She mocked concern.

Even though Sophie was making fun, Boy knew he was probably being ridiculous. "Okay," he finally conceded, "you're right. I'm being silly. I'll drop it." After a pause he added, "For now."

Though Boy knew Sophie meant well, he wished it felt safer to talk with her about this. He might try WJ, but WJ's love of conspiracy often went too far for Boy's sensibilities. Boy hoped, if any of his experiences were true, Sophie would see the reptiles as well, so she would believe him. He had to admit that it was suspicious that no one else knew what he was talking about, or could verify what he'd seen.

Sophie gave a surprised look of a cheesy murder-mystery sitcom actor. "What if they all live in the undergrounds, and they are actually just waiting to take you away and replace you with a robot so they can have another figurehead to control?"

Boy knew Sophie was unlikely to let up, or take it seriously, so he joined her in ridiculous claims to exaggerate the experience, as good a route to levity as any other he might try. "Yeah," he said, pretending to think really hard, "yeah, and...and the Bush, Trump, and Clinton dynasties are really some of their leaders...GW planted bombs in the Twin Towers so they would explode...to start a war and push the first domino pieces in a chain reaction to destroy the economy...funneling wealth into fewer hands...to make the middle-class lose its financial footing...reinforcing their oligarchic leadership over the world....But!" He squinted, looking around like someone might be listening. "The rich are actually aliens who are run by computers put into their DNA by an alien overlord who oversees all their undertaking so the reptiles can harvest all of the natural resources and ship them to an alien planet hundreds and thousands of light years away." He glared at her, mocking epiphany, and she glared back.

"Watch out, Boy," Sophie said, "you're starting to put even WJ to shame."

They broke smiles, abandoning the conversation, becoming distracted by the large buildings appearing around the train. They were pulling into the city. It felt like they'd only just left Pudong, and they were already arriving in Shanghai. The Grand Hyatt was on the far side of the Bund, in what was called the 'New City', just east of the Huangpu River, in the middle of the flashy high rises that were the modern cityscape of Shanghai.

As they were driven from train station to hotel, Boy wondered how all this capitalist wealth came to this so-called communist country. The city center was bigger and flashier than most of the US. The streets were full of businessmen in three-piece suits running from building to limo. Skyscrapers spilled into the river. It was the poster-child of what capitalist society idolized, mixed with a 1960's sci-fi futurist dream cityscape. These weren't the endless rows of hovels, three families to a house, steaming street food, and dirty-faced kids the movies had promised China to be. This was modern, big, and far more than he'd expected.

The hotel was the most over-the-top, impressive and oppressive he'd ever been in. A central corridor stretched up through the building, going on into infinity. He felt vertigo gazing through the winding, florescent-lit balconies. This is China?

When he got to his room and looked out over the large expanse of Shanghai, he couldn't understand what he was looking at. It wasn't that he'd never seen sprawl before, he had grown up in New York, after all. In Manhattan, however, the sprawl was contained by the Hudson and the East Rivers. In New York there were big buildings scattered in areas, then the boroughs, and towns, all collected in such a way it didn't feel sprawling to him. He had also been to LA and Las Vegas, but even in these notorious megalopolises there was something that didn't feel so endless in their expanses, there were borders where the city met the land again, where the mountains rose up, ending the suburbs. But here, in this bourgeoning industrial center of commerce, Shanghai went on forever, in all directions save the sea. And it sprawled in a tight-knit, over-dense, and dauntingly-impacted manner.

Meeting in the dining hall for regrouping, orientation, and first-impression filming, Boy was surprised others who hadn't been to China before weren't as shocked. Most, to some degree, were impressed, overwhelmed, and intimidated by what they had seen, but no one seemed quite as astounded as he. WJ thought it was funny Boy was so taken aback. From WJ's perspective, China was the true economic powerhouse behind the international monetary system at this point, so what else could one expect?

That night Boy decided to ask WJ about everything he had been experiencing. WJ listened intently.

"There are so many things at play in our world today that we don't know about," WJ offered. "The more famous we get, the more likely we are to start running into the hidden underpinnings of society. I don't believe everything Ike says, but I wouldn't be surprised if there are reptilian overlords at least influencing, if not controlling, society. Sometimes, when I take mushrooms especially, I feel like they're offering me extraterrestrial information as well. It wouldn't surprise me if it were actually the mushrooms running the whole shebang. Did you know, the largest organism alive is a mushroom pad nearly the size of the state of Washington?"

Boy was glad WJ had taken him seriously, but he drifted off as WJ entered into the esoteric arenas. Boy loved hearing WJ's wild opining, but ultimately felt they were no more grounded than a good sci-fi book. He fell asleep as WJ gently continued his gentle rant about the 'true world' beyond our socially-constructed reality. The last thing Boy remembered was WJ describing Plato's cave allegory, naming who he thought the modern shadow puppet masters were. Boy wasn't sure if it was a dream, or if WJ had actually named Boy's mom as one of the most significant shadow casters while Boy was drifted in and out of sleep.

29

The next day the Chinese audience was huge and full of energy, emulating the type of excitement one might expect from a Beatles performance circa the mid 19060s. People were literally fainting against the barrier between the crowd and the performers.

As a contingency for the performance the production team had been required to hire many of the city's otherwise off-duty police to guard the stage. Requiring so much security, while sounding overkill, now made sense, even if it was also a way for the local government to line the pockets of some of their officials. The crowd was fanatic, the performances amplified by the frenetic energy.

Sophie was impressed when she watched Boy perform. He got better as the crowd grew wilder. She saw the deep passion of his inner performer in his performance. She saw surprised how bright his charisma could get. She understood in a deeper way than she had previously why he had always wanted to do this. He was made for it, and it suited him.

That night the elation turned into an undulating puddle of debauchery, the party ended up at the pool. The hotel manager had been bribed to not call the police. All the entrances to the pool but one had been locked. That night the pool was the hottest club in Shanghai, with the most exclusive list..

Cameras in a waterproof cases caught started in the hands of camera operators, and eventually were passed around by anyone inspired to pull them up from the bottom of the pool. There were impromptu a cappella sing alongs, sex in the plastic bushes lining the poolside garden, drugs being consumed with not nearly enough discretion. ego-clashes, near-drowning, chicken fights, and splash brigades; Dionysian revelry par excellence.

At the peak of his inebriation, while looking for a lost camera, Boy thought he caught a glimpse of another human-sized reptile, treading water in the bottom of the pool. But, even in his intoxicated state, he wanted someone else to be the first to say something about it, so he waited. But the dino-businessman swam into the shadows without stirring any response out of Boy's co-revelers.

Sophie happened to notice Boy from across the pool as he stared blankly into the water, head swaying, brow crunched in concentration. She followed his eyes but didn't see anything under the water where his inebriated gaze fell. She crossed to where he was sitting and plopped down next to him.

"You okay, Boy?" she asked, leaning against him slightly, noting he had the tensile strength of an earthworm.

"You saw it?" He swiveled his head around to look at her, overshooting her face, shaking his head to regain focus.

Oh shit, he is really fucked, she thought to herself. "Saw what?"

"The alligator in Versace who just disappeared into the bottom of the pool."

His eyes were rolling back into his head.

"Oh, right, that. Yeah, he seemed pretty drunk too. I hope he finds somewhere good to get that suit cleaned." She played along, sure that there was no point to opposing him in his state.

"I fucking told you," he said, his glare returning haphazardly to the pool.

She knew he was past the point where he would remember anything that happened for the rest of the night.

"Let's get to bed, Boy," she pulled him up, flung his arm over her shoulder, and started walking towards the door.

Just then her phone rang.

"You going to get that?" Boy asked, awkwardly dancing to the ringtone.

"Uh..." she hesitated, knowing only one person who'd be calling.

She looked at the caller ID, then at Boy. He was extremely intoxicated, so she decided it was safe to take the call.

"Hey...don't worry, I got him...he'll be fine."

He looked at her confused, his eyes widening in an effort to see her more clearly.

"Who's that?" he managed to slur.

She ignored him, continuing the phone conversation, "No...Of course...I've always taken care... Why would this be any different...Yes, he's right next to me...Yeah, he can hear me, but he's so wasted he won't remember anything, I promise...I haven't seen him this drunk since the day they took the record contract...You're right." She abruptly hung up and put the phone in her pocket, adjusting his arm over her shoulder as she did so.

He was squinting at her incredulously, as though he didn't recognize her.

"What?" she asked, mocking his incredulity.

"Well?" he inquired, frowning slightly.

"Well what?" she was calm, knowing he was far too gone to process any of this with reason. "Boy, you're wasted. You have no idea what you are talking about. Come on, let's get you to bed."

"But you did see it?" He said, his mind returning to the reptile.

"Sure bud."

She helped him to his bed. The whole way he was lost, trying to remember how he had gotten so confused. He couldn't quite remember what had spurned the confusion, but he was sure it had something to do with Sophie and a huge pool lizard. He fell asleep his pants half off, one shoe on, his brow furrowed, mumbling, "I fucking know you saw it."

Sophie fell on the bed next to him, not wanting to struggle to get Boy out of more of his clothes, hoping she wouldn't have to hold his tie back in the middle of the night. Though it was unlikely he would remember anything from the night, she found herself wishing he wouldn't forget, so she would finally have to tell him everything. Even so, as she tried to lull herself to sleep, she planned a lie, hoping never to use it, and erased her phone records.

30

Boy awoke with an familiar pounding, inside his head, and at the door. The PA knocking at the door didn't stay to make sure he was awake. He knew it was time for everyone to be up, eating, caffeinating, packing, shuffling onto the bus, and heading out to the train station. Boy grimaced, looking down at his tattered outfit as he heard Sophie laugh.

"Fuck off," he coughed.

"Good morning to you too sunshine," she said as she rolled out of bed and opened the curtains.

Boy looked out over Shanghai as he packed, struck by the rubble he imagined was old China, crumbling around hideous, skyscraping apartment blocks. He recoiled as, even so early in the morning, there was a thick, brown haze lifting out of the streets, into the sky. His stomach turned as he noticed similarities between his coffee and the treacle color of the river lugubriously winding its way through this flashy façade-riddled city.

Sophie had slipped out of Boy's room, packed, showered, was already three coffees deep, and in much better shape than Boy as he staggered into the seat next to her. She handed him a coffee, a water, and a packet of electrolytes.

"Thanks," he said.

"Sure."

"And for getting me to bed." He tried to smile but it made his head throb.

"You were fucking wasted," she laughed. "Do you remember anything from last night?"

"No. Why? Did you take advantage of me?" He laughed, but winced immediately. The pulse of pain through his temples and behind his eyes turned his smile into a grimace.

Seeing his recoil Sophie offered, "Drink that electrolyte, it hurts to watch you right now."

They sat quietly as Boy worked through the distraction of his headache, sipping his enhanced water and coffee intermittently.

Today they'd journey from Shanghai to Beijing, transferring onto the official train at the official launching point for 'The Trans-Mongolian Festival Express'. Excitement was enough, fortunately, to pull most out of their biochemical fog. There was relatively little chatter as the team slowly entered the buses that would carry them from China's most populated city to its capital. As others boarded their bus Boy's memory started offered brief glimpses of the previous night.

"Wait…" He said, searching for clarity in his recollection, unable to sift swiftly through the haze of hangover.

He turned to look at Sophie, who seemed suddenly nervous, or was it curious? She was about to divert his attention when he asked, "Was there another reptile, in a suit, swimming in the pool last night?"

She laughed, relieved. She responded through a wide smile saying, "Oh, yeah, that…You were so wasted you saw another one of your dragons." A single, short push of breath burst through her nostrils as her grin widened.

"Fuck, they're here too." He said, letting his forehead fall against the back of the chair in front of him. He was trying to sound sarcastic, but his compromised state made his words sound indifferent. The doors closed on the bus and they pulled away.

After a couple of minutes listening to the rustle of people around them, and the rumble of the big diesel engine, Sophie asked, "Remember me dragging your ass to your room?"

"Why? What are you hoping I don't remember?" He was trying to be funny, but again his demeanor killed the humor. His eyes were closed, but if they hadn't been he would have seen remorse cross Sophie's face. Trying to conjure more from the dark abyss of his black out, a faint vision of her taking a phone call skimmed near the surface. Thinking little of it he asked, "Did you talk to someone last night?"

Thinking quickly, and hoping to sound amused, she said, "Besides you and your reptile boyfriend?"

Boy's eyes were still closed but the corners of his mouth curled up. He moved his head from its uncomfortable position against the hard seat back, and onto Sophie's shoulder, and he fell asleep.

At the Hongqiao train station, she handed him a thermos of coffee she'd had in her bag. He thanked her, feeling much better even after such a quick and uncomfortable nap.

The journey from Shanghai to Beijing would take just over ten hours, and as the day had started so early, the first half of the trip almost everyone slept the harsh morning off. Accordingly the camera crew was able to get some embarrassingly amazing shots of whole bands asleep in their seats, dribble down their cheeks, mouths agape, hair in a hot morning mess.

As people started coming to, there was a buzz of worry that the whole trip was going to be this cramped, both physically, and time wise. Boy's mom came to him, telling him he had to explain how things would be different from Beijing to Moscow, to quiet his restless masses. Tired and reluctant, he knew she was right. He considered what he might say.

At their next stop he called a whole crew meeting. Grabbing a bullhorn, and finding his way onto a concrete bench he held court.

"Hey everyone." After everyone was looking his direction, and relatively quiet, he continued, "I hope you've all been having an awesome time."

There was some minor clapping and cheering, with the enthusiasm you might expect from a swarm of zombies.

"I know the trip's been pretty rigorous so far, but I want to assure you, it's not all going to be like this, so cramped, and rushed. As a reminder, in Beijing we will have an entire train to ourselves, plenty of room, plenty of space, and no more packing and unpacking until Moscow."

People's cheers grew a little louder, and a little more engaged. As the crowd's energy grew, Boy's became more alive and more captivating.

"Each car has its own shower, and we've designed the train to make sure the sleeping arrangements are comfortable. Everything is going to be much easier from here on out." He smiled and winked at the crowd. Boy's charm had won them over. "Thanks for bearing with us for these first few days. Tonight and tomorrow night will be our last nights in a hotel, so enjoy the stable ground. And more importantly..." He searched around as though he were looking for something he'd misplaced, finishing his speech with, "Where the hell is the whiskey?"

He had read his audience well, and an enthusiastic din ensued. Boy didn't want the drink, but he knew how to please his crowd. As the roar continued, a bottle of whiskey was passed up to him. There was a minor ebb to the noise as Boy took a hearty slug from the caramel-colored firewater, and as he lowered the bottle the cheers reached crescendo.

Boy looked up to see his mom. He felt an impulse to hide the bottle. Lowering it to his side he thought he could see her version of pride hidden behind her cool stare. She'd seen his speech, had asked him to make it, understood his intentions, and perhaps was now appreciating his execution. She'd seen him successfully manipulate a restless group of onlookers, and he could tell that she knew exactly what he was doing. He was reticent to admit that she felt pride in his capacities as a leader.

This might be the first time she's ever been proud of me, he thought to himself. He realized that even this thought was a dismissal. His mind raced with myriad examples of her disapproval, moments of her disappointment, her resignation, and his need for approval. He returned to his seat, receiving high fives and pats on his back as he went. He wondered if he would be able to take it all in better if he weren't hung over. He guessed it was unlikely.

The rest of the ride returned to a level of party that would appear indulgent to onlooker, but was sustenance to the rock stars involved. There were more sing-alongs, make-outs, anecdotes, dramas, heart-breaking and heart-warming stories, fueled by inhibitions abandoned by exogenous alteration. There were expressions, and repressions. Artists hard at work in artifice.

They arrived in Beijing, another endless grid of electrified masses. The sky was dark, but the lights of city made it hard to tell. Lost in their self-abandon, they barely noticed. They stumbled through checking in with the idea to regroup for a late meal in the hotel restaurant. Less than half came for the food, and most of those left before being swept into another sleepless night.

It was silly to be halfway around the world, staying in fancy hotels, emulating ever other fancy hotel, eating hotel food, augmented to the pallet of the observer, comfortable, and in so being, bland.

Boy felt they ought to be roaming the streets,

taking advantage of the opportunity to see and interact with something completely outside what they were used to. However, after a day of sitting and drinking on a train, and a previous night with barely any real sleep, Boy followed the general momentum of the evening and was ready to call it a night. He fell asleep as soon as he was under the covers of his king-size bed, emulating ever other king-sized bed, in his uncomfortably familial king-sized room.

He ran through subway tunnels from reptiles always just out of view. He made it out of the station under his house in Manhattan, and past the receptionists, who he avoided. He rushed out of the elevator, running up the stairs and down the hall to his bedroom. As he opened the door he was instead entering his mom's office. She was at her desk, mug in hand, looking down at papers. "Mom!" he called out. He swung the door closed, sure the reptiles were close behind. She looked up from her paperwork, oblong pupils of red-yellow eyes glaring back at him.

He gasped awaked, kicked off the blankets, convinced the paranoia of his dreams was the result of his drinking and drugging. He told himself he was quitting. He lay awake until low light crept in through the windows. He knew he needed sleep, this only made it harder. Sometime just before the sun cut across the horizon he dozed back off.

31

The next day Boy rallied Sophie and WJ to go check out Tiananmen Square. Arriving at the grand plaza they noticed the huge painting of Mao that hung between the two arched entryways to the ancient 'Forbidden City'. It was the image of Mao that they had been seeing everywhere since entering China, but this was the largest they'd seen so far. The archways on either side were monumental, grand opening into the area that had previously been the primary residence of the King.

Boy had always felt his home in NYC was ostentatious, but he was impressed how much more ostentatious a home could be. He was taken with the layout of the palace complex, and noticed a prevalent theme of reptiles and dragons throughout the architecture. It seemed to him that almost all the railings of the many stairways leading up to buildings were the ridged backs of serpents. He wondered if Sophie, or at least WJ, were also noticing the reptilian themes scattered throughout this ornate abode. He imagined Sophie telling him he was only seeing so many because looking for them. He couldn't help but wonder if these ancient dragons might be earlier representation of the same reptiles he kept seeing. He started to spin out thinking about how many different ancient cultures had dragon or reptilian lore. He asked WJ about it, and was offered a cascade of entertaining ideas.

WJ knew an incredible amount about the dragons. He claimed dragons were always on the high-ranking official buildings because the dragons were seen as power, and were even the mythological henchmen of the ruling class. WJ told Boy he believed dragons had actually existed, and they likely still exist. Dragons were the only things the ruling demigods of the past had feared. They were a revered secret society amongst the rulers. The ruling classes were the only ones who had direct contact with the otherwise invisible dragon race. WJ suggested that the old stories or most cultures supported many of the more recent theories of secret societies of reptiles who covertly ran the world. WJ suggested the reason the reptilian societies kept so well hidden was that most human minds could only perceive in three dimensions, and that the reptilians were able to move in the forth, or likely even higher dimensions. WJ explained that being unbound by three-dimensionality, the reptiles could evade any attempts at being caught or even seen in the third dimension.

Boy listened intently to WJ's conspiracies, though he worried they wouldn't help his paranoia. He decided to enjoy his surrounding, enthralled by the ancient buildings of the Forbidden City, and all the history held within them. He was captivated, imagining back when these buildings housed the ruling class of the Chinese Empire. If Sophie hadn't been there to remind them they had to get back for sound check, they likely would have stayed all day.

Sophie acted as wrangler, and before long they were back at the hotel. WJ left to his room, and Sophie followed Boy to his.

As Boy was getting ready he asked her, "Isn't this place wild?"

"Yeah." Sophie said passively, her attention on her phone.

"Who're you texting?" Boy asked, surprised to see her on her phone.

Sophie didn't change position, didn't show Boy her phone.

"Why?" she asked, not looking up, shrugging as though the question was absurd. "You getting jealous, Boy?" she asked, still keeping her gaze down, playfully smiling.

"Jealous of what? I'm asking because you're not

paying attention to me, and it probably costs a lot to text from here, which makes me curious about who would be worth the money, that's all." He realized he did sound jealous, which caught him off guard. Am I jealous? He wondered.

To divert his attention Sophie said, "You protest too much." She smirked, still not looking up at him. "And I was paying attention to you. I answered your question, didn't I? This place is fancy. What more do you want from me?"

"I wasn't talking about the hotel, I was asking what you thought about China."

Thank god his attention got diverted, she thought to herself. "Sure, China's wild. WJ told me that rural Chinese are limited to only a few days visit to the cities, for which they have to basically get a visa. That shit's really crazy. Can you imagine growing up in the sticks and getting arrested because you overstayed your visit in a city? Do you actually think that's real?"

"You never know with WJ." He finished buttoning his shirt and grabbed a thin black tie from the bed. "What about the fact that you can own a building, but the land is still owned by the government, to whom you have to pay rent for the lot?"

Sophie wanted to make sure she got him to sound check on time. She truncated the conversation by saying, "That doesn't sound so different from property tax and eminent domain to me Boy. Now get your ass dressed and let's get down the Birds Nest so you can sound check with the rest of the fellas, who are probably already there."

"What about all that dragon stuff?" he asked cautiously, not wanting to sound too enthused, as

Sophie was already over the conversation.

"Oh god, Boy. Just get dressed already. We gotta go."

She looked annoyed, he didn't push, but his mind reeled with everything WJ had told them.

At sound check Boy got into performer mode. Again the crowd was wild, and again he gained energy from his audience. Even so, he was glad this would be the last performance in a major arena on this leg of their trip. He was excited to see how performing on the platform at the train station, or random stops along the railway was going to work out. He was excited and nervous about the train, his daydream come to life.

He saw Johnny T. after the show, and the actor was impressed, which pleased Boy more than he could explain rationally. Johnny T. convinced Boy and some others to join him and see what the Beijing nightlife was like. He told Boy he had heard great things about a place called 'White Rabbit'. Boy forgot his conviction from that morning that he was going to quit the party, and was swept up in the momentum.

The club wasn't so different to those of Tokyo, Europe, or New York. The music was entertainingly bad, and it had the essentials, namely whiskey and a dance floor. Uninhibited by the booze, they gyrated opulently a while, before deciding to take the party back to their amazing suites. It became another blurry night, as much as any of them had hoped for.

Boy was glad to connect with Johnny T., yet there was something confusing about the strange actor. Boy still couldn't place why he was so familiar, and yet somehow off, as if Johnny T. was perpetually imitating himself, never actually authentic. These thoughts flooded Boy's mind a few drinks deep, and were gone as fast as they came.

The night ended predictably, Sophie escorting Boy back to his room. Even though he could barely speak, he insisted on taking his drink with him. As they walked through the door he accidentally spilled the leftovers of his cranberry vodka all over himself and Sophie.

Sophie went into his bathroom to rinse her shirt off and take a shower. When she was done Boy was already passed out on the bed. She was exhausted, and didn't want to walk down the hallway in her bathrobe, so she pushed him over, his face squished against the pillow, sleeping, and slightly-pickled.

Sophie cared for him too deeply and worried that if he found everything out before she had the courage to tell him, it might be the end of their friendship. Yet, if told him, he would likely push her away for good as well. She didn't know what to do. Luckily, she was sober enough to know she wouldn't solve anything right then, and let herself fall asleep.

32

Boy awoke and rolled over to find Sophie next to him. He noticed how comforting it was to see her in the morning. He adjusted the blankets, and found that Sophie appeared naked under the covers next to him. He didn't realize she was wearing a bathrobe that had come open in her sleep. They had been naked in hot tubs and skinny-dipping together, but never alone, and in bed. His mind raced for a logical reason why she would be naked. His face flushed wondering if they had been sexual and he had forgotten. He started to feel simultaneously feel turned on, and ashamed. He didn't have anything against the idea of sexual intimacy with Sophie, as his body was clearly conveying, but he didn't want to it be something he didn't remember. He especially didn't want it to end up compromising their friendship, which he was more and more realizing was perhaps his most important.

As he continued searching his mind for evidence of the end of last night he realized he was still fully clothed in the previous days garb, even socks on.

She stirred and he awkwardly pretended to be asleep. She didn't say anything but got out of bed. He opened his eyes a slit expecting to see bare body moving across the room, hoping, while again feeling guilt and confusion. He was disappointed to see her suddenly in a robe, and not naked at all. She turned around and he closed his eyes.

"Why are you pretending to be asleep Boy? Fucking awkward," Sophie laughed.

"Huh?" he grumbled, trying to keep the charade.

"Give it up. I saw your eyes close when I turned around. Why lie about it? You're so weird." She was being playful, and he tried to calm his involuntary arousal.

She smirked to herself as she turned to the bathroom. Before she closed the door she called out, "Get up, it's time for our train!"

I have a crush on Sophie? Boy wondered. Is it a crush? He was sure it was a bad idea. He was not lacking in romantic possibilities, why muddle up things with the only real friend he had. He hadn't felt attracted to anyone in a long time, and it was exciting, and annoying that it happened to be her.

There was a loud knock on the door. Boy called to Sophie to get it, but she was already in the shower. He huffed lazily, and got himself out of bed, stopping briefly at the mirror in the hallway to make sure he didn't look like death. He pulled his fingers through his hair a couple of times, chuckling to himself at his vanity, before opening the door. He expected a bellboy or PA, but it was his mom. She stared at him until he moved aside so she could enter.

"Good morning," he offered, confused by her unexpected visit.

"Since my room was next door, I decided to make sure you were awake." She looked at him curtly before continuing, "I would have already left, but when I heard the shower running I decided to meet the person showering in your room."

"It's just Sophie, mom," he said, thinking it would dissuade her from needing to stick around.

"Sophia, eh? I thought you said she wasn't your girlfriend." Her gaze was piercing.

"She's not." He looked back, hoping to match her intense calm, frustrated that he could feel his cheek rouge.

"Who is your girlfriend, then?" It was not like her to probe.

"What do you want mom?"

"Or boyfriend," she added, keeping her cutting gaze locked on him.

He figured she must have something else in mind as her questions were so out of the ordinary. "Are you ok?" He ventured.

"I want you to be happy, Boy, that's all." She almost looked like she was going to express emotion.

"Your speech was good the other day, keep up the good work. I think the show we're making is coming along nicely." As suddenly as she had arrived, she departed.

Boy was perplexed. He wanted to like that she had shown concern for his happiness, but it was so unusual he figured there must have been something he missed.

When Sophie got out of the shower he told her about his mom's visit. She seemed surprised, even a little concerned. This further shocked Boy, as he had expected her to think it was funny, not concerning. Sophie left hastily, saying she needed to get back to her room to pack. Boy thought he must be reading into things too much.

He finished packing and went to breakfast. Just as he was sitting down with a cup of coffee, Johnny T. arrived. Boy was impressed with how chipper Johnny T. was, especially considering how hard he'd partied with everyone the previous night.

"You look like you got a full night's sleep. How the hell does that work?"

"It's all in your 'tude, dude," Johnny T. replied. "If you want to know how to feel great in the morning, wake up feeling excited about the day."

Boy figured Johnny T. had already been blowing lines, he was a little too exuberant, though he didn't seem jittery at all.

"How's your day been so far, Boy?" Boy second-guessed his conclusion, as Johnny T. seemed actually interested in something other than himself, not a common effect of morning after coke consumption.

Boy was surprised to find himself telling Johnny T. the whole story of his morning. He felt a comfort he couldn't place, and it felt great to have a confidant to discuss his confusion with that wasn't Sophie.

After Boy was done Johnny T. asked, "How

well do you know Sophie?"

"What do you mean? She's my best friend."

"Right, but how well would you say you really know her?"

After a moments consideration Boy said, "I guess it's hard to know how much you actually know anyone, but I do trust her, if that's what you're asking. Why?"

"Well," Johnny T. replied, looking ruminative, "I'm not claiming I know what's going on, but…here's the thing Boy. Your mom has been rich and famous for a long time. You have been too, by default. But now that you're coming into your own, finding your personal fame, people will start changing how they treat you. You can't trust everyone you meet, no matter how nice they are. Most people probably want something from you."

Though Johnny T. was being pretty pessimistic, his voice stayed bright, a non-ironic smile between his nose and his dimpled chin. Boy wondered if this was early morning drug induced paranoia, or if Johnny T. was just trying to offer sage advice from a long life lived in the spot light. Boy was more uncomfortable believing that latter.

Since Boy had grown up in the shadow of his mom, none of this was new to him. He was certain Sophie wasn't someone he had to worry about. She'd always been his talisman in that regards. "Sophie was my friend way before I became famous Johnny T., that's part of why I have so much faith in her."

"Yeah, but…hasn't she always been aware of who your mom is? And how did she come to be one of the official photographers for this trip?"

"She has never tried to get me to do anything for her. Never even asked to have any of her pictures put in a magazine, or anything. In fact, it was my idea that she be photographer. She has hundreds of potentially compromising pictures of me, and I don't think she has ever even done so much as show them to anyone else." Realizing what he had just said, Boy couldn't help but feel a tinge of anxiety. He shook it off. If he couldn't be sure of Sophie, whom could he be sure of? "I appreciate your concern, I really do, but I'm sure Sophie's someone I can trust."

"Well, all I'm tryin' to offer ya is this, kid. Your mom has been around this block many more times than you. It sounds to me like she doesn't trust Sophie, that's all I'm sayin'. Make of it what you will."

He grabbed Boy's coffee cup and took a swig. "Damn that's good. I think I'd better get myself a cup." Johnny T. unceremoniously got up and walked towards the coffee station.

Boy was baffled. He wanted to be on good terms with the guy, so he called to him as he walked away, "Thanks for your advice. I'll think about it."

Johnny T. didn't turn around, merely tossing his fist in the air and pumping it as though showing solidarity with a Black Panther somewhere in front of him.

What a strange fellow, Boy thought.

He finished his coffee and went to reception, where he found nearly everyone waiting. Spotting Sophie, he wanted to tell her about his conversation with Johnny T., but as he moved across the room toward her he realized the light it shed on her, and decided against it. He hated keeping things from her, and they were piling up.

The production coordinators and a team of PAs started checking that everyone and everything was accounted for. These were the people who had everyone's passports and visas, knew where the luggage was going, and knew which train car everyone would be in. These were the people who kept everything running, and Boy realized he hadn't met any of them. Some of their names might not even make it into the credits, and yet without them it none of this would have been possible. Boy smiled as a woman came by checking him off a list, giving him a card to wear around his neck.

"Thank you," he said. She blushed at his unsolicited appreciation and walked on without responding.

"What was that about?" Sophie asked.

"It's because of people like her that we're able to be the belligerent rock stars we are. They keep this machine rolling. I was just appreciating that."

"You know, Boy, sometimes you can accidentally be a sweetheart."

Boy gave Sophie a half smile back and bumped her gently with his shoulder.

33

In Boy's dilated moment of appreciation he took in the impressive feets that everything had been loaded onto the train, things in their appropriate spaces, people assigned to their cars, a crew cohesive. Somehow the train had nearly been converted into fully furnished apartments, considerably more comfortable than tour buses, with so much more space. Boy hoped that his compatriots appreciated all this luxury.

The lobby cars were particularly well organized. The bars were fully stocked (even hosting the strange alcoholic preferences some of the more eccentric stars had asked for—rare absinthes and the like). The most impressive part of the whole train was the 'fold-out-flat-bed-stage-car'. It was a train car that unfolded to become a covered stage, equipped with highest-end sound and the highest-quality lighting array Boy had ever seen in such a compact space.

His mom was with him as he got the tour. "Where the hell was all this made?"

"China, of course," she replied, as though it was a silly question.

"Who engineered it all?" Boy continued, still in awe despite his mom's condescending tone.

"It was a couple of our stage people from New York working with a couple of our local manufacturers here. Why does it matter Boy? It's the best we could buy. Don't you like it?" Something about her gaze reminded him of the dream he'd had a couple nights back, which he'd nearly forgotten about. He shook it off, turning his attention away from her unblinking stare.

"Do I like it?" he asked. "It's blowing my mind." He was slightly distracted by the lingering thought of the dream vision of her yellow eyes.

"Good," she replied. "I think it will do." She walked away.

Boy was relieved when she left. He ventured to his cabin, which was in the car next to his band's. The band had one car with separated bunk spaces, but he had a special cabin all himself. It was one-third of an entire car, and consisted mostly of a comfortable looking bed and a desk. There was a computer on the desk with a note explaining he'd have access to the video feeds from any of the cameras that had been installed in all the common spaces to augment whatever the film crews picked up.

Boy wanted to check in with his band, and with Sophie; he also wanted to lay down. He opted to check the computer first. It had satellite Internet access. The Internet didn't surprise him, but the number of cameras on board did. They hadn't just rigged the common spaces in the common cars, but all the 'common' spaces, even in the private band cars.

A pop up window explained he was to keep this computer, and the camera-viewing secret, as it technically might be breaking the contract agreement of some of the bands on board, and that the any sensitive footage was for archival purposes only, and would not be publicly used.

The vast camera network made him uneasy. He liked the idea of getting the footage, and was even guiltily compelled by voyeurism, but he knew it was a infringement on privacy, and would be a breach of trust were it discovered. He would be pissed if he were one of the people being recorded without knowing. Before he came to a conclusion on how to feel there was a knock on his door. He clicked a button that appeared on pop-up window, and was exited from the camera surveillance, a safety precaution he was startled by, but impressed with.

"Come in," he said, closing the computer.

Sophie entered, looking around. "Wow! What the fuck? You got the penthouse suite."

"Shut up, I'm sure your place is great, too."

He started to say something about the cameras but decided against it. Another secret. He would have normally told her, but had the intuition it might be a better not to, at least for now. He didn't like that this was the second thing he was keeping from her in one day.

"Where are you?" he asked instead.

"Right down the hall, but it's only got a single bed, and the space is about a fifth this size." She made a fake scowl.

"Whatever. You'll probably spend most of your time partying anyways, so why does it matter?" He wanted to say she would probably spend most the time in his bed, but again stopped himself, afraid he'd sound thirsty.

"Yeah, you mean I'll probably spend most of my nights walking you back here?"

His heart rate increased, so he pretended to be annoyed. "Shut up, Sophie. You're the lightweight in this friendship and you know it." He knew he was being juvenile and playing games by saying friendship, but he wanted to deny the crush he still didn't want to admit he had.

She looked at him as though he were a young student who'd just said something idiotic to his kind-hearted teacher. "Right, Boy. I'm the lightweight," she punched his arm.

The train's whistle blew three long, deep chirps, and a familiar voice came over the intercom, "All aboard the Trans-Mongolian Festival Express. Last call. The train is leaving the station in five minutes." Was that Johnny T.?

The train shifted. Boy guessed it was just the engines turning on.

"Let's see how everyone else is faring," Sophie said, grabbing Boy and pulling him out of his room.

They stopped for a long time checking in with the band. Everyone took shots of bijou that WJ said he bought in Shanghai, in celebration of the trip beginning. The alcohol tasted like vodka strained through cow manure. The train started moving, secondary shots were taken to send Beijing off, and the group decided to roam through the cars together. As they went Boy tried identifying where the cameras had been placed. Their locations were so covert, and his inebriation so quick, that he forgot all about them.

They stopped in to say 'hi' to pretty much every car they passed, building a cognitive map of who and what was where. They found the bar car, and it's adjoining lounge. Enthusiasm for these cars was only slightly outshone by the excitement at the meal car. An overhead sign explained a buffet would be available twenty-four hours a day, and a kitchen staff at normal meal times for specific requests.

After the tour, they headed back to their respective cars. The fellows from the band all agreed they ought to conserve some energy for the rest of the trip, and decided against welcoming the dawn. Sophie fell asleep next to Boy after explaining he either had to share, or trade rooms. He restlessly eventually fell asleep fighting an urge to kiss her.

He wandered aimlessly through a strange, undulating field. It was bright, and the brightness became so overwhelming he couldn't make anything out. He was suddenly freezing cold, surrounded by ice, in a frozen landscape. He thought he could almost make out a person in the distance, but they never got closer. He yelled for them, but they were so far away he couldn't be sure they heard or saw him at all.

34

After a relatively brief but relatively deep sleep, Boy restlessness got the better of him, and he decided to wake Sophie and wondered their way to the party cars. They were delighted to see the party was still rolling. Those still lingering in the morning hours were of an intoxication there was no chance of catching up with.

The party had been an eager, drunken marveling mass. Drinks had been spiked, and nearly everyone still participating by dawn found themselves embarked on a psychedelic journey they may or may not have connected to. He could tell by the remittance that it was the epic kind of party Boy had envisioned, and it had only been the first day on the train. Among the many was WJ, who Sophie found her way over to. Boy offered to gran them coffee from the bar.

Boy was impressed to see Johnny T. behind the bar, among the diehards that weren't letting the night end. Johnny T. poured old fashions and brought one over the Boy.

"You missed a good one," Johnny offered, handing Boy his libation.

"Looks like it." Boy wasn't sure starting his day with an old fashioned was the choice he needed to make, but he didn't want to refuse Johnny T.'s offer, so he accepted.

"Were you shaking it up with you're lady?" Johnny T. asked, winking, inebriated.

"What? Sophie? We're just friends," Boy blurted a little too quickly, taking a chug off the drink in his hand.

"Thou dust protest too much my dear sir." Johnny T. offered a sympathetic grin, as though a zookeeper sweetly disappointed in a stupid monkey. "Have you checked her phone?" he asked.

Boy was suddenly tipsy and maybe even a little high from something he hadn't realized he'd taken. "Why would I check her phone?" he asked.

"That's how you find out if they have a partner." Johnny T. said in as close to a whisper as he could manage through his drunkenness.

"If they have a partner?" Boy asked. He was trying to let the conversation play out, but he was also having a hard time not feeling defensive of Sophie.

"Look, if I'm wrong, and there's nothing on her phone, then you won't have to feel weird about it. That's all I'm saying." He was looking across the room like a bad actor overplaying a spy in a low-grade, big-budget action movie. His gaze was obvious, overly relaxed, dissociated.

Boy stared at Johnny T., trying to decipher his intentions. "I appreciate the advice," which he didn't, "but Sophie's okay."

"Just check her phone, that's all I'm saying." Johnny T. had stopped paying attention to the conversation. A waitress, one of his mom's models, came walking by with a tray of green liquid. Johnny T. got up abruptly to grab her and her drinks. He didn't say good-bye, reminding Boy of how his mom would just split in the middle of a conversation.

Boy scanned the room and saw Sophie laughing with WJ in a corner. She turned, looked at him, and smiled. Her smile was warm, he felt the rush of his crush surge. Fuck. He meandered over to them.

Just before he got to their corner, Sophie pulled out her phone, looked at it, looked up at him, and quickly put the phone away again. Her expression subtly shifted. Despite himself, he felt uneasy. What if Johnny T. is right?

"Who was that?" he asked when he got to her, trying to pretend like he wasn't suddenly paranoid.

"Who was what?" she asked back with a sincere smile.

He didn't want it to be true that she was hiding something. He wanted to ask her, but Kevin walked up handing everyone shots of the green drink the waitress had been passing out. Kevin made a toast to the most epic adventure of their lifetimes, and they all drained their small glasses. It tasted of licorice. It was something Kevin had called, 'The Green Fairy', an ancient recipe for herb-infused liquor, with supposedly psychedelic attributes, including an increased libido.

Boy tried to let go of the phone thing, but became fixated on it. Finally, as he could tell they were coming up, he tried playing it off like it wasn't a big deal. "Does your phone get reception here?" he asked.

"No, but it gets the Wi-Fi, which is amazing. Why? Doesn't yours work the same way?" She looked at him innocently.

"Who was calling when I walked up earlier?"

"Calling me?" she asked, confused again. "I haven't gotten a call since before we got on the train. What are you talking about?" Her sincerity was off putting in this moment of distrust.

Why would she look like that if she wasn't trying to hide something? Boy thought.

"A text?" he asked.

"When? Not today. What are you talking about, Boy?" Her upper lip curled under, she was getting upset. He persisted, feeling like she had to be lying. He had seen her do something with her phone, and now she was trying to say nothing happened.

"Can I see your phone?"

"Why do you want to see my phone? You're acting so weird." Despite her anger he couldn't back down now.

"You're acting weird," he was loosing hold of his emotions. "When I was walking up you took your phone out of your pocket and looked at something on it," he said, trying to regain his control. "I don't get why you're being weird about it. What are you hiding?"

"What am I hiding? What the hell are you talking about, Boy?"

"That's what I'm saying. Why would you feel the need to hide anything from me?"

"I don't. I don't feel a need to hide anything." She knew this last part wasn't true, and it showed in her voice.

"Then what were you doing on your phone, and why won't you let me see it?" Boy's altered state wasn't helping him not freak out.

"I don't even remember looking at it, and it feels like an invasion of privacy. If you trusted me you wouldn't need to look at it."

"And if you were trustworthy, it wouldn't matter if I did. So we're in a bit of a bind."

She remembered looking at her phone and smiled.

"What's so funny all of the sudden?" Boy asked.

"I was looking at the time silly. I just remembered."

"Then you won't have any activity in your phone's call and text logs." He'd committed, and held firm despite the sinking feeling he was being a jerk.

"You're right." Her smile was gone as she pulled her phone out and showed him there had been no calls or texts that day.

Boy felt like an asshole, which was somehow relieving. The relief made it easy to quickly admit he'd been wrong.

"I'm sorry, Soph." He was tempted to tell her everything Johnny T. had said, but couldn't for some reason. "I think I'm getting paranoid. You know I trust you right."

"Of course," she said. He could tell she was still off, but didn't know what to do.

"I love…" he caught himself. Why would it be weird to say he loved her? He adjusted, "…how awesome you are." He felt ridiculous. "You know I know that."

"Yeah, I do." She smiled, looking at him sideways. "Were you going to say you loved me?"

He ignored the question and hugged her. As he held her he realized how high he was getting, the colors of people's faces a three-dimensional, high-definition plasma screen adjusted to bring out the oranges and reds, their skin undulating slightly, the particles unsure where to be at any particular moment.

"You can let me go now," Sophie chuckled after some time.

He had no idea how long he had been holding her. It could have been a short moment, or a matter of minutes. He could tell the conversation had shaken her. He wanted her trust back, but didn't know how to regain it. He couldn't focus on it currently, he wasn't even sure what he wasn't focusing on.

They were swept into other interactions, and the day unfolded. They had passed Hohhot some hours before, but no one knew where they were. The party was down to the all-nighters, never-stoppers, and the belligerent drunks, not mutually exclusive groups.

Boy realized his fatigue as bright blue poured through the window. He decided to go return to bed. He noted that Sophie didn't offer to walk him. He said adieu to everyone in his immediate vicinity before stumbling away.

When he got to his room he opened the computer to look at the camera feeds. He found the lounge he had just left, hoping to see Sophie. He couldn't find her. Either she'd left, or she was out of frame. His feelings were getting complicated, and he wished Johnny T. had never implanted this paranoia in him.

Boy lay back onto his bed and stared at the ceiling a while, until finally he passed out.

He ran through puddles, unsure of what he was running from, a sinking feeling in his stomach. His feet became wet and heavy. When he got to the subway entrance below his home he stopped, trepidation building as he felt discomfort in all choices--"Boy", his mother's voice came from somewhere behind him. He turned to see reptilian shadows stretching across the tunnel walls and the sound of a train approaching. He ran out of the tunnel, to find the barren, frozen wasteland he had only ever seen in his dreams. He fell down on the ice in exhaustion. He started to shiver, waking to find himself cold and uncovered.

He struggled to take off his shoes, but gave up, wrapped himself in blankets and fell back asleep.

35

The land passing by through the windows of the

train had been barren since before they'd left China. Many hours of high desert finally broke when small shacks started to sprinkle the landscape, the air thickening with smoke of diesel engines and burning garbage.

Boy couldn't remember much of the night before, but something felt off, as Sophie wasn't lying next to him when he awoke. He was disappointed her grumpy face wasn't there telling him to shut up and let her sleep more. His mind snapped to the camera system. He felt compelled, and guilty for the compulsion, to see what the cameras could show him. His curiosity overrode his guilt.

He found Sophie's room. She moved the covers like she might be getting up and Boy was torn. He wanted to watch, and he knew how invasive and weird it was that she didn't know he could see her. Just as she peeled the covers back he forced himself to avert his eyes.

He knew he would keep this from her, another strange secret. He didn't want secrets. He'd always appreciated, almost needed, their candor. Was it him who was becoming untrustworthy and dishonest?

He needed to eat. Nico, Stanley, and WJ were about to head to the food car when he passed through the band's room, so they became a troop. They shared stories from the previous night, and as usual WJ's was the craziest. Somehow he ended up on the roof of one of the train cars, getting yelled at by the border police when they crossed from China into Mongolia. He didn't have any pants on when he finally came back down, and he still couldn't figure out what had happened to them.

The scenery change as they approached Ulaan

Bataar. These changes were difficult to integrate juxtaposed against the lavish experience of the big cities in Japan and China, let alone the expectations Boy had developed being from the wealthiest part of the western world. What was craziest to Boy was that no one else seemed affected by what he saw as an extremely underdeveloped urban landscape. People merely continued chatting about how glad they were the next performance wasn't until the following day, how fucked up they still felt from the night before, not reacting to the miles of yurts and non-permanent structures they were swiftly passing through.

Everyone's vapid, apathetic nature made Boy particularly miss Sophie, as she was different. He knew WJ would probably understand, but it wasn't the same kind of understanding Sophie would offer. WJ saw the inconsistencies in humanity, they just didn't bother him. Even now WJ watched the world, delighted by the marvels, rather than captured by bleakness.

Just as Boy's spiral turned downward he heard Sophie's sardonic voice ask, "Can you fuckers make a little room?"

"Of course," replied WJ, pulling back the chair next to him.

"Thanks," she replied.

Boy looked over at her, nodding in attempted nonchalance.

"'Sup, Boy?" she replied to his awkward nod.

"Hey, Soph," he said back. He was no longer thinking about the people passing outside the train, the people living in small, but sturdy veritable tents along the railway. He noticed how quickly his attention became myopic onto Sophie. He was no better than any one else who'd been talking about their hangovers instead of discussing the hardships of the locals. Witnessing his own self-centered nature he craved candid interaction. He was compelled to address the awkwardness between he and Sophie.

"Look, Sophie," he said, not caring that his band-mates were at the table with them, "I'm sorry if I was an asshole last night. I could say I was really wasted and I don't remember much, which is actually true, but I know I was being an idiot."

He paused hoping she would say something. She glared at him blankly.

He continued. "I'm trying to let you know that I remember being an asshole, and I'm sorry for it." The fellows all stopped moving, trapped by the sudden vulnerable sincerity of the moment. WJ grinned and gazed out the window. Sophie still gave him nothing.

"I really value you…" He was squirming, feeling the group cringe with him. He persisted, "…and your friendship. Sophie. Come on," he implored, waited for a response, deliberately ignoring the shocked and awkward looks of his band-mates (save WJ, who seemed to be passively enjoying the exchange and the morning view).

"Don't worry about it butt-face," Sophie offered, quickly redirected the conversation, "How fucking crazy are all these shacks, or uh, yurts maybe?"

WJ's grin broadened, "aren't they awesome? I love a proud nomadic culture," WJ gushed.

Boy imagined WJ was amused by the irony that bringing attention to poverty could be relieving for affluent people uncomfortable with emotional expression, that everyone felt safer looking at extreme poverty and displacement than dealing with two friends' relatively shallow emotional drama. Boy loved WJ for this, even where it was an uncomfortable reflection for him to hold. Boy was disappointed by how glad he was for the diversion from his vulnerability. He was, however, happy that Sophie wanted to talk about the yurts, which had inspired his desire for genuine interaction in the first place. He smiled to himself looking at her, and even though WJ wasn't looking at him Boy could feel that WJ had noticed. Boy loved that WJ was the kind of guy who notices most everything without needing to comment. Boy realized WJ was the best kind of friend to have, and very few of his friends realized it. Boy saw something similar in Sophie, felt pride in these strange people he had gotten close to.

36

Ulaan Bataar was nestled in a valley between two looming ranges. The yurts littering the basin went for miles, punctuating into a downtown that looked to have been modern in the late 1980s, and had largely gotten stuck there. Most of the bigger buildings were neither new nor particularly well maintained. There were business districts within the metropolitan area, small quadrants dissipating quickly into the never-ending yurts, which wound alongside the meandering river that cut through Mongolia's most notable city. It was hard to imagine a time when the Mongolian empire was the strongest and largest on Earth.

Rome fell, why shouldn't we? Boy thought as he stared out into the crumbling buildings.

Apprehension arose in Boy regarding the way

the show was being shot. It misrepresented scenarios to the benefit of a dramatic outcome. He was aware there was some element of this in all 'documentary' filmmaking, but he'd never realized to what extent the canned shots played a roll. He couldn't imagine very many of the other rock stars, let alone the models, would really be enjoying themselves in this underdeveloped city. Yet, when the cameras were on, everyone was having a great time. It was everything Boy hoped to avoid. It was fake, it was for profit, and he worried it didn't forward any kind of deeper understandings about the human condition.

Boy tried hard to resist this disappointment, so overwhelmed by the disingenuous nature of the situation that he headed back to his bunk early. He wrote heavy-handed poetry he knew he would never turn into song, only exacerbating his sense of frustration. In his mind everything was falling apart, a complete failure, and he started to wonder if he might be bipolar. He noticed how sharply his mood had swung since his morning interactions with Sophie and WJ. He wanted to feel proud of the project, but he was feeling more ashamed. He realized he wasn't doing this for the people whose countries the train would be traveling through. This was all for him, for a feeling of accomplishment in a project he could hold ownership over. He no longer felt in control. The show had been co-opted, and he was lost. This was merely a project he'd helped organize, the momentum of it had taken over, and now he was mostly a spectator to the unfolding.

Boy knew he was fibbing himself, but thought partying might pull him out of his funk. There was a group of people in the party car already, perpetually. He ordered himself an extra-strong tequila sunrise. Thinking the metaphor might lift his darkness. He wanted to restart the day. He wanted to rejoin the jubilant.

When his posse arrived they found him in a stupor, unable to articulate how he had arrived in such a disordered state. He had departed sobriety with a vigor, leaving him incoherent. His inebriation led to rants. At first his antics were entertaining, but he didn't stop drinking, and soon the laughable became the wallowing.

"You know?...Don't you know?...You guys..." People around him chuckled uncomfortably. "No, seriously—look...We are pretty, sure...Sure...But we are the ugly ones here. I mean...We come here all high and mighty...All my and highty...Wait...All sure of this pretty little life...Bullshit...Fucking bullshit...You know, too?...Don't you?...You don't feel pretty, do they?...They aren't ugly...We are...We're ashamed...Look...Why don't you come to my house all pretty and tell me how much better you are...And I will be in awe...Because you have everything...But I don't...I don't have a goddamn thing...I'm fucking useless...What good does any of this do? What good does any of us do? Anythin...thing?...Nothing!...Goddamnit!...It's all the same fucking lie..."

Against her better judgment Sophie finally cut in, "Ok Boy. Why are you so upset?"

"You," he replied, interrupting her. "I don't even know." He stumbled and she caught him.

"Here," she said, putting his arm around her shoulder. "Let's go to bed." She'd never seen him so upset.

"It's all bullshit, Sophie. My mom. All these

pretty fucking assholes." This was the last thing the lounge heard as she walked him out. She hoped his diatribe hadn't been caught on film, sure it had, and smart enough to know this was juicy enough to show up in the show.

"You know," he continued as they ambled awkwardly down the hall, "I really want to trust you, Sophie, but everything is so full of bullshit that I don't know what to trust."

"Yeah, and I don't know either." She knew he was drunk enough he wouldn't remember, She wanted to muster the courage to tell him everything she'd been holding back. "I…"

"I think…" he interrupted, "I think I might be a little bit in love with you, Sophie." His head bobbling as he spoke. She wasn't sure he knew what he was saying. She remained silent. "Did you hear me?" he looked up at her, but his eyes couldn't focus.

"Sorry, what?" Sophie asked.

"I FUCKING LOVE YOU, SOPHIA!" He was looking right at her as he said this. "In this world full of shit you have always been good."

Sophie didn't know what to say so she just kept trying to move him towards his room. "You're drunk, Boy," she finally said.

"I am not just drunk," he replied. "I am drunk, but I am not just drunk. Listen to me, Sophie, I have been freaking out a little bit about this, and maybe it's the alcohol letting me be so honest, but I love you, and I know you know it."

Sophie knew fighting his conviction wouldn't do anything, it never worked, even when he was sober. She took a different route, "I know, Boy, and I love you, too. You're my best friend, of course we love each other. I hope you know that's true, no matter what." She felt the weight of her dishonesty.

"But I think I don't only love you as a friend, as a best friend, but also I think I am in love with you."

Sophie was shocked. She wanted him to sleep this off. She had purposefully tried to never pay mind to the complex feelings between them, and the inconveniences those feelings wrought.

"Do you hear me, Sophie? I'm trying to tell you I'm in love with you." Boy's eyes were nearly rolling back in his head, his balance still needing her to stay upright.

Boy's movements were getting sloppier as they arrived at his room. Sophie dropped him onto his bed, took off his shoes and pants and listened as he mumbled on about being in love with her, occasionally responding, "Thanks, Boy, I know," or, "You're sweet." She told herself she was only staying with him to make sure he didn't fall asleep on his back. She was afraid to admit that she was also staying because she loved him too. She shushed him until he passed out.

37

Boy woke up, a rockslide in his head. Even through the pain, he was happy to discover Sophie's sleeping face. The previous night a haze, he hoped he hadn't compromised the social ease of the rest of the trip.

He noticed his computer open and was taken by fear he may have shown her his observation capabilities. Withholding information, and blacking out to the point of not knowing if the information remained withheld, swept Boy into anxiety. His hangover was no help. He knew the most likely resolution to this anxiety waited on the far side of honesty. He could rid himself of this discomfort if he were merely stopped hiding from her. And yet, when Sophie started to stir, he knew he would keep the secret if it were still a secret to keep.

"Morning," he said.

"Morning," she grumbled, opening an eye to leer at him. "How you feeling this morning champ?" she asked. He could tell she was amused at how shitty she expected him to feel. Not a great sign.

"Feeling like a champ. How's you?" Boy faked, not want to give her the reward of his actual discomfort.

She shut her eye and smiled, "Probably a billion times better than you. How much do you remember?"

Fuck, he thought, what did I do?

He assumed he had told her about the surveillance. Just in case he hadn't, he asked, "Why? What did I do?" The pounding in his head, and his fear, made it nearly impossible to play off with levity.

She could tell he was having a rough one and chose benevolence. "You expressed your deep affections for me," she said, smiling broadly, her eyes still closed.

He couldn't tell if she was teasing, but he was relieved that she didn't say he'd shown her the surveillance. His relief was short lived when he realized what she had said might be true. "What?" He stumbled, trying to contain embarrassment.

"You got exceedingly drunk and proceeded to express your undying love for me." She chuckled playfully.

Boy froze. Divert. "Wow. I must have been

wasted."

She snorted at his poor attempt at diversion. "You told me you're in love with me." She was elated at how uncomfortable this was making him.

He was glad her eyes were closed, his cheeks going crimson. He decided to pretend like he didn't really believe her. "Oh," affecting sarcastic, "is that what happened? And what did you say?"

"I told you I thought you were sweet," she said playfully. "Are you trying to pretend like it isn't true?" Her lips pursed stifling a smile.

"Why would I?" Trying to sound over the top, he added, "Obviously it must be true, if I said it when I was sooo wasted." He punctuated this statement with an unfortunate forced laugh.

"It's okay, Boy," Sophie continued, "I already knew."

A knock came at the door. "Who is it?" Boy hollered, wincing in pain at the loud knock and his loud response.

The door swung open and Boy could see his mom standing in the entrance. "Do you realize what time it is?"

"Morning, mom," Boy said.

"If it was morning that would be good," she responded. "Boy, you have the first platform performance to be overseeing." Even though she was obviously irate, she wore the same emotion she always showed; stern, cold, barely expressive.

"What?" A rush of adrenaline, his heart rate increased, his vision blurred, the pain in his head pulsed. "What time is it?"

"Get up, Boy. I am not your secretary. This is the last time I'm going to save your ass on this trip." Without closing the door she walked off, yelling down the hall, "Get him out of bed, Sophia, if you know what is good for him."

Boy scrambled out of bed. He looked back at Sophie, her eyes were wide, frightened. "If I have to get up so do you," he said.

"I didn't even think your mom saw me until she yelled back," Sophie said, trying to make light of the situation.

"Get up."

He rushed through his band's cabin on his way to the performance car and growled, "What the fuck, guys? How come none of you came and woke me up?"

The answer was obvious. None of them were out of bed yet.

"Get the fuck up, we have our first train performance, like now!"

They rustled themselves out of bed. Sophie arrived, following Boy as he rushed towards the 'stage coach'.

On his way, in an attempt to calm himself, he reached for the serpent and moon pendant hanging from his neck. Holding the necklace settled his nerves.

Turning fast around a corner he ran into Johnny T. Boy had nearly forgotten Johnny T. was on the trip.

"The big day. You ready?" Johnny T. asked.

"Honestly? No. But I think it'll be great," Boy said, a game face on.

"Let me know if there's anything I can do. I'm actually quite the MC, if I do say so myself." There was something endearing about Johnny T.'s arrogance, something in Johnny T.'s charisma felt almost paternal.

"Thanks, Johnny," Boy rushed. Then, upon consideration, he continued, "Actually, if you wouldn't mind, it might be really great for you to do a bit of the introducing today."

"You got it, kid." Johnny T. was exuberant. He followed Boy and Sophie to the stage, which had already been set up. Boy was relieved to find the opening band getting set up, and the sound guy getting the levels started.

There weren't many locals gathered for the show. Boy assumed it was because there was actually the better part an hour left before the music was scheduled to start. The few stragglers seemed to be there by chance.

Boy's eyes darted around for something to do. He noticed Johnny T. was leaning over someone, his posture flirtatious. Boy wondered whom Johnny T. had set his eyes on this time. He was taken aback to see it was Sophie. Boy was even more shocked to see her flirtatiously averting her eyes in response to something Johnny T. said. A rush of jealousy surfaced, and the nausea he would have been feeling without the adrenaline from his mother's jolting wake up call, and his tardy appearance at the stage.

Boy's sight blurred, he saw a strange green undertone to Johnny T.'s complexion. He wondered if this was jealousy. He didn't care. He even felt slightly betrayed. His hand started to hurt and he realized he was gripping his pendant so tightly it was about to break the skin of his palm.

Why the fuck is Johnny T. flirting with Sophie if he thinks she's my girlfriend? It would be bad enough if he didn't think that. And flirting with her right in front of me, what an asshole, Boy thought. *Fuck that guy. And fuck Sophie, too. Oh god, I'm going to hurl.*

Boy's vision was so misty with rage he had a

hard time stumbling behind the stage to find a good place to puke. Just before he burst he, through his blurred vision, he saw another large reptile in a suite, which shook him so intensely he erupted. Done releasing the contents of his guts he looked back in the place where it had been, it was gone. He was having a hard time seeing through the tears that had formed while vomiting. Through his distorted sight he saw nothing, not even a normal person.

Am I going crazy?

He wasn't used to this much stress, off kilter from the drugs, drinking, lack of sleep, responsibility. Let alone the discomfort of feelings for Sophie, a vulnerability he had never allowed himself to feel with anyone. He decided to disregard his perception, assuming it a hallucination due to his compromised state. He knew it wasn't the best choice, but to function well that night he needed a hair of the dog.

He found Johnny T. flirting with some groupies who had shown up for the first band, and asked if he had a flask. Johnny T., of course, had one, which he was delighted to share with Boy. Boy was hated how much the first sip relaxed him. He knew this was a bad sign, but now wasn't the time to think about it.

He drained the flask, not caring how Johnny T. might react. His focus returned. Tension he hadn't realized he was holding left his body. The stage suddenly looked great. A few more locals had arrived to watch, and the crowd was filling out with people from the crew who weren't otherwise occupied putting on the performance. Boy also knew that, if they were crammed in close, the cameras could work magic to make the crowd look full. He disliked the fallacy that filming in such a manner could create. It could feel so blatantly oppositional to the authenticity he'd said the project was about. But right now he was mostly just glad to no longer be freaking out.

Pulling Johnny T. aside Boy shared, "You'll never believe what I just thought I saw behind the stage."

Johnny T. smiled and inquired, "What's that?"

"A huge reptile, dressed in human clothes." Boy laughed a little at the absurdity of the claim, but Johnny T. looked concerned for a second before he joined in Boy's laughter. He wondered if this was just another of his paranoid delusions.

Let it go Boy, not now, he demanded of his newly relatively relaxed state.

"That is crazy," Johnny T. replied, "You see stuff like that often?" Johnny T, acted amused, but Boy sensed a seriousness to the question.

Again Boy ignored his instincts, deciding instead to open up to Johnny T. "Not often. Actually, the first time was when Sophie and I were on shrooms at that party we ran into you at. I saw the same reptile-guy disappear into the wall. That's why Sophie and I were staring at the wall for so long that night."

Johnny T. laughed, appearing relieved, replying, "That makes so much sense. So what did you take today? And do you have any to share?"

These questions put Boy at ease. Johnny T.'s solicitation for substance made him Boy's peer again, not someone judging from the outside. Boy replied, "That would be nice. I wish I was high and had something to share." This wasn't actually true, but Boy wanted to appear badass, save face in front of Johnny T.

Johnny T. produced a small strip of paper from

his pocket. It looked like paper ripped off any slightly thick stock. "You wanna take some of this acid with me?"

Boy was trapped. He wanted to remain cool in Johnny T.'s eyes. Johnny T. ripped off two small squares, put one on his tongue, and offered the other to Boy. Boy didn't know what to do. Someone on stage called his name. As he turned to look he felt Johnny T.'s finger push into his mouth.

Boy immediately turned back to look at Johnny T., who was smirking, mischievous, put the rest of the strip back into his pocket. Johnny T. said, "Have a nice trip Boy, I wont tell if you don't." He winked in the corny manner of a old Hollywood actor, and darted away.

As soon as Johnny T. was gone Boy spit the little piece of paper out and ran to the stage to see who had called for him. What Boy didn't realize was that LSD dissolves into one's system seconds after contacting the tongue.

Boy was quickly absorbed in the show. He was sober enough to coordinate the rest of the set up, but by the time the first band was actually performing he was starting to get high. It wasn't out of control. Time became a squishy, fungible substance. He lost himself to the music, thoroughly enjoying each of the bands as they played. He would have missed his band's sound check if he hadn't still been standing backstage, elated at the depth he was finding in lyrics he'd heard many times, but never really listened to.

Each band was only required to play four songs, which made the sets quick. Fit to Burst's set was awkward. The band was on, and it wasn't that Boy was completely off, it was more like he was hitting everything at the very last moment possible, which gave the music a strange tension. Boy thought he was really getting into it, but his altered delivery put the band on edge. He hadn't explained what was going on, and the only person that knew, without being told, was WJ, who didn't mind, and enjoyed riding the wave of Boy's high vicariously.

After the set was done the band was pissed, which confused Boy as he had felt so 'in it'. Fortunately, they didn't get too down on him, because it would've merely turned his pleasant trip sour. Instead they did what they knew to do, catch up with Boy, and start partying for the cameras.

Boy was in no space to drink, and instead went wandering around looking for Sophie, getting distracted along the way, following the fractals of fascination as they blossomed in front of him. After the eighth hour Boy started to wonder how long this trip would last. He'd gotten sidetracked investigating how the wheels and under-workings of the train worked.

Sophie pulled him out from under the train and suggested they go watch the rest of the music. He was overjoyed to see her and tell her everything he had realized about the train's underpinnings as a macrocosmic representation of the brain. She listened with a tender affection he was too intoxicated to observe overtly, but was subconsciously drawn to.

They wandered back to the stage where they stayed until after breakdown. Boy tried to help, wandering around, picking up already wound up cords, puzzling at their ability to transfer sound from instruments to amps and out into the minds of the audience, then putting them back down in completely different parts of the stage where they didn't belong.

Eventually he found himself in the dark of night, in his room alone with Sophie, waxing philosophic, falling in and out of something like sleep, the seams of dreams and the geometric shapes he saw on the back of his eyelids when the closed melting into one and other. It had been one of the best trips of his life. He didn't notice when Sophie left.

He fell into a dream of *the undulating field. A figure walked towards him, becoming more out of focus the closer it got. Boy felt soothed by the figures presents, but averted his eyes due to the figure's brightness. He noticed the ground was a maze of interconnected threads, all moving together. There was no independence in the movement, and his feet had no clear distinction from the ground he was standing on, as though he was becoming part of the interwoven fabric of the field surrounding him. He trusted this integration, and felt a deep sense of interconnectedness and peace. He could feel the figure, a gently nearing warmth. He released into rest, knowing somehow he would be held.*

38

Boy woke with a haze of enthusiasm, both from his dreams and the previous day's adventure. He was surprised Sophie wasn't with him. The train was moving. They were probably near, if not already in Russia, Boy had no real idea of how far they had gone.

Wondering at Sophie's whereabouts, his focus fell on the computer. He hadn't done much observation since that first day. After a little searching the only two rooms he didn't find were his and his mother's. He took this as proof it was his mother that had orchestrated the whole thing. He found his band's room, everyone in bed, except WJ meditating on the sofa. He knew all this tooling about was distraction from his true motivation. He was trying to resist the urge to look at Sophie's room, but broke, expecting her to either be asleep still, or not there. Instead she was talking to someone who was standing just out of frame, in the hallway. She was gesticulating wildly, but without sound it was impossible to tell what was being said. She looked angry, or was it defensive.

He felt uneasy watching her move so violently in silence. He searched for a volume knob, but couldn't find one. Sophie was becoming increasingly upset. He needed to protect her.

He shut the computer down. Dashing for the door he realized he was naked. He tossed some things on but stopped at the door. His vanity wouldn't allow him to leave so disheveled. He primped himself as quick as he could before entering the outside world. It was only a couple minutes before he was out the door, hurrying down the hall to Sophie's room. He passed Johnny T. in hallway, merely slapping him a high five and a, "Mornin'".

Boy didn't stop to engage as Johnny T. said, "Someone's in a hurry."

Continuing down the corridor, he wondered if the person outside of Sophie's room could have been Johnny T. Johnny T. had been calm, not like someone who had just come from an argument, but Boy remembered the older man flirting with Sophie the night before, remembered his jealousy. The bliss he had woken into became tenuous as discomfort flooded him.

When Boy finally got to Sophie's room he knocked frantically on the door.

"What?" Sophie hollered.

"It's me. Open up." Boy hollered back.

"The door shouldn't be locked." Sophie's voice seemed calm, despite the amplified volume to make it through the door, which was indeed unlocked.

When he entered Boy found Sophie lying in bed. He couldn't be direct, because he would have to explain how he knew she had been having an argument.

"What's up? You're on a rampage this morning. Did you sleep alright?" Her voice had a hint of grit, as though she had just woken up.

"Huh, what? No. I, uh…I mean, yeah." He was having a hard time parsing what to do. She wasn't in danger, nor was she consumed with the frustration he'd seen on the screen.

"Did you just come to wake me up?" She was disarming.

He remained silent, stunned.

Sophie continued, "What's your deal, Boy?"

"Have you seen Johnny T.?" he asked.

"The T-Bomb?" A coy smirk nudged its way onto her face. She looked at Boy curiously. "Not since the party last night. Why? What did that weirdo do?"

He didn't like that her smile triggered jealousy. "Just trying to find him is all." He felt like a complete idiot, and knew he sounded like one too.

"Yeah?" She looked at him in disbelief. "And you rushed here to see if I knew where he was?" A large grin suddenly spread itself across her face. "Are you being jealous?"

He scoffed at her, "Of what?" He felt like a 12-

year-old. How did this always happen with her when she called him out? He blushed.

"You're jealous!" she exclaimed. "You have a little crush on me, Boy?" She asked playfully.

"What are you talking about Sophie?" Boy wasn't convinced. Sophie wasn't either. He tried diversion. "Did you just wake up?"

"No. I've been lying here for a bit. I'm super hungry. But don't change the subject, Boy. Is there something you need to tell me?" She shook her shoulders and teasing him.

"About what?" He looked at the ground. "Shut up, Sophie. Get up and let's go get some breakfast." He heard Napoleon Dynamite in his voice. The embarrassment felt better than the jealousy.

"That's so cute. You like me." Though she was teasing it didn't feel mean. "You think I'm sexy." She started doing a little dance under the blankets, continuing to wiggle her shoulders back and forth, batting her eyelashes and making playfully flirtatious eyes at him.

"You're so ridiculous," he said, annoyed that he liked her teasing, and double embarrassed to realize he was getting turned on.

"You already admitted you were in love with me the other night." Her smile was so broad it seemed like all her teeth were showing. "There's nothing to be ashamed of, Boy. I'm a real looker, and you're not denying it? Don't worry. I wont tell anyone." She jumped out of bed, gave him a big kiss on the cheek. "You're not so bad yourself kid."

He smiled, falling onto the bed as she got dressed. Neither of them spoke again until they left the room. The tension a thick muggy air just before a thunderstorm. Boy forgot his earlier concern, his jealousy, the fear that Sophie had been in danger.

His earlier enthusiastic undertone returned. He felt tingly, and felt cliché for it.

They left to get breakfast, picked up the band on the way. They returned to a familiar banter, as though nothing had happened. Boy knew he was grinning more than the morning usually gave him excuse to, and caught a knowing eye from WJ.

The train slowed. Boy realized they must be only now arriving at the edge of Mongolia, the beginning of Siberia. They were entering Russia again. Boy shivered involuntarily. What a rollercoaster to be at the whims of all these feelings all the time, he thought. The real rides inside. He laughed at himself.

39

As the trip progressed to Irkutsk things started to become routine on the train. Everyone fell into habituated partying protocols. The models always arrived during the most significant filming times. Scenarios played out as though real, all for the purpose of 'documenting' the 'real' experience aboard this 'festival express'. The organic excitement became the performance of performers fulfilling unspoken expectations of what they thought they were supposed to be.

Whether it was because of the perpetual partying, or because they found a rhythm on the train, the trip started to fly by. Boy was shocked at how developed Irkutsk was, and how indifferent the people seemed. He tried to venture out, to regain a sense of excitement, to break out of the routine of it all. However, barely any of the locals spoke English, making it very hard to interact. Boy also noticed he was hyper-vigilant being back in a Russian speaking environment. Nevertheless he wanted to try to broaden his perspective, and if he smiled the locals usually smiled back.

Boy was grateful that more people arrived for that nights show, a trend that continued for the rest of the trip. Even though they didn't speak much English many somehow sang along with at least the more popular songs. The audience was thrilled, which gave Boy a sense of pride and hope. There was something worthwhile in all the effort of this endeavor.

They passed Lake Baikal on their way to Novosibirsk, Russia's third largest city. The world's deepest known lake was breathtaking. Boy wished the trip had allotted more time for exploration. There was so much they were rushing past. As they passed the lake he overheard WJ telling someone that it was so deep that they had never actually found the bottom, and that some believed that there were secret underwater tunnels connecting Baikal all the way to Antarctica. Boy smirked at the delightful conspiracies WJ played with.

Novosibirsk was dauntingly industrial. It was where the road came up from Kazakhstan and the rest of the southern ex-soviet 'Stans', and met up with the Trans-Siberian. It was major shipping hub and cultural center because of its location at such a significant crossroads.

Seeing the relative poverty of the places the train passed through Boy started to churn in frustration against the corporate element of the journey. He had always struggled with the privilege he had grown up in. It was arrogant, and he was accidentally arrogant as a consequence. He had become sensitive to the ways in which wealthy people often thought the little things they gave were enough to make up for everything they took. The people who had signed on as executive producers the 'festival express' were drawing a monetary benefit from this venture they had framed as an altruistic endeavor. The bands wouldn't have signed on if they weren't getting paid. The funding would have come if it weren't for the prospect of making money on the back end. They were actually making money on the trip itself. Sponsors were footing most of the bill just to have their products incorporated into the show. Soda bottles everywhere, tobacco, labels on the food, clothing, shoes, instruments, and especially the booze. Comparing their lavish living upon the train to the lack of resource that flashed by outside, Boy's dissolution pulled him back into a familiar depression. Boy was one of those producers he was criticizing and he squirmed recognizing it.

By Yekaterinburg he was so far consumed by his self-loathing and seemingly inescapable dissatisfaction that he even lost motivation to go out and try to see something new. From the window of the train Yekaterinburg looked like any other big, dirty, industrial city to him, and he needed a break. It appeared another example of humans exploiting humans and disregarding everything else along the way.

Boy hadn't been interacting with his mom much, which he didn't generally mind. Nevertheless, he started to wonder where she was. He knew she was around, working from behind the scenes, the executive producer, silent, hidden, her fingers in every pie. She probably wouldn't even be in the movie at all, and she probably wanted it that way. He wouldn't even be surprised if her name didn't appear anywhere on the show, her anonymity somehow commensurate with her fame. He wished he could look at a camera of her room to see what she was up to. She was likely at a desk, writing something, talking on the phone, drinking from that ceramic mug of hers that she had likely brought from her office at home, or telling someone somewhere what to do.

One day he opened the computer to see if he could find her anywhere on the train. He looked in the food car, the only place he could imagine her if she wasn't in her room. She wasn't there. He checked the lounge, not expecting her, but no harm in looking. No sign of her.

He had an impulse to view Johnny T.'s room. Johnny T. was alone. He looked like he was asleep standing up. He had one hand pressed against the wall, but it didn't look as if the hand was supporting him, it appeared more like a limp cord connecting to a wall socket. He watched Johnny T. rocking gently with the movements of the train. Just as the limp rocking of Johnny T.'s body started to become uncomfortable for Boy to watch, Johnny T.'s head turned and looked up at the camera. Boy figured Johnny T. must know about the cameras, and he must either know someone could be watching, or he was playing it up for the sake of the documentary, in some awkward attempt to get more camera time. Boy was uncomfortable with the way Johnny T. stared at the camera. Johnny T. grinned. Boy shuttered and turned off the computer.

After a moment's pause Boy turned the computer back on and found Sophie's room. She was standing in the doorway talking with someone. Again very serious, and again, he wanted to protect her though he didn't know why. He couldn't see whom she was talking to. He noticed this time she was holding her camera, and it looked like she was showing some of the pictures to the person standing in the hallway. Who the hell could it be? He wondered. It clearly wasn't Johnny T. this time, as he had just been in his own room. Sophie turned away from the door and back into her room. Just before the door closed Boy thought he saw the shadow of a huge reptilian tail departing in the hallway.

Boy told himself it had to be the shadows playing tricks on him, his mind wanting to see something that wasn't there, as it couldn't have been real. He knew when he got into this kind of state, this depth of despair and mental fatigue, the best thing for him to do was to take some time off and keep his eyes shut for as long as he could. He decided it would be best if he stopped watching the hidden cameras, as he was obviously only digging himself into a hole. It also felt dishonest, an extra emotional pressure he didn't need.

He tried taking the next day off, to get a full day's rest on their journey from Yekaterinburg to Moscow. But just as he was starting to fall asleep, Sophie knocked on the door, bursting in, grinning, and asking why he was in bed. He told her he was exhausted, and she told him not to be such a wuss, entreating him to get his sorry ass up, as partying would be more relaxing in the long run. He resisted. She relented.

After Sophie had gone, and despite his need for rest, Boy's fear of missing out kicked in causing sleep to eluded him. He considered how time, when he wanted, or even more, needed sleep, became awkward and irregular. His mind raced over things he wished he'd done different until he accidentally started to slip into the strange thoughts of near sleep. Then, again, on the edge of slumber, another knock shook him alert.

His mom pushed opened the door and asked, "What is the matter?"

"What?" He asked.

"Why are you laying in bed? Are you ill?" She was matter of fact.

"No, I'm not ill mom. I'm just wiped. And I need to get some sleep before we got to Moscow." He flopped his head back onto his pillow, squeezing his eyes closed with considerably more vigor than was necessary, in protest to the demands the waking world was making of him.

"We don't just get to take breaks when we want," his mother persisted. "I know you've been mostly doing everything out of enjoyment, but it is your responsibility to make sure there is always a party happening, and right now, without you, the lull is taking over."

Boy listened, confused and angry. Why couldn't he just take a moment for himself? He couldn't believe how much this journey had turned into simulacra of fun created for the fulfillment of marketing obligations. Was there anything real in documentary at all?

Boy's mother's voice cut through his contemptuous thoughts, "So. It is time to get up. It is time you went and started the party." She promptly closed the door, which she hadn't ever come all the way through.

How many people had their parents tell them they weren't partying enough? Though this was about the show, and though Boy knew she was right, he hated her and the project for it. He didn't want it to be out of fear of his mother's wrath, so he told himself he was getting up because he was a professional.

He put himself together, light black suit, thin slate tie, over a burnt cream linen shirt. He rallied the band to parade down the corridor starting a chant as they walked through the other bands cars towards the party lounge.

"You can sleep when you're dead! So party with us instead!"

They pulled many of the other rockers out of hiding. Before long the party was renewed, Dionysus invoked, praises to revelry engaged. Boy's enthusiastic mask so convincing as to only not fool WJ, who found the process entertaining, watching someone fake fun, convinced that this was mostly what humans seemed to be doing everywhere anyways.

Boy drank, but drunkenness that night was a dark and distasteful drunk, the type of place reached when the party has gone on too long and too hard, and not because you love it, but because you can't stop. Offering cheers, feigning laughs, pantomiming participation, inside spiraling further and further into dissolution, disgust, and mistrust of himself and the world he had created around him.

Once the momentum of the necessary roistering had been achieved, and his control over his outward expression started to sleep in intoxication, Boy started to wallow, a complex bitterness astringent enough to curl his lips. Sophie found him there and led him back to his room. In the sanctuary of his room he embarked on long rants about the lack of authenticity in art and in the world at large. He berated himself as just another bullshit cog in a machine merely created to sell overpriced garbage to the desperate, distracted many. He had become the circus to keep the masses passive. In his stupor he admitted he had been watching her on the hidden cameras.

By this point he expression had become incoherent. Sophie wasn't sure how much to believe, and how much was inebriation. She decided to let most of it go, though she did check the computer, unable to get past the opening screen without a password she wasn't about to ask for. She wanted to believe he was being drunkenly delusional, but the little she was able to understand sounded too close to home for her to feel comfortable. She put him to bed, and, seeing he was safe, left to sleep in her own room as he wasn't such pleasant company.

They arrived the next morning in Moscow. Boy, consumed by hangover, couldn't piece together the previous night. He could tell they had arrived as the train was no longer moving. He didn't know how long he'd slept, or how long they had been stopped and adrenaline of 'things needing to be done' pulled him from sleep. He knew he would be bothered if he didn't rouse himself and make sure that set up for the day was underway. He was pleased to see things well underway, and to hear that the previous night was largely a success for both participants and production.

Moscow was their most successful show from the platform. Despite the resounding successes, Boy's complex inner state, and the fog of prolonged chemical compromise, kept him from taking much of it in. Boy was so distracted by his haze that he didn't even think about what he had been through the last time he had visited the city.

After the show was done, and people started talking about going out into Moscow, Boy started to feel uncomfortable. Boy's nerves got the best of him and he became afraid to leave the train, concerned the cops might mug him again, or worse. WJ knew this, and after the crew had done their obligatory filmed visit to Red Square, WJ convinced Boy he needed to address his fear. WJ was probably the only person that could have gotten through to Boy in this moment.

Boy saw the value in WJ's perspective and allowed himself to be convinced to split from the group and wandered the long way back to the train, trying to find the place where the officer had allegedly died. As they rounded a corner near the spot they noticed a group of three cops ahead of them. Boy wanted to turn around, but when he looked at WJ, motioning to retreat, WJ just beamed and continued to walk towards their potential assailants. Boy took a deep breath, forgetting to breathe again as they passed the dark figures, who merely offered smug scowls and disregard.

Once the train yard was in view, WJ said, "When you address your demons, they lose their power." Boy offered only a sideways glance, still trying to regain even a modicum of composure. "Those guys seemed nice." WJ commented, seeming to be speaking to himself more than Boy.

"You are such a trip, WJ." Boy was always impressed with WJ's faith in humanity despite his knowledge of how corrupt everything was.

Back aboard and on their way from Moscow to St. Petersburg, Boy noticed he hadn't seen Sophie much since the party. When he reflected on it, even in the brief moments he had seen her she was distant, even cold. He started to worry he might have said something weird to her during the part of the party his mind either didn't want to, or couldn't remember. He wish that circumstance weren't keeping them apart, but he never seemed to find a chance to check in.

He didn't know if it was the excitement that the end of the trip was nigh, or if it was the glorious city, but something started to shift in him, everything abuzz as they arrived in the Village of St. Peter. He suddenly had energy to go out, and go out they did. They ran in large groups through the streets, in awe of the architecture, enjoying their revelry in Russia's intellectual and artistic capital. They drank vodka like water, and water like vodka. The city received them. Bars welcomed them, cameras and all. People smiled at their antics. Boy wasn't sure if it was real, if his improved mood was just helping him see the better side of things, or if a little bit of WJ's optimism had rubbed off. Or maybe it was the relief that the trip, his project, seemed to have accomplished at least it's production goals. Maybe he was proud that he would have something he could point to as proof he could bring an idea into reality, how ever distorted the lenses might be. Whatever the source, he was the happiest he'd been since that first night in the Tokyo. He didn't question the happiness, despite recognizing the rollercoaster.

Their performance for Pete, the last performance of the tour, was perhaps not the most professional, as many of the musicians were wasted, but it was definitely the most fun. Everyone seemed to have a great time. The show was punctuated by a large free-for-all, as many members from as many bands as possible rotating in an impromptu jam. Their anthem a medley of: 'The Weight', by The Band, 'Let the Sun Shine In', from the musical, Hair, 'Atlantis', by Donovan, and, 'Black Water', by The

Doobie Brothers. They bridged from one to the other, punctuating seamlessly into a free form, which only shut down when authorities insisted the show be over.

The show ended but the revelry lasted through the night. Though many nights of the tour had become celebrations of Bacchus, this was the biggest. It was as though Dionysus was there and deemed it indulgence worthy of his name. It was pure debauchery.

In the peek of Boy's altered state and revelation, out of the corner of his eye, he saw two figures interacting with another reptile. At first he ignored it, not wanting to loose his bliss. WJ came to his mind, "If you address your demons, they lose their power." He had to look. Turning his gaze towards the figures he was amused to see no reptile, but merely his mom and Johnny T. deep in conversation at a high cocktail table with a lamp on it between them. This was the first time he'd seen his mom at a party. He wondered if they were sleeping together, laughed at the ridiculous thought, and let the whole thing slip away from his mind.

The next day's flight home was rough. Many of the musicians and crew expressed sadness to be leaving the 'Festival Express', though they were so hung over they barely brought themselves to say good-bye. Boy wondered how many were as secretly relieved to be done as he was. He sat with his mom, Sophie, and Johnny T. on their private flight home. They slept the better part of the journey. Contained in his seat, alone in his evaluation of the mad adventure they'd undertaken, he was unsure of where to start the conversation, and too tired to try. He was glad no one else seemed to need one either.

40

New York was cold, but Boy liked where he was living. He liked that in the morning he could wake up and see something familiar, and something new almost invariably. Boy had expected down time, a few days to rest and rejuvenate. He hadn't asked, he had simply assumed it. It was in this wishful thinking, and the expectation therein, that his resentment at its lack of reality lay.

After less than a days of recovery, his mom knocked at his door early in the morning, before letting herself in. Skipping pleasantries she started, "May I remind you, Boy, our work is not over. Just because the filming is done, and just because we are no longer on the train doesn't mean we are finished. We have editing, and post-production to start on. More importantly, you need to start the nighttime entertainment circuit. You really ought to have started promoting the project publicly even before we left, but I won't chastise you for it, as I know you're still learning."

He glared at her with a mixture of sleep deprivation and anger.

She continued, "You're tired, Boy. Everyone is. Signifies a wonderful trip. I'm going to give you the rest of today, but we are going to start work in the morning. This is what the life of a professional is like. You want this project to succeed, this is what you do." But even before he could attempt to respond she added, "Of course you want it to succeed. We all do. I am proud of you, and I think all of this could become something great."

She glared back at him a moment before finishing, clearly not expecting a response. "Okay. Good. I'm glad we had this talk. Come down to my office to work out details when you're ready." Without Boy saying a word she was back out of the room. Though his fatigue was to the bone, and though he wanted to spite her for her curt reflection, he knew that she was right, he had to keep the momentum. He wouldn't even give it the day, he would start now, which he knew was really what she had expected.

Boy got dressed and walked down to her office. His mother acted like it was natural that he hadn't taken the day to rest. They made a plan of action and he engaged it. They started the hype machine, and the media world became abuzz about the new project from 'The Wonder Boy', as the media spin had been instructed to refer to him. People were getting excited merely because they were being told to, and he was telling them to. He felt they were building expectation with no foundation outside the words he spoke. He was shocked at how easily people seemed willing to following him. He wanted people to enjoy his art because his art was enjoyable, not because they'd been coerced by him, by the mind control of suggestion, by the machine of the media.

As Boy's notoriety and momentum grew so did his resentment towards the industry. He began experimenting with making no sense when he talked about the project, to see if anyone would notice. What he found scared the hell out of him. When speaking incoherently the project was spun as more artistic, and the hype got stronger. When he acted awkward the media spun him as an intoxicated and dedicated artist, building hype that the show would be the best party the world had ever gotten seen. When he brought focus back to his original intention, to bring music to the underprivileged, the media spun it as an altruistic venture, something he had come to realize was far from the truth. No matter what he tried, he felt trapped, supported on a life raft floating I a sea of bullshit, perpetually spinning in one direction, to glorify and venerate him and whatever endeavor he was engaging. He couldn't wag his tail; his tale was wagging him.

Boy found the editing process infuriating. He hadn't realized what a big role his mom was going to play, and he felt frustrated with her choices and influence. He would see footage, gritty but honest, tapping into the harsh, and therefore compelling part of the experience. It felt like every clip Boy was excited about would get cut because it made the 'characters less popularly accessible', or 'was too dark for popular consumption', or 'would get push back from the personalities publicist'. He watched the footage get manipulated for the maximum corporate plugs, slanted towards the fashion, and glorifying the parties, without showing that they never ended as beautifully as they began. Everything he'd hoped to accomplish was squashed in order to mold the show into something that idealized the elite upon the train, especially him, turning it all into something that would bring in more money. He was disgusted.

On his way home from the editing studio one night a cop car rushed up on Boy. He was startled, unsure of what the problem was. His first thought was that something must have happened to his mom.

"What's the matter? What's happened?" he

asked as the officers burst out of the car.

One of the officers yelled, "PUT YOUR HANDS WHERE WE CAN SEE THEM!"

Boy anxiety peeked. Everything slowed, like he was in the middle of a car accident happening. He noticed the cops' hands were on their guns, and his hands shot up before he could even process the movement. After realizing his arms were up, he wondered at his body's intelligence that was faster than his thoughts. It didn't want to risk getting shot. "What's going on? What's happened!?" he yelled back as the faster of the two officers was grabbing his upraised arms and throwing him against the wall.

"You have the right to remain silent," said one officer as the other yanked his wrists into handcuffing.

"You have the wrong guy. Don't you know who I am?" Boy asked, repulsed by the words as they left his mouth, but indignant nonetheless.

"Shut up Boy," snarled the other cop as he actively pushing Boy against the wall. "We know who you are. Make this easy. Where are they?"

"Who?" Replied Boy sincerely.

"Don't fuck around, it'll only make it worse. Where are the drugs?"

Boy was dumbfounded. His couldn't make sense of the situation. He scanned his memory to make sure he wasn't carrying, and realized he might still have a few hits of blotter Johnny T. had given him at the end of the trip, but they looked like a normal small piece of ripped white paper. It was safest to deny. "I have no idea what you are talking about," he tried. "What's happening?"

"Pockets," said the officer who had just mumbled the Miranda Rights hurriedly. When the cop holding him pulled his hands out of Boy's right jacket pocket he produced a baggie of white powder.

"What's this?" he asked, shoving the bag into Boy's face menacingly.

"I have no idea. That's not mine," Boy said, becoming dizzy from fear and adrenaline.

"Bull-honkey," said the other cop. He looked at Boy in disgust and spat, "Don't you know who I am?" in a high pitched, nasal voice. "These goddamned rich kids. Blow or dope, every fucking time."

"Spoiled shits," the other officer replied as he jerked Boy into the back of the squad car.

"Seriously! I don't know where that came from…"

The first cop cut Boy off, "Enough, you entitled piece of shit. Just because you're famous doesn't mean it's okay to do drugs, let alone distribute them. No one carries that much heroine for themselves." Then turning to the other officer he said, "That's probably how he actually makes money, because you know no one's listening to his crap."

The squad-car door slammed shut. Boy trembled, on the verge of tears, overwhelmed, and suddenly powerless. He was already feeling flooded by resentment from editing and the bullshit he was having to do for promotion of the project, and now this was going to ruin all that hard work. His stomach contracted, and he closed his eyes. Everything he had been doing was now nothing more than a big waste of time. He ruminated on idea that he'd been doing things that didn't serve him, doing things that went against everything he wanted to be, and now even those things he hadn't wanted to do would be lost because of something outside of his control.

He couldn't figure out where the drugs had come from. He knew they weren't his. He hadn't loaned his jacket to anyone, and hadn't even taken it off that night. In fact, he remembered having his hands in his pockets until the police officers told him to put them up. He thought hard, trying to reconcile the situation in his mind. Nothing made sense. The only conclusion was that the cops had planted the drugs. Though that was nearly as far fetched as any other stories he desperately created.

His mind returned to Moscow, how disempowered he'd felt, a pivotal moment in his understanding of entitlement and the illusion of absolute power. When he'd made his way back to New York after his first trip to Russia, he had been so grateful to be American. He felt reassured that, while US had its faults, at least he knew he wouldn't get mugged by American cops. He wanted this idea to feel immutable. He wasn't sure it was.

Things flipped upside down. He was in a holding cell, with drunks and who knows who, waiting for his phone call. He became more and more certain this was a set up, but he didn't understand by who, or why. Who benefited here? The officers who arrested him put him in the system, so how would they benefit? Why the fuck would anyone, let alone these two randoms, want to frame me?

His mom's voice, loud, sharp, clear, snapped him out of his otherwise unresolvable mental spin cycle.

"Release my son this instant." The responses to his mom's request were muffled and Boy couldn't make them out. Again he heard his mom's voice, "I don't care what you think he did, or how much of what ever it is you claim he had on him, bring him out here immediately." Her last words were staccato, each one almost a sentence unto itself.

Quicker than made sense the door to the holding cell swung open and Boy was called out and into another room. His mom was there with one of her expensive suit-wearing lawyers. They were sitting at a table. His mom looked unperturbed. The lawyer asked the officer to leave, as he needed time with his client. After the three of them were alone Boy's mom looked at him.

"Boy?" she asked.

"What mom?" Boy replied. "I got arrested. But the drugs weren't mine." He wanted to share everything that had happened, but didn't trust that they weren't being watched by cameras. He hated that he now had more evidence to reinforce paranoia.

His mom's voice cut the silence, "I believe you."

She looked at the lawyer who interjected, "Don't say anything else yet. We can talk about all of this later. I believe you too, of course." The lawyer handed him some papers across the table. "Your release forms. We can post bail for you as soon as you sign." The lawyer produced more papers, "Assuring payment of your lawyer fees, and releasing the money from your account for the bail."

Boy's indignation started to take hold, he couldn't believe he would have to pay as a result of being framed. *I shouldn't have to pay anything. I was set up. The cops should be the ones paying, the ones in jail.*

As though reading his mind, or perhaps seeing

his hesitation around the papers, his mom broke his train of thought. "Don't worry about the money Boy, you have plenty. We will go over everything once you're out. Sign the papers."

He wanted to yell, he took an angry breath instead, not nearly as satisfying. He signed the papers, was immediately released, and left with his mother and her lawyer. He no longer felt safe in his own country, in his own city, with the very people imbued with authority who were supposed to serve and protect him. He hated that this was something he realized so many people must feel every day, and his umbrage was an undeniable sign of his privilege.

He felt this irony as he approached the limo waiting for them, as he looked up at the crowd of paparazzi and reporters lining The Tombs detention center steps. Cameras flashed, reporters yelling questions and accusations. The crowd was way bigger than made sense to Boy and the world started to spin.

"He has no statement at this time!" His lawyer hollered over the horde.

As they left the police station a small group of bodyguards surrounded them, and his mom stepped away. He looked for her and saw she'd been safely shuffled around the back of the crowd by more incognito bodyguards. His guards pushed him directly through the swarm and into his car.

He struggled with how comfortable he felt in the back of the limo. The comfort, however, let him feel safe enough that he started to cry. His tears weren't sadness, they were the twisted tears of stress. His mom had always been honest about the negative aspects of fame, even giving him training for it in his youth, but this was the first time he'd been so confronted with it. He hadn't become used to rushes of fans yet, which happened with greater and greater regularity. A group of thirsty journalists was a whole different level of mob.

Though his mom seemed to understood what he was going through, she offered no sympathy. The closest she came was stopping the lawyer from talking for the first couple of minutes in the car while Boy collected himself. He appreciated this, despite his anger and overwhelm.

Once he'd calmed his mom asked, "What happened, Boy?"

Trying to tell her, he got choked up again. This time the tears were frustration. He couldn't remember the last time he cried. He felt weak. His shame bubbled up inside of him. He wished his discontent toward the world would push him into nihilistic relief, but this time it didn't.

Eventually, he pulled it together and told his side of the story. He spoke and she listened without judgment. He was surprised, taken aback even, but glad for to have her listening ear.

"I believe you, Boy," she said. He believed her. "And I think I know what's happened," she continued.

"What?" he asked. The word sounded like teeth clenching.

She didn't speak immediately. When she finally did her words did nothing to quench his curiosity or mounting rage. She merely offered, "Before we get into speculation, I would like you to listen to Mr. Weismann."

Boy interjected before the lawyer could speak. "No, mom! What do you think happened? What do you know?"

"I didn't say I knew anything," she replied, her

voice piercing.

He knew she would win if he took her to battle, so he swallowed his frustration and stopped.

She motioned to the lawyer, who had been waiting silently. Weismann explained the details of what Boy was being charged with, how they were going to address the charges, and the details of a first offense out-of-court settlement. He also explained what he thought the best plan of action would be for interacting with the media.

Boy was sick. He was glad he was siting as he became light-headed he likely would have slumped to the ground had he been standing. He wished he could throw up, release the sour pill he was being told to swallow for a thing he hadn't even done.

"Boy," his mom called for his attention, "this isn't bad."

"What the fuck are you talking about mom?"

"When was the last time you talked with Jimmy?" she asked. The question was strange and out of context.

"Jimmy? I don't know. Why?"

"When he was just starting in the business, he told me an gimmick he'd used for generating press," she said.

"How long have you known Jimmy? I thought you two didn't really know each other." Anxiety flooded his angry, confused his body. He kept his eyes shut. Was Jimmy just another hired gun on her team this whole time?

"We have known each other for quite some time. Impossible not to, in our positions. Beside the point. Just listen." If his eyes had been open, he would have seen her snake-like gaze, unblinking, staring at him. "Back in the day, if someone needed more publicity they would intentionally get themselves busted for something petty, like drugs."

"Are you saying I did this on purpose? Seriously? THEY WEREN'T EVEN MINE! Don't you get that?" He was so flustered he wanted to break something.

"Mind yourself Boy," his mom persisted.

"Mind myself? You're fucking accusing me of setting myself up," he replied, grabbing at her with his angry tone, his arms limp at his sides.

"I'm not accuse you. I'm suggesting it was Jimmy." She spoke as if it wasn't worth saying anything because of how childish he was being.

"The drugs weren't mine..." He spat back, having not listened.

When what she had said finally sank in the car was quiet for a moment.

"Jimmy? You think The Gun did this?" Boy's voice quivered.

She allowed silence. Weismann kept quiet, looking as though he were trying to blend into the seat and out of the line of fire. Eventually she offered, condoling, "Yes, Boy. Jimmy."

"But why the fuck...Why? We don't need the free press, we can buy it. Why not tell me?" Boy spilled.

"It worked for the old rockers. People still do it all the time. It's a way of promoting artists by giving them extra, and basically free press. Glorifying them, and even pseudo-deifying them." She looked at him a moment to see if he was following. "Where this little fiasco is going to cause you a little monetary setback, the amount of publicity you are going to get will far outweigh the cost, and increase your mystique."

Boy sat silent, trying to take it in, recalibrating into a new, deeper rage. If it had all been planned for his benefit, maybe the world wasn't the worst place ever, just really fucked up. He wanted to hold this feeling, but the trauma was too strong, too fresh, and before he knew it he was reeling again.

"How the hell does this glorify me?" he asked.

"You are part of the rich and elite, for whom the law bends, conspicuously. Every one of those reporters is going to comment on how you got out of this pinch with not even a blemish on your record, which will be true. The only reason you're going ay everything politely, as Mr. Weismann has outlined, is so the authorities don't attempt to make an example of you. Though, someone of your profile, they wouldn't try in a first offense, or really ever. It's a demonstration of fealty that everyone knows is a lie, and everyone pantomimes anyways. " She took a drink from her ceramic mug. She brought that with her? "This makes you a demi-god. You can carry drugs, get busted, get a slap on the wrist, and come out shinier than ever."

Boy could feel a wave of disgust rising inside of him and in an attempt to distract himself asked, "Isn't this going to fuck up the show?"

"Not at all, Boy. The show is about rock stardom. You have just been busted for being a rock star. There is no such thing as bad publicity. Not to mention, you now have your compulsory, 'celebrity mug shot'."

Boy wished this was relieving, but it left a familiar bad taste. No matter what he did, no matter how honest his intentions, he kept discovering himself a cog in the big synthetic wheels of an industry he had so desperately tried to avoid being consumed by. He opened his eyes, his face pursed. He looked at his mom. She held his stare, unblinking.

For the remainder of the ride no one spoke. Boy's hard gaze only broke when they arrived home and the car stopped moving. He got out and took the elevator, his mom staying behind with the lawyer.

He wanted to call Sophie. He wanted comfort, but all he could do was find his way to bed. He landed, face down, and let the slow tears of stress, angst, and disillusionment spill gently into his pillows. Eventually his exhaustion won and he fell asleep.

Again the subway. He was being chased by the reptiles. This time, when he found the entrance under his house it offered no solace. The beasts were bearing down on him and he had nowhere else to go, so he ran up the stair. He turned to run down the hallway to his room, though he was unsure of what sanctuary it could offer, and there, in front of his mom's office door, was Jimmy. The Gun turned, minacious, laughing. Boy pushed by him and into his mother's office. She was there, behind her heavy desk, leering at him, eyes large and yellow, pupils vertical slits instead of round spots. He screamed, running back past the still laughing Jimmy, to the end of the hall, and launching himself out the window. Instead of falling to the street he fell only a few feet into a snow bank, the building was gone, replaced by a barren, frozen landscape. He shivered, stuck sunken into the snow. He lifted his head, searching for explanation, seeing nothing but ice tundra to the horizon. His legs ached from cold. He gave up, his head falling back into the snow.

41

Boy awoke, shivering, still belly down. He had not

covered himself before passing out. He was still wearing the clothes he'd had on in jail. The pillow under his cheek was wet. His neck was sore. He could tell it was day through his eyelids. Not the soft light of dawn either, but the bright midday light he couldn't ignore even with his eyes closed. He had lingering, foreboding feelings from his dreams, which were rapidly fading as waking life distracted. If his already racing thoughts hadn't stolen the memory of his dream, his shock, when he opened his eyes, to find a face staring back at him, would have.

It was Sophie. She was lying on her side next to him, eyes open, quiet. He nearly fell off the bed before he realized who she was. She laughed, which she stifled quickly with an apology. "Sorry, Boy, I didn't mean to scare you. I thought you heard me come in. When I laid down you made a little noise, so I figured you knew I was here."

"Holy-fucking-shit, Sophie," he said, trying to calm his breath. He was glad to see her, but his didn't know how much more shock he could take.

"Sorry," she playfully pleaded.

"Ok, ok, ok," he exhaled. "I'll be okay," he said as much to himself as her. "Fuck I'm fragile right now." He hadn't meant to say it, but it was honest. He took a couple of deep breaths.

"I bet," she replied, reaching out a hand to rubbed his back. "What the fuck happened?"

Sophie's voice was soothing. He realized how much he'd been missing her since the trip had ended. He needed to cry, repressing it at first, but couldn't hold it back and quietly burst. She pulled him into her arms, hugging him. He sobbed. She listened, tender, holding him.

42

Hours of eternity later, as though lifting above the clouds, Boy returned to the present to find Sophie asleep next to him. He felt horrible, which was somehow an improvement. As though at a distance he witnessed his brain turned back on. As soon as his mind started turning his thoughts began to spin out so fast it felt a fall, even though he never gotten up from his prone position. His body shivered in discomfort, his teeth clenched.

Sophie awoke. Tentatively she whispered, "Tell me."

"What's the point?" He didn't move.

She was quite a moment before replying. "What do you mean?"

"It's a fucking hoax."

"What is?" She was slow, deliberate.

"Come on, Sophie. I need honesty right now." As he said honesty his jaw clenched involuntarily.

Sophie too a long pause, contemplating something before she responded. Then, "You're right."

Boy unclenched his jaw.

"Boy," she continued, "You've always known this was a façade. What isn't?"

At first Boy's breath sped up, but then he let out a big sigh. With a sudden movement he reached for the phone in his pocket. The battery was dead.

"Can I use your phone?" he asked.

Sophie handed him her phone. He opened his bedside drawer rummaging through it, eventually pulling out The Gun's card. He dialed the number, expecting Jimmy not to answer, as he wasn't calling from his own phone.

Boy was surprised when Jimmy answered, "Hey."

Jimmy sounded like he'd been expecting the call, and Boy froze.

After a beat Jimmy asked, "Boy?"

He considered hanging up. How the hell did he know it was me? He wondered.

As if psychic Jimmy said, "I'm pretty sure Sophie wouldn't call me on her own account."

Boy's anger finally moved him to speak. "Why?" was all he could say.

Jimmy paused. Boy wanted to yell, but didn't have the energy.

"You've been going through it Boy. I could try to guess at what you're asking. I don't want to insult your intelligence, so I'm not going to pretend like I have no idea, but I'm also not exactly sure. How can I help?"

Jimmy's voice was sincere, which made Boy even angrier.

"My mom told me everything," Boy spat into the phone, "so cut the shit, Jimmy."

Sophie had never seen so much anger in Boy's face.

"I get why you would do it, but why wouldn't you talk to me about it first?" Boy asked. "Don't try to make something up. I can't take one more lie. My mom already told me, so just be real. I fucking respected you, can't you do the same for me?" Boy was pleading as much with the world as with Jimmy.

"What did she tell you Boy?" Jimmy asked, almost sounding amused. Boy could hear wariness and calculation in The Gun's voice.

"Come clean Jimmy. If I'm ever supposed to understand what's going on in this bullshit business, you gotta be real. Do me that honor at least. Don't be another piece of shit like everyone else." Boy immediately regretted this last statement.

"Do you have any idea what you are talking about?" The Gun asked.

"Don't give me that..."

"Shut up, Boy." Jimmy's voice stayed quiet, but gained a harshness that frightened Boy, even through his animosity. "You want truth?"

Boy had heard a similar tone from his mom before. Something hard was coming. He braced himself.

Jimmy was too calm as he said, "You want a piece of the fucking truth, kid? Chew on this; it was all her."

Boy could feel it was true. It felt like someone had reached into Boy's chest, taking out his organs. His breath left. A belly flop off a high dive, the air knocked out, a desire to punch the water back for the sting it gave. He wanted to scream, but you needed air to do that. He wanted to slam the phone against the wall, but this anger was so deep, so old, all it did was tear at his heart, until the only thing he felt was the grimace that had formed on his face. Eventually he dropped his arm, and the phone, to the bed between him and Sophie, exhaling, "Fucking bullshit."

Sophie was a desert hare in headlights, eyes wide. She stayed unmoving.

Boy shot up out of bed and headed for the door. He was going to his mom, ignoring the potential fall-out that would result from such haste.

Sophie called to him, "Wait. Boy." But it was too late. Even if he could have heard her, he wouldn't have stopped.

He raced down the hall, using all of his will power not to knock everything off of the walls as he went. He slammed open the door to his mom's office, as she set down her ceramic mug with one hand, and her phone with the other.

"You," he snapped.

She was unfazed. His upper lip tightening to a snarl, his jaw clenched. She looked at him, through him, and said, "I'm not sure what you mean, but I can guess."

"You know," he spat at her. "Don't try to fucking play me like you play everyone else, mother. You know." He wanted to throw something at her, he wanted her to get defensive, he wanted some kind of emotion to emit from her cold, stone face. Anything would have been better than the serene stoic gaze she always held.

"So you talked to Jimmy. He told you something that upset you very much." How did she know? Had that been Jimmy on the phone when he stormed in? If he hadn't known her his whole life he might have thought she was mocking him.

His emotion continued to escalate as he glared at her. He felt like he wasn't even talking to a human being. He thought about the lizard eyes she'd had in his dreams. He could almost see them now, hidden behind her calm, collected irises.

He continued in a harsh, hushed tone, "Admit it. Admit it was your idea to send me to jail." He wanted to run, wishing she would reassure him somehow. If she wasn't to be trusted, being the only person with real vested interest in him, how would he ever trust anything. He stayed still, awaiting an answer, which came slowly. The silence felt precarious. He had never spoken so sharply to her, and fear was seeping in.

"That's what he told you, Boy?" She looked away from him and back at the phone on her desk. "That, I can assure you, is not the case. I would never have done that, even for your career, with out asking you first. I would never…"

Boy stopped listening to her, trying to understand what Jimmy had said. He knew she wasn't lying, but The Gun hadn't been either. Had he misinterpreted Jimmy's words? His mom seemed relieved by this false accusation, which suggested there was something she was afraid he'd discovered, something she was hiding. The dark storm clouds of his mind burst with electricity as his neurons fired trying to put the pieces together.

What else could Jimmy have been talking about?

Despite the chaos in the storm, no conclusions were coming. He tried to remember the exact words Jimmy had used. It was all her. Boy realized he didn't know for sure who the 'her' was, or what 'it' was that she had done. Maybe the 'her' Jimmy was referring to wasn't his mom. As fast as this thought came it left. There was no other 'her' Jimmy would have referred to. Or wait. Could it have been Sophie? But that made no sense either.

It had to be his mom. But what was the 'it' that she was responsible for. As he thought through what could have been his mom's idea he tensed, realizing Jimmy meant 'all of it' was her idea. Everything. Boy's entire music career. His entire rise to fame. He hadn't done it himself. She'd shaped him, guided him, with her name, her fame, and her ever-present, if sometimes hidden hand.

He became deliberate, looking directly into her eyes, saying, "You?" His lips turned down in revulsion, as much at himself as her, as much at his lack of sight as at her stealth.

"No Boy," she said, sure of herself.

"Jimmy's been on the payroll from the start. Or at least you pushed his hand."

She didn't respond. He knew he was right. This time his anger was so strong, so vehement, all he could do was stare; his vision was white with rage.

"You made the music Boy. You wrote the songs. You created the band. You came up with the idea for the show. Don't try to make this a sob story just because you're worried that I helped you along." He didn't speak, couldn't say anything, so she continued. "He liked your music, and was glad to do it. He's been laughing all the way to the bank, but I didn't pay him, I didn't have to. You're music was good enough to make him more money than I would have been willing to pay. And, it was your band mates that sent him, and every other major producer your demo disc, not me. He did come to me asking if he ought to take you on, but really all I had to do was give him the go ahead, and assure him I wouldn't get in his way."

He couldn't listen to anything coming out of her mouth. He left the room, stumbling back down the hall. Sophie was still in his room but he didn't see her. He collapsed onto his bed, supine this time, silent, reeling, unable to move, a long blank stare at the ceiling. How much further was this rock bottom he kept thinking he was hitting? How much more could this silly and surprisingly fragile house of cards collapse? His exhaustion sent him into a strange dream state, not awake, but not really sleeping either.

He was stuck in the frozen landscape. He ran, but never got anywhere. He saw a figure on the horizon. Was it Johnny T.? He stumbled towards the figure as another, and then another appeared, until he was surrounded by a swarm of people snapping pictures and asking for autographs. He was suffocating. Someone in the crowd asked how it felt to be his mother's child, how grateful he was to have such an amazing woman for a mom, how much better his life was because of her. He yelled at the crowd to leave him alone, but couldn't break free. He would die if he didn't get fresh air. Out of breath he started awake.

43

Boy awoke full of feeling: fear from his dream; sorrow in his solitude; scared at the lack of things he felt he could trust; and least comfortable, but more empowering, rage towards a world he wanted to feel anything but rage towards. It was a rage he didn't know how to direct. It was a rage at the privilege he had been born into, a privilege that stifled him. It was rage at the fact that he couldn't do anything without it being influenced by who, or what, his mother was. It was a rage folding in on itself, a rage at being enraged by petty things while there were people struggling to merely survive in the world. It was a rage that perpetuated itself in the knowledge that this rage was based in abundance and yet was something he felt no control over, something he even felt ashamed of. Because this rage fueled shame, and because it was directionless and out of control, it was unsustainable.

After what was either forever, a couple of minutes, or a few days, Boy fell into depression, an emotion he felt much more comfortable in. Before he knew it, and because he didn't know how to address it, this depression nearly incapacitated him. If he couldn't do anything about his feels, complacency seemed as good a solution as any, and a horrible one at that.

This rage-fueled shame spiral of depression would have kept Boy bedridden if it hadn't been for Sophie. She always seemed to save him. She pulled him out, brought him to appointments, got him to the parties, dragged him to the clubs, attempting to scrape him out of his funk. He went with her, the only reason he did anything. He didn't even have the will to stop her direction. He observed everything from outside himself, or somewhere deep inside, shut down, and hiding; a robot, completing syntactic commands, but removed from the semantics of his reality. He knew himself merely as a result of instructions, not as an individual impulse, not as a personal drive, not as a human at all.

Boy had been depressed before. He had shut out the world, but he had always pulled through. He didn't know where to begin this time, or didn't care to try. He couldn't fathom the long, arduous climb out of this deep valley of dismay. He didn't know who to trust, or if he could trust anyone at all. He wanted to be more upset that his mom didn't try to console him, but knew she was staying away for his sake. He knew she was wise in doing so and hated her even more for her wisdom.

The show finished, a huge success. Because he'd become so disengaged, the project became something far from what he'd hoped, another commercial idealization of a false, rich, rock-star life. He was the star, and he was more famous than ever. His trip to jail only aided his climb to the top.

He was now something even more than famous, something archetypal, a myth. The story woven by the media only slightly resembled the truth, but it was picked up and disseminated at a speed he could never catch up to, let alone stop. He saw this unfolding, and it only made him worse.

He'd known fame his whole life, seen the façade of the glamorous life, the life he'd been raised in, surrounded by. He felt the binds of this fake life, the web he so desperately wanted to escape, wrapping around his present and future even more tightly than it had his past.

He started to hate everyone around him, even his old friends, seeing only the sickness the power of fame bestowed on those it was bestowed upon, the curse of turning to gold. The only one who seemed untainted was Sophie. She was the one thing he couldn't find a way to not trust. He didn't know what he would do without her, didn't know how to thank her.

Boy retreated more and more into himself. Hating himself for all his hatred. Loathed his self pity and stuck in wallowing. He fell further and further into the bottle. He knew he had to pull himself out, which he tried to by attaching to the goodness he saw in Sophie, to the honesty she represented.

At the beginning of Boy's increased fame he used to love reading letters from fans. He had them kept in a special file, responding to them, time permitting, until there was no time permitted. He was flooded now with mail, finding it petty. The only envelopes that caught his eye were the shiny gold-leafed invitations from that exclusive club, Atlantis. He would occasionally hearing whispers about the place, and it sounded like another exclusive trap of fame. He was disgusted with himself that the secretive nature and fancy invites lead him to be curious about it. He tried avoiding the curiosity, but wouldn't throw away the invites.

One day, as he threw the flashy Atlantis invite into a pile of letters he told himself he would eventually throw away, Sophie noticed and asked what the bright envelope was about. He pretended he hadn't noticed it. She grabbed it, peeled it open, and gawked at its elegant interiors. Boy feigned disinterest. Boy could tell Sophie's interest was primarily a desire to support him, a desire to pull him out of his funk.

"Come on, Boy. It'll be funny. Remember when we took mushrooms and went to that swanky party with your mom? Maybe we should get high and go to this silly club," Sophie suggested.

Boy could tell she was trying to help. Some part of him even kind of liked the idea. But he was also afraid of where his mind might go if he took psychedelics in his compromised psychological state. Part of him was worried he might realize he needed to just run away from everything. Part of him loved the idea of disappearing. Most of him was scared to leave, scared to be away from everything he had ever known. Accordingly, he persisted in disinterest. He could tell Sophie knew he wasn't being fully honest, and he loved that she didn't push.

"Let's just go to The Boom Boom Room," he suggested, hoping to find solace in the numbness alcohol occasionally delivered. Even then he knew drinking would only drag him down further, but he wanted to hit that bottom, to feel the sharp pain of the rocks he'd been falling towards ever since he could remember. Hitting rock bottom would be better than the apathy covering his rage.

Sophie relented. Boy couldn't tell she was disappointed, afraid nothing would change, and wishing Boy would be willing to do something about it. He wished that himself.

That night he got particularly drunk. It was a sloppy inebriation only useful for releasing demons (or maybe calling them in), and primarily just a poisoning of the body. He was reckless. He wanted it to feel good. In his chaotic state he tried to kiss Sophie. He had only held back before because he didn't want to lose her. He had been even more afraid she might only not stop him for fear of loosing him, which would be worse than just loosing her. But when he tried now, sloppy and drunk, even in his compromised state he could tell that she loved him back, which was the primary reason she dodged his attempt. He turned to the despair he was trying to escape, and knew he couldn't, at least not the way he was trying now. Tears formed, held in his eyes, warping his already intoxicated vision.

Eventually Sophie walked him home. He tried to kiss her again, this time thinking it was for the right reasons, not recognizing he was trying to use her to avoid himself, and again she turned her face away, even as she hugged him tight. In his emotionally compromised state he was shivering in the night air, and Sophie put her jacket on him.

"We'll talk about this in the morning, Sophie, I promise. I'm sorry for being an ass." He couldn't look her in the eye, which scared him. He could feel his fear rising, wondering if he had screwed up the only good thing in his life, his last piece of self-sabotage.

"Don't worry, Boy. You're an ass for waiting

until you were trashed to try to kiss me, but you're not an ass for wanting to. I'm pretty hot shit." They both laughed. He couldn't tell, even in his desperate state, that she wanted him to feel safe.

He finally looked up at her as she tucked him into bed. He felt warmed by her care, and hated that there was something else, a fear perhaps, in her gaze.

"Stay," he asked.

"Where the hell else do you think I'd go at this time of night," she responded, plopping down on the far side of the bed.

Boy stayed turned away from her.

"I'm sorry," he whispered, as much to himself as her.

"Shut the fuck up Boy, I'm trying to get some sleep over here," she gently chastised him, more caring than collusion would have been.

He drifted into oblivion.

44

A vibrating phone, pressed between Boy's body and the bed, woke him. He patted the bed next to him, finding it empty, and instinctively answered the call without opening his eyes. When he went to talk only a hung-over, early-morning squeak came out, no proper greeting.

Boy was confused when his mom's voice responded to his squeak with, "Sophia? Are you with Boy?"

"Huh?" he chirped, his voice still not returned, his vocal chords still stuck in the delirium of sleep deprivation and exhaustion. He opened his eyes with some effort, looking at the device in his hands, and noticing he had answered Sophie's phone.

He heard his mom voice again, "Sophia?"

The caller ID said, 'the dark mistress', and had a picture of his mom. Why would Sophie have his mom in her phone? Maybe that's not weird, he reassured himself.

"Mom?" he asked, having to force his larynx to work.

The call disconnected.

What was that? Boy wondered. Why had he had Sophie's phone in his pocket? Looking down he discovered he was wearing Sophie's jacket.

The call having been cut off, screen of the phone showed its recent call list. 'The dark mistress' appeared to be the most frequent caller. He tried to apply logic to this, but no easy story revealed itself. Boy started to look through Sophie's, phone trying to understand. He was startled when he heard the toilet flush and the sink turn on in his bathroom. He realized it must be Sophie. Confused, he felt guilty for invading her privacy, but also wanting more time to look through her phone. He made sure the ringer was off and put the phone under his pillow.

Sophie exited the bathroom. He pretended to be asleep. She asked, "Who were you talking to Boy?"

"Whuh?" He pretended she'd just woke him, which might have been pretty convincing, as his face was still puffy, and his eyes hadn't adjusted to being awake.

"I heard you say something when I was in the bathroom. Were you talking in your sleep?" She smirked at the idea.

Boy was glad Sophie seemed oblivious. He tried to smile, it felt too forced, instead asking, "What happened last night?"

"You know," she started, "the usual." Sophie looked like she was trying to suppress disappointment. Or was it embarrassed? He couldn't tell.

"You got wasted," she continued, "and started trying to kiss me. Telling me that I was the most amazing thing that ever happened to you." She gave a coy smile.

Though he guessed there was truth to what she was saying, Boy was glad it also seemed a pretty funny joke to Sophie as well. He was relieved he wouldn't have to defend himself at least, if she hadn't taken it too seriously.

Boy wanted to laugh, but winced instead. His mind returned to what he had just seen on her phone. His confusion regained its hold on him. He asked, "Do you talk to my mom much these days?"

Sophie seemed nervous, and trying her best not to let him see it. "What? Not any more than usual. You probably see her more often than me. Why?"

Fuck, he thought. Something off. She was acting weird. He felt as though he were being lifted, twisting, out of his skin. What the fuck in going on? Am I dissociating?

Maybe she was just lying because she knew he was mad at his mom. Maybe they'd only been talking because his mom knew he wouldn't talk to her unless he had to. Maybe Sophie was merely giving his mom updates on how he was. He hoped all of these things, and something in his stomach told him none of it was what was happening. He needed to throw up, the lingering alcohol in his system churned by the sinking feeling that even Sophie, his last safe place, might be tainted by deception.

"You okay, Boy?" Sophie asked.

He scrambled out of bed and stumbled into his bathroom, projecting what was left of last night towards his toilet.

Sophie was there, behind him. Normally this would have been comforting, but now it only made the spinning worse.

He didn't know what to do. Tears streamed down his cheeks as he lay on the bathroom floor. He asked her to leave. Her nervousness became obvious as she tried to take her jacket off him. He hoped it was to protect it from his sick, but realized it was at least as likely that she wanted her phone back. He shrugged her off.

"What's going on?" she asked, panic in her tone.

"I'm sick," he replied. "I need to be alone." He paused, wanting to contain his venom, but unable to. "Just leave, Sophia." The name erupted from him. He saw her face drain of blood, then flush.

"Your mom called while I was in the bathroom." She finally said, her tone controlled.

"You lied?" he asked, crumpled, broken on the bathroom floor.

"When?" she said, recognizing the mistake immediately.

"Well. When have you?" he asked, his heart in rapid syncopations. All the extra blood pumping the remnants of intoxication through his system re-engaged his nausea, and he threw up again, surprised there was anything left to purge.

After he'd finished she asked, "About your mom and I talking?"

Boy spat into the toilet trying to clear the vomit from his mouth. "Why does everything in this fucking world turn to shit?" The words felt like part of the toxins he was expelling.

"Boy," she said, wishing she could say something that would make him feel better. "I love you," she tried.

"Bullshit Sophia. Bull-fucking-shit. Love is about trust, and you are just like everyone else, fucking liar."

"No, Boy."

"There you go again." He couldn't look at her. He sobbed, his jaw clenched in anger.

"Okay. You're right. Is that what you want?" She was crying too.

"No, I never wanted that from you. I never wanted that to be true. You were the only good one. I know I tried to kiss you last night Sophie. I know I loved you, and I thought you did too, and now I feel so fucking afraid and fucked up." He slumped into a corner, behind the toilet.

"I've wanted to tell you, Boy. I tried. So many times, I tried. I was afraid. I know things have been hard, and I didn't want something else to be hard, so I kept it from you, but I swear that I love you. I have for a long time and you know it." Tears poured down her face. "You know that," she begged.

"I don't know that Sophie. I don't know what I know." He took a deep breath. "Why have you been talking with my mom?" He frowned.

"She asked me to keep an eye on you, to make sure you were okay, that's all."

"For how long?" He asked, feeling she was still holding back.

"Why does it matter?"

"Why won't you just tell me? If it doesn't matter, why wouldn't you just tell me?" He shook, wanting and not wanting the whole truth, and feeling sure he was unlikely to get it. "Get out!" he finally yelled. "Just get the fuck out of here." His face pinched. "Of everything, not fucking you too!"

She fell to the floor. "Please, Boy, I'll tell you everything. I never meant to hurt you. I really care for you, and I have since we met." She sounded desperate. She was desperate.

"Then the truth," he replied. "All of it."

"Your mom asked me to watch out for you since before we met."

"What?" His wished this was the lie, and could feel that it wasn't. "Before we even met? You're just another hired hand?" Another wave of nausea, but with nothing for it to bring up. After a moment he continued, "Why, Sophie? Why even you?" He simultaneously wanted to fall through the floor and jump out of his skin. He could feel his heart trying to break free from his chest.

"From what I've been able to put together, your mom was worried about you after that first time you were mugged, when we were kids, so she looked for someone to watch over you, but she also knew you wouldn't take a bodyguard. I needed help getting into school, and I had won every grappling event I had entered, even against kids much older than us. She found me, got me into the school, all I had to do was keep up with my martial arts, befriend you, and watch out for you. But I promise, I have always been real with you."

"How can you say that, Sophie? You were working for my mom! You're one of them and you know what that means." His eyes rolled back into his head in pain. His voice became barely audible, "Get out."

"I took her help before I knew you, but as soon as I met you I honestly liked you. I thought I had lucked out. The job she'd given me was something I would have done for free."

"She paid you." Boy felt the last morsels of his guts pushing their way up. Sophie stopped talking. He was disgusted by her silence realizing what it meant. "She still pays you." As words left his mouth, she sobbed audibly, reaching her hand towards him.

"Don't fucking touch me," he said too calmly. "Don't you dare fucking touch me." There was a short silence. "Out."

"Boy."

"Get the fuck out of here!" he yelled. "Get out! Now!" His vituperation stung him as much as it hurt her.

"Please," she pleaded.

"Out." He shut his eyes and wept like he had never wept. He realized he'd been holding on to Sophie as the hand that would be waiting for him when he hit rock bottom, when in fact, she was another of the sharp rocks waiting to smash him to bits. He knew now that there was something bellow rock bottom, made of quicksand, an even darker place for him to fall.

He shut down. He didn't notice Sophie leave. He remained on bathroom floor, falling in and out of a hopeless and fits of restless sleep.

45

When Boy finally fully awoke from his haphazard slumber he couldn't place where he was, nor tell what part of the day he had awoken to. Despite his discomfort, defeat nailed him to his crumpled state on the floor. His eyes didn't open. Waking life taunted him, cold and abrasive, until he was pulled back into a tumultuous dreamscape.

He was wrapped in residue of the pain his mind was torn by, but there was calm as well. He was back in the undulating field, more ambiguous than ever; not made of grass and dirt; a single cohesive substance, pliant, resistant, alive. It became brighter, and as it did Boy's heart quickened until he awoke, confused. The weight of his body sank in, the pain in his mind returned.

He fell like this, in and out of sleep, until his body stopped cooperating. When this pseudo-slumber no longer held him, he still wouldn't move or open his eyes. The first few wakeful moments he thought he heard Sophie breathing somewhere near him, but now, in his shut down state of dormant consciousness, he knew she was gone, he was alone.

When he finally peeled opened his eyes he wasn't sure he actually had, it was dark. Regaining awareness of where he was he didn't know what to do with himself.

He saw his discomfort as a blessing, it offered distraction from his aching heart and restless mind. He contemplated going to bed for what must have been hours before he made the move.

The transition was laborious. Finally reaching his destination, he fell with all his weight, his face hitting something hard in his pillow. Sophie's phone. His stomach churned. He wanted to fight the urge to open it, wanted to stop himself from finding more fuel to feed the pain, but he knew his resolve would eventually give in, so he didn't wait.

She must have recently erased her call log and text history, because there wasn't much past the previous day. In that short amount of time there were myriad calls from his mom, and texts asking how things were going, whether or not Sophie had been successful in certain tasks his mom had assigned.

He threw the phone across the room.

As it arched over the accumulated chaos of his floor the screen illuminated something golden before smashing against the far wall. Boy focused his eyes though the darkness. A gold-leafed envelope.

An ignored invitation to that pretentious sounding club. In need of distraction, Boy slithered out of bed, to examine this shiny something. He spun the envelope around in his hands. Even in this dismal state, he couldn't help but be drawn by the beauty and detail in the simple, ornate sleeve. He opened the back gingerly and withdrew its contents, even more simple and ornate. Three words: "Welcome to", and underneath, in much larger, but still elegant type, "Atlantis".

The back of the card had a QR code which lead to a simple website, which gave brief directions, and explained his new V.I.P. status put him permanently on the list. Normally this pretense would have triggered distain, but in this particular moment, so desperate for anything different, he entertained the idea of going.

He was sure this club would be full of the inauthentic people he had always been surrounded by, who riddled the world of fame. In his desperate state he had a moment of empathy wondering if their façades were from the same sense of isolation he now felt mired in. This almost tender moment of grace passed and quickly the negative feedback loop of frustration and mistrust resurfaced, returning him to his state of incapacitation.

He realized he hadn't looked at the time on Sophie's phone before destroying it. Thinking of

Sophie sped up his rapid tailspin into deeper depression. He lay limp on his bed, a bag of lead, his eyes soggy. Eventually sleep retook him.

The bright undulating field; the strange ground. Awkward anxiety, and calm, rushed over him. In this place he knew nothing would hurt him even as everything he had known was falling apart. It was comfortingly psychedelic, an aliveness in the field, one unified thing breathing. Light radiated rather than reflected; a glowing, bright, amber hue; orange, red, and brown. The light came from the ground, not the sky. Someone, or something, was approaching. He wasn't afraid, but couldn't help a rising sense anxiety. Or was it excitement? Again his rapidly beating heart brought him back to his waking life, to his bed.

46

The activation from his dreams distracted his waking depression for a brief moment. His gaze fell to his hands, which still held the card from Atlantis. His racing heart kept him from his previous contempt. Looking at the card before remembering the oppression of his emotions, for an instant he liked the card, its golden sheen. Was the card emanating light as the field had? As reality flooded back in, somehow the card, and the club, became the only things not completely horrible. A seed of positivity was planted, despite himself.

This seed grew throughout that day, and the next. He started coming up with reasons why it might benefit him to go. Maybe it was time he embraced reality as one of the world's elite, seek solace in the company of others who shared burdens similar to his own. Maybe, at the very least, he'd find some companionship in people with whom he could commiserate. Without realizing it, he imbued the club with hope, the only hope he had access to.

He had effectively isolated himself, not even his mom was able to break through his isolation. He turned his phone off, kept away from his computer, ignored the couple of times there had been knocks on his door. Finally, after a couple of days of gestation, thoughts of the club became so compelling as to inspire him out of bed, out of his room, out into the world, to see what Atlantis might offer.

He waited until his house and his mom's office ha gone quiet. It was a Tuesday night, which he expected would be safest, a mellower introduction to this new and supposedly exclusive experience. His first impulse was to go in his current state, un-showered, disheveled, indignance embodied. His vanity won.

He found one of his simple, elegant, vintage suits, donned an understated baseball cap to cover his hair, and stepped into a clean pair of comfy sneakers to demonstrate how hard he wasn't trying. This gesture set a part of him at ease, and he hoped would make it easier to brake through the first walls celebrityhood can create in people. He wasn't convinced he cared to push past those walls, but wanted the option. Still, part of him wondered if his going was more to be reckless than for any hope of finding genuine connection. This idea also seemed a protection against an expected disappointment. He just had to go.

He decided to drive himself, something he almost never did. It was uncomfortable at first, but he eased into it. He was confused by the address, as it was familiar, yet he was sure he'd never been.

Boy was familiar with most of New York's VIP lounges. He thought he knew all the secret hidden rooms within parties where the elite would congregate to consume the cleaner, more illicit substances. But somehow, though it was so apparently well known by entertainment's upper echelons, this club, Atlantis, had eluded him.

He got close, found a lot a few blocks away, and wander to the door on foot. As he approached, it looked like any other Manhattan club: a long line, people trying to look important, a crowd around the bouncers trying to explain why they ought to be let in, even on a Tuesday. He realized quickly he had been here before, and had to double-check the address. As he arrived the address was correct, but the name of the club was not Atlantis.

47

It was The Dream. Normally this type of place repulsed Boy. He found it hard enough to enjoy the few places he frequented, as they hosted rich, 'important', inauthentic people, but he had always considered the Dream Hotel particularly fake. He felt the people who wound up here did so when they hadn't made it through the more prestigious doors. This was where people pretended to be important, which was even more dismal than 'important' people pretending their importance mattered. These people wanted to be something that was only exciting because they wanted to be it. The shimmer of fame was only there by people not having it and wanting it. His misanthropy pulsed.

Boy was embarrassed to be there. Even more

embarrassed to realize he was worried it would sully his image. He was taking himself too seriously. But somehow, in realizing this, he laughed. He laughed at his hypocrisy. He laughed noticing how much he was just another fake. He laughed, and it felt amazing. But as he laughed his broken heart gushed its poisoned blood back into his system, back up into his brain. He still didn't want to be there.

As Boy turned to leave he noticed a symbol on the wall of the building he'd never noticed before. The symbol printed on the Atlantis invite. Something so simple it could be everywhere and no one would notice it. It was three dots, arranged to make a triangle. In this strange context, with the secretive element to this silly elite club, the simple symbol conjured thoughts of the illuminati, the eye in the pyramid, secret societies, and conspiracy theories.

A chill rushed over him. Curiosity piqued. Boy had come this far, and now he had to go in, had to follow the symbols. The doorman moved to stop him, then, without a word, realized who Boy was, and the entry ropes opened.

The Dream seemed full for a Tuesday night. Boy wondered if he might have been off. Maybe it wasn't Tuesday. He became nervous he'd be noticed. He ducked into a crowd of people moving through the entrance. He found himself whisked into a hallway with elevators.

The movement of the crowd pulled Boy along. As the amoeba of bodies was about to head out of the hallway into the barroom he noticed a guarded door with three dots above it. He stepped back from the group hoping to be left alone to follow the symbol. The crew left and he walked over to the door. The bouncer was a huge man that someone could disappear in a small hallway. He didn't even look down as Boy approached, but merely pushed the door open saying, "Welcome, Boy."

Boy passed through the door and into a little room. The room housed a small table with an ashtray, a large mirror, and the entrance to an elevator that looked like it may have been built in the gilded age, the golden dots on the door. He considered a moment before he pressed a button beside the ornate elevator. The doors opened swiftly and with an unexpected grace given their apparent age. He shrugged to himself, why not, and entered.

The doors closed behind Boy as swiftly as they had opened. He guessed they must be motion censored or remotely controlled. He didn't see any indication of how to choose where to go. It was dark, and it looked as though the walls of the evaluator were made out of glass. He'd expected to go up, and was surprised as he felt the glass box start to descend. He was even more surprised at the distance it seemed to descend. Then, abruptly, yet smoothly, it stopped going down and started to move laterally. He'd never been in an elevator that moved in any directions other than up and down. He looked for tracks, but was unable to see any, neither above nor below.

The strange trajectory and lack of clear means of propulsion was so distracting that Boy almost didn't notice he was approaching a lit area. It was like being in the front car of train moving through a tunnel as it approached daylight. It started as a fixed point of light before growing into the entire view out what he now considered the front of this see-through box propelling him through space. It was a well-lit entryway, a square in the darkness, three golden dots on an otherwise bright white plane.

48

Where the hell am I? Boy wondered.

Boy realized how jaded he'd been. He'd thought there was nowhere new to discover in this city. He'd believed he'd been everywhere worth being. He let a cynical attitude disrupt his enjoyment of the chaos he'd grown up in.

So there still are things to discover, Boy mused to himself.

The elevator slowed, rotating one hundred and eighty degrees. The doors opened. Boy stepped out onto a platform. The entrance was similar to the invitation. Boy saw that he was in a long tunnel that punctuated into the bright wall. Boy couldn't identify the source of the light, which he guessed must be inset into the dark walls of the tunnel. It was as though the wall were nearly glowing. He thought of the undulating fields in his dreams.

Almost seamless, Boy noticed a square door in the middle of the wall. Looking closely at the black tunnel walls surrounding the bright entryway Boy noticed what looked like subtle inlay of vines and snakes, easily missed by the stark contrast the white wall gave. This detail would easily have gone unnoticed if Boy hadn't been so hyper-vigilant.

Despite Boy's vigilance he somehow didn't notice the extremely large bouncer standing silently next to the wall until he moved. The beast of a man was dressed in a black suit, which Boy attributed to his previous near invisibility. Something about the man's appearance made his skin look like it was part of his outfit. He never spoke and with a elegance that stunned Boy, he swung the door open before stepping aside.

The tunnel had been silent, save Boy's breathing. The wall of sound that emanated from the doorway as it opened was jarring in contrast to the tunnel's stillness. There was a deep-bass sound, electronically crunched, a particularly grimy drop that vibrated through Boy's body. It was a sound Boy had only heard at the latest of late-night dance parties at the better European summer festivals. It was electric, and yet, felt organic. His body moved to it subconsciously. The music moved through him in a wave as he stepped out of the tunnel, through the threshold, and into the club, not noticing as the door closed behind him.

Boy crept slowly into a throbbing mass of bodies on the dance floor, undulating in blue light show. Liquid smoke clung like tule fog, a rippling ocean on the ground. The room was huge, and packed. The quality of sound was amazing considering the brick walls and square dimensions of the space. Before he overthought it Boy's body started the rhythmic movements of uninhibited dance. Boy forgot everything for a moment, compelled beyond control, free. He heard something familiar in a song, an incidental baseline he couldn't quite place, his mind returned, and his misery flooded back in. His body stiffened. He needed a drink, anything that might let him release again. Searching he saw a door at the far side of the room. He swam through the crowd and out of the throng.

The adjoining room was much quieter, dark-sanguine motif, subtle 1920's jazz playing. This was more what Boy had expected. A swanky prohibition-era speakeasy, rounded booths, black velvet trimmed in gold, impeccable. The tables, large, dark wood flats, were adorned with candles in delicate hand-blown glass balls. The walls, brick, exaggerated by of the lighting, gave the room its dark red color. The lights above the tables were soft, large, and also looked handcrafted. The filaments inside the bulbs were ornate. The bulbs themselves were considerably larger than modern lights. The walls were adorned with tasteful taxidermy of wild cats, birds of prey, and reptiles. It was a museum.

The room was full of the people Boy had expected to see at such an exclusive scene: debonair, bourgeois, elite. These were the people he had been stuck going to parties with his whole life; the people his mother had made him rub shoulders with. The men wore suits and smoked cigars, sipping brandy from snifters, or drinking peat-laden scotch on the rocks. The women wore elegant gowns, their cigarettes held away from their faces by long, illustrious holders. They looked trapped in a time that only existed in the movies. Even the smoke in the room was somehow different, older, thicker, more yellow than grey, and sweeter than the pollution from cigarettes in a normal bar. Boy started to wonder if this were just a dream.

Then all the pretense started to turn Boy. The distraction he'd been harboring so delightfully was turning back into a more familiar distain. His mouth returned into the grimace his face muscles had grown accustom to. Yet, he was still somehow mesmerized; enchanted by the subtle allure this stuck-up elegance exuded. He hated them more for it. He watched them, wondering if there was something special about these people, or if they simply thought they were special, making them appear so. If this was a dream, it was turning into a nightmare, a reminder of a cage he wanted to pretend he wasn't in.

He wanted to leave, but couldn't bring himself to. Instead he found the bar. Without asking the bartender served Boy an absinthe, room temperature, with a sugar cube on fire in a silver holder above a delicate glass of the strange green liquor that turned milky as the melting sugar entered. Boy didn't have the patience for the sugar to finish melting. He stirred it in early, blew out the flame and threw back the drink as though a shot, beckoning for another before the first was done. He decided to see if the Green Fairy might guide his way out of his labyrinthine hauteur.

A switch flipped. He would drown his disgust. He would trash himself to so his outward presentation might more closely resemble his internal turmoil. He would re-break his broken heart so he could at least have a sense ownership over the pain. He requested a third.

After the third glass of serpentine liquor Boy's gut burned. He wanted to keep going, but his body wouldn't let him. As the burn moved through his body, the effects started to kick in.

Before things had started to fall apart, Boy had loved the way absinthe made him feel. It was an uplifted drunk, not the sluggish drag most alcohol created. It had always felt a little like psychedelics and drinking together. He'd felt particularly creative and even inspired by the highness in the intoxication. But now he only felt woozy. He started spinning, which caught him off guard as he'd only just started drinking. His vision started to blur, going subtly in and out of focus. He decided he needed to go dance it off.

As Boy stood his body mechanics were as off as his vision had become. Historically, he might have found this incredibly entertaining, but because of his downtrodden state, and because of this new environment, he became a little confused and scared. The fear triggered his anger, indignant. His indignation became conviction and he wobbled his way to the door he thought lead back into the dance party, determined to sweat out his buzz.

50

The door opened just before Boy reached it. A voice, emanating from nowhere, said, "They've been waiting for you."

Boy paused, turning to look at another looming bouncer, nearly 7 feet tall yet somehow nearly invisible in his dark suit. There was something unworldly, and familiar in the man's eyes. They looked like contacts over something brighter, brown over the gold of a lizard's pupil. Boy realized he'd been staring at the man for a long, awkward moment.

Boy closed his eyes and shook his head hoping to lose the mounting confusion of his decidedly inebriated state. The bouncer didn't smile, though there was something understanding in his expression. Boy nodded a thanks to the Goliath for opening the door, patting his huge arm.

Distracted by the intimidating, yet lovable beast of a doorman, Boy hadn't noticed he wasn't headed to the dance floor. He had instead entered a small room with a staircase leading to a new, all-white door. Intrigued, he shook his head to make sure he wasn't hallucinating before he laughed at the ridiculousness of the circumstance.

Boy's balance compromised, he became amused at the difficulty in the task of ascending. The walls were matte black, black marble stairs, and he made good use tasteful golden handrails up either side. He appreciated the large surface of each step, and the sturdiness of the rail.

Halfway up, leaning against the wall, Boy noticed the stairwell was actually subtly inlaid with Egyptian looking artwork. It looked like it depicted a story. Trying to discern its meaning, in his inebriated state, paranoia grasped for his mind. The art appeared to tell a tail about humans interacting with non-human creatures. He was too intoxicated to focus, and instead regained his drive to reach the top.

After an eternity of Sisyphean effort, Boy reached the white doors, which opened away from him as he approached.

The room beyond was crystalline, with windows looking out into chaos. The large men at the entrance looked so similar that Boy wondered if they were the same bouncers from the other doors somehow. He chuckled to himself realizing the ridiculousness of the thought.

As if choreographed the two ominously large men simultaneously said, "Welcome Boy."

Boy's bewilderment by this recurrent welcome turned into a furrowed brow and a frown. He squinted against the brightness of this seeming VIP lounge in a VIP lounge, trying to regain focus. As his sight returned he found the room full of the 'A-list' famous people who were never seen anywhere. Those that other people spent time wondering about, trying to imagine where they partied. The elite's elite, in fame and more importantly wealth. A cast of such notoriety, even Boy couldn't help but be taken aback. It wasn't the rich and famous that struck him, it was seeing so many gathered together in one place, and not for a specific event.

"You're wasted," came a friendly voice.

Boy turned to find Johnny T.. He started to smile, but remembered that Johnny T. had known his mom before they'd met, that Johnny T. was likely just one of his mom's plants, not Boy's friend, but just another person on his mother's payroll.

Johnny T. caught Boy's awkward mood immediately. "That bad?" he asked concerned.

Boy tried to focus on Johnny T.'s face with little success.

"I know what you need." Johnny T. took Boy by the arm and led him to a table where a slew of flashy folks gathered around a ridiculously large pile of white powder. Boy wasn't sure of what was happening when Johnny T. said, "Try that on for size, Boy, I think it will snap you out of it," gesturing with a rolled up bill to a line of the dust on the table presumably just cut and waiting for Boy.

Perplexed, Boy looked from the line, back up to Johnny T.'s face, and back down to the line. Boy'd never done coke, but had heard it was the best cure for premature drunkenness. After a sloppy moment of consideration, he took the rolled money from the entreating hand. He breathed in hard, but was unable to insufflate the whole line. His eyes watered and he coughed. He was worried he'd looked like a rookie, so he switched nostril and finished what was left. He looked up expecting some sort of reaction, but no one was paying him any particular attention. He saw those gathered around the table captives of the pile in front of him.

The powder ripped through his nasal passage with a sharp burn. His vision crisped, the sound in the room became sharper, more acute. Subtle electronica played in the background along to the intoxicated chatter of a room full of half-drunk, half-high limelight lovers.

Snapping back into clarity he turned to find a genuine smile on Johnny T.'s face.

"Helps, don't it?" Smirked Johnny T.

"Fuck," Boy responded, taking a deep breath, his eyes opening wide, his jaw clenching.

Johnny T. chuckled gently. "Glad you finally made it, kid."

51

Boy was impressed at the speed with which he lost the feeling of incapacitated inebriation. He also became acutely aware he'd just broken his probation. Everything he had been fighting all night rushed back. He didn't want to explain himself to Johnny T. He wanted to leave, but didn't really understand how he'd even gotten to this room. The cocaine had brought back his capacity to focus, but this more aware mind was what he'd been trying to escape.

"If you're worried about not passing a drug test, or something like that, fear not my Boy," Johnny T. offered, having watched Boy's opaque emotional transition. "This shit is so pure they wouldn't even know what to look for in your system. And anyways," he continued, winking at Boy, "that drug bust was a smart media ploy, so what's to worry about?"

Boy watched Johnny T.'s focus return to the pile of coke, his eyes twinkling. "Another bump," Johnny T. proclaimed, cutting two lines. Boy oscillated between wanting to punch the guy and wanting to dive head first into the mountain of white powder before him.

Where the fuck am I? Boy thought. This is fucking ridiculous. I forgot how much I swear when I'm fucking high on this shit. Shit. Fuck it.

Boy's jaw clenched as his sorrow turned to anger, turned to despair, turned to apathy, turned to recklessness. His face in a snarl, he leaned over to rail in unison with Johnny T.

Johnny T. punctuated the experience by giving Boy a firm pat on the back and saying, "That's my boy."

Boy winced, even though he knew Johnny T. was speaking colloquially. "You just need to cut loose a little," continued the strange man. "Here. Come check this out. I think you'll dig it."

Johnny T. walked towards the window. Boy followed. The window looked out onto the writhing dance floor he had entered through. He unconsciously bounced to a beat he wasn't actually hearing, in unison with the rippling mass he watched ungulate to music that somehow wasn't coming through the glass in front of him.

"Pretty fun, right?" Johnny T. was smiling. "It's a one-way mirror so we can watch them, but they can't see us. They even figured out how to make it matte, so it doesn't reflect down into the room there."

Boy thought he saw Sophie trying to move through the crowd. He flinched. Then he saw something that made him second-guess what his eyes were telling him. One of those reptiles he hadn't seen since Mongolia was moving along the back wall. He could only make it out when the strobe flash reached as far back as the creature's path. Then it was gone.

He realized the non-human figures on the stairwell and corridors he'd passed through on his way here must be representations of these creatures. Maybe it was the coke, maybe because he didn't give a shit anymore, maybe he just wanted to trust the man standing next to him, he blurted, "Did you see that fucking reptile thing?"

Johnny T.'s grin didn't change as he said, "Yup. I must be as fucked up as you are." He turned to Boy, "Were you drinking the green stuff from downstairs?"

Boy's eyes got wide. He suddenly feared he'd been drugged, which he found amusing as he'd been willingly drugging himself all night. He laughed out loud.

"Yeah, me too," continued Johnny T. "I always see shit when I drink that stuff."

Boy thought about how Johnny T. had denied knowledge of the reptiles back on the train.

"I'm sure it has nothing to do with the lines we just railed," Johnny T. said sarcastic, before laughing at the situation. Boy laughed too, breaking his train of thought. It wasn't the laughter of levity Boy might have had without the influence of the substances; it was dark, heavy, angry. It still felt good.

After the moment passed, Boy's short attention span brought him to another window, which looked down into the red room. It was calmer, less immediately entertaining, but ultimately more intriguing. The dance room was blue in tone, chaotic, yet more simple in its rhythmic pulsations. This red room was subtler, darker, more political; façade and pretense; a high-level game of chess to the overt battle of the blue room.

Boy noticed the bouncer in front of the door to the staircase. The large figure grabbed someone who must have been trying to enter without proper access. He set the person down some feet away from the entrance before returning to his post. A woman. Sophie. Boy's stomach dropped. His dopamine studded half grin returned to a more unfortunate, comfortable scowl.

Johnny T. had followed him over from the other window, startling Boy by asking, "Hey, Boy. Isn't that your girlfriend?"

Boy started to unravel.

"Did she come with you? She probably can't come up. They're pretty strict. Trust me. I've tried so many times, all for naught," Johnny T. continued, eye's locked on Sophie, oblivious to what was happening for Boy.

Boy spun and stumbled toward the bar.

"Hey. Where ya goin', bud?" Johnny T. called after Boy.

Boy didn't respond, staying his course. Johnny T. watched Sophie a moment longer before following. In the time it took Johnny T. to get to the bar, Boy had already downed a shot of something unfamiliar and was about to take another, which Johnny T. pulled out of his hand.

"Whoa, buddy…"

"What the fuck?" Boy gave no real effort to retrieve the drink.

"I think we're fucked enough kid. Let's cool it." He was surprised by Johnny T.'s serious, almost stern but still kind tone.

"Don't fucking try to control me. I know what I'm doing." Boy motioned for the barkeep. "Give me another boss," Boy hollered.

Johnny T. grabbed the shot and drank it before Boy could.

"Hey. Fucking quit it, dude." Boy said, stealing his neighbor's drink and gulping it down as quick as he could.

"You trying to kill yourself, kid?" Johnny T. asked.

"Fuck you," Boy replied belligerently.

"Suit yourself." Johnny T. walked back to the coke table.

The bartender started to pretend to ignore Boy, while also protecting other patrons' drinks. Boy was still aware enough to realize he wouldn't get anything else out of the bartender, so he got up.

Boy still had jitters from the coke, but the drunken wobble was fighting its way back into his legs. He wandered aimlessly around the room. He didn't want to go back down the stairs, afraid he might run into Sophie, but he didn't want to talk to anyone up here either.

Much of the VIP lounge was made up of discreet areas. Small groups sat in conversation around counter tops covered in powders for insufflating. Boy knew many of the characters, and was beckoned by some, but he was hell bent to avoid more interaction, desperate to find a secondary exit.

Eventually Boy was pulled into imbibing, inhalation, loud self-promotions by association, awkward attempts at companionship. He said nothing, but simply stopped resisting. He was like a stick in a river, listless, occasionally snagged or caught in an eddy, to be released back into the stream, steadily moving down the path of least resistance. In this aimlessness he lost himself to intoxication.

Through the fog of chemicals glazing Boy's brain, after an intoxicated immeasurable amount of time, he was dragged by a crowd into a different elevator than the one he had arrived in, behind a wall he hadn't noticed was a door, though, in his state he wasn't tracking any of this fully.

As swiftly as Boy was swooped into the elevator he was out again, and on the street alone. His awareness was only coming in spurts, then he was in his car, barely keeping tears at bay, head nodding in exhaustion. He didn't want to be alone, but he didn't want to be with anyone either.

The only person Boy could think of that he thought might have insight without judgment was WJ. Boy realized what a horrible friend he could be, as he hadn't seen from or reached out to WJ since their return from Russia. This was not out of the ordinary for his relationship with WJ. WJ almost never initiated contact, and was just as likely to not answer his phone. Boy tried anyways.

WJ's voicemail was sardonic. "I'm probably not picking up because they got me. Or maybe I finally joined 'em. Either way, you can leave a message, but I might never call you back."

Boy listened through the beep, wanting to laugh, but was unable to muster the energy. He hung up without leaving a message.

Boy knew driving was a bad idea, which made him want it more. He wanted to get the hell out. Out of the city, out the country, out of the world, out of his mind, out of this reality he was trapped in. He turned the engine over and drove.

Boy made it out of the city, something he only realized after the road had become lined with trees instead of buildings. He guessed he was upstate, or in Jersey. His vision was inconsistent. He was somehow still moving further from sobriety, as the alcohol trapped in his gut soaked in.

There was a loud bang, a slamming against the driver's-side-window as he crashed through a railing. Slow motion. The seatbelt clenched, the windshield exploded, the airbag released. Each impact flinging him about, a rag doll. Free-fall. He'd gone over a cliff. He watched the macabre ballet of broken glass dance around his flailing arms as the car plummeted. Then he black out.

52

Garbled sound of a TV, as though from down a long corridor. Slowly the noise sharpened; a news broadcast. It was hard for Boy to focus, but his attention was pulled out of its haze.

"In other news," the broadcaster announced, "the poster child for rock and roll appears to have died last night in what is being called a substance-induced car accident. Boy, front man of world-famous 'Fit to Burst', and son of fashion mogul…"

Boy focus dissolved. He couldn't understand what he was hearing. He tried to move, but was unable. His attention returned to the broadcast, "…The young rock star's car was found at the bottom of a cliff in upstate New York after a night of what witnesses describe as reckless partying. The accident occurred sometime near four in the morning. No further details are available at this time. Boy had been arrested earlier this year for possession of narcotics. All of this only weeks after the release of the docu-series Boy himself produced, 'The Trans-Siberian Festival Express', which stands to become one of the most successful docu-series of all time…"

Boy could no longer maintain the arduous state of concentration required to listen and the noise returned to a fuzzy distance as he re-lost consciousness, returning to a dreamless state.

53

Boy came to, voices talking over him. His eyes wouldn't open, or he didn't want to open them, he wasn't sure which. One of the voices above him sounded like Johnny T. Another, to Boy's bewilderment, sounded distinctly like Elvis.

"I think he'll be fine," said the Elvis voice, "don't beat yourself up about it."

"I didn't realize he would just take off like that," Johnny T.'s voice responded. "I thought we were just having a good time, and then he was gone all of the sudden. I figured he had gone down to get his girlfriend." Johnny T. sounded genuinely distressed. This confused Boy.

"Just set the water down on the bed stand," replied the Elvis voice, "and get back to work. I'll stay with him."

"Thanks, buddy," Johnny T. said. Boy heard footsteps coming towards him. "I didn't know he'd taken off until I went down stairs and found the kid's girl, still waiting by the VIP entrance, all messed up because she had followed him to the club as requested, but was having a hard time tracking him inside, only to be denied by one of her goons."

Who is Johnny T. talking about? Sophie? Someone else? At who's request?

Johnny T. went on, "Those bouncers were supposed to give her clearance, but they claimed they didn't recognize her, so she'd been blocked down in 'prohibition'. When I found her she told everything that had been happening, and I couldn't believe that I had been updated."

Again, confusion. *Is this yet another person? Updated by whom? Bouncers were told to give Sophie access by whom?*

"Poor kid. Not having an easy transition," The Elvis voice added.

What are they talking about? Boy wondered. *Where the hell am I?*

"I ought to go." Footsteps moved back across the room. He wanted to ask Johnny T. for clarification, but it was too hard to open his eyes, still unable to move.

"Thanks for watching the kid, Prez. It means a lot to her."

Prez? Boy wondered as the door opened.

After a pause Johnny T. added, "And me too."

"I know," replied the Elvis voice. "Get back to work." The door closed.

Mustering all his might Boy was able to barely open an eye and make the smallest of noises. His vision was fuzzy. He saw a figure that indeed even looked blearily like Elvis walking over to him.

It looked to Boy like he was in a hospital room. There was a TV in the corner, to the right of where he lay; a small table with flowers at the end of his bed. The walls were a warm, off-orange hue. He was in a slim, adjustable bed. An IV bag hung on a rack next to him, with a tube connecting to his arm. A bedside table on the other side of his bed had food on it, and the glass of water Johnny T. had brought. The rest of the room was bare.

Upon seeing Boy stir, the man came over to the bedside, "Hey kid." The low timbre of his voice so much like the icon. Seeing the TV reminded Boy of the broadcast he'd heard. *Had that been real?*

"Where," he tried, but his voice broke.

"You're in Atlantis, Boy."

What? Am I still at the club? Who the hell is this guy?

He concentrated hard and focused his eyes. "Elvis?"

"Funny thing about being someone," responded the man, "you often get mistaken for who you are."

Boy couldn't help but smirk at the funny Elvis impersonator. Then his smile left as he thought again about the broadcast. *Wait, what if this guy really is Elvis? What if I am dead? Am I fucking dead?*

He mind started going over the previous night, everything that had lead up to now, everything falling apart. He started to convince himself he must be dead, even playing with the idea that he could have died some time ago.

He wondered if that was maybe what Johnny T. had meant a moment ago when he said Boy was having a hard time getting used to everything. He realized the VIP lounge had looked how he could imagine some people might think heaven would look. *Only, if I were already dead, why would the news report say I just died? Why would I feel this shitty? And why the hell would I be in a hospital?*

"Am I dead?" he finally blurted out.

Elvis chuckled. "I guess it depends on what you

mean. If you want, you can be dead. Most of the world thinks you're dead. But if you mean, 'is my body no more?' Well…that's obviously not the case."

That didn't help at all. Boy wished something would start making sense. *What the hell is this guy talking about?*

As though he noticed Boy's confusion Elvis offered, "Look, kid. You are in Atlantis."

In? Not at? What?

"This is where we come to live when we're ready. The question of your aliveness is a particularly confusing topic to explain, but I'll try. Take me for example. You think, or have thought, that I, that Elvis, was dead. Sure there have been fun rumors that I was still alive, but most people never believe it. And here I am. My body is in excellent condition, and will be for as long as I want. So, I am dead to the world, but I am also very much alive. I, as with many here in Atlantis, was done with the invasive nature of the fame I'd stumbled my way into. You are now faced with a choice that I had to make some time ago. Do you want your anonymity back, or do you want the world to continue to experience you as the famous person you've become? McCartney tried the dead thing, decided he wasn't ready for anonymity, and went back. Lennon waited longer to come here, but he's never gone back. You get to make the choice as well. Many return, and many stay. There are ways to do both. The only time pressure is that the longer you stay, the more difficult it is to manage the return story."

What Elvis was saying wasn't hard to understand, but Boy was finding it very difficult to believe.

Boy asked, "Who was in here before talking with you?"

"When?" Elvis replied.

"Just now. Before I woke up." Boy's energy was waning.

"You mean your dad?" Elvis asked.

"My what?" *This has got to be some fucked up dream.*

"Your pops. Johnny T.?" The man was sincere, only aiding in Boy's mounting bemusement.

Could this be true? I must be asleep. Or is this some kind of hell and I am actually dead? Fuck!

Boy had always been able to wake himself from dreams in the past, but this didn't feel like a dream. He'd always realize he was dreaming the second he thought it. He didn't know what death ought to feel like, but he could still feel his body aching all over, still very much there, and worse for the wear. *But Elvis? Johnny T. his dad?* The infamous choosing whether or not to be publicly dead; none of this made sense, at least not enough to passively believe it.

Boy wanted to hit something, wanted at least to yell. He mustered a growl, "Fuck you man," his eyes welling with angry tears. He was sick of this, sick of having everything he understood uprooted from underneath him. He just wanted something consistent, something he could hold on to.

Elvis turned some knobs on the machine regulating Boy's IV drip, and a drowsiness overtook him.

"Sleep a while longer, Boy. You'll feel better when you wake."

Maybe this is just a dream, Boy hoped to himself. His vision phased out, his eyes closed. Part of him was relieved to pass out, and another part of him didn't want to loose consciousness, loose any sense of control. This part wanted to run. There was nothing he could do either way. He passed back into a drugged and dreamless semi-coma.

54

When Boy woke it was sudden, as though he hadn't slept at all. His trepidation was strong so he hesitated before opening his eyes, hoping the crazy story swirling in his mind had merely been a dream. He didn't want the pain of his body, or the beeping sounds nearby to indicate anything. Maybe he was still in a hospital, maybe he had crashed, but maybe Elvis wasn't his nurse. He hated that he couldn't believe what he felt was the clearly more realistic of the two possibilities.

Finally Boy forced his eyelids to part. He was still in the off-orange glow of the same hospital room. The chemicals of resignation released from his hippocampus. Unsure of where this hospital was located, and if Elvis had been telling the truth, he tried to get up. Movement caused a wildfire of pain to spread through his body. He was wearing a hospital gown, arms still connected to an IV. With some effort he was able to move himself to the edge of the bed. Scanning the room he noticed his clothes folded neatly on a chair by the door, his shoes tucked underneath.

With care Boy pulled the IV out of his arm. He stood but was unable to balance with ease. He slowed down, taking time to reestablish a semblance of equilibrium before moving to retrieve his clothes. Despite smelling as though they'd been cleaned, his outfit was still tattered in places. It must have been a pretty bad crash, Boy reflected. He was exhausted from the effort of bottoming his shirt and pulling his pants on. He knew he wouldn't make it far if he tried to leave in this state. He decided to return gingerly back to the bed, unintentionally fell back asleep, but this time arrived directly into dreams.

He floated through the undulating field, perpetually approaching a form that never came into focus, never getting close enough to touch. He looked to the ground, which shifted from amorphous texture to hardwood. He looked back up; his mom's office. She sat behind her desk and he tried calling to her. She couldn't hear him, never moved. All he wanted was for her to be real, for this nightmare to be over, to be home.

55

Boy's heart beat a rapid, syncopated polyrhythm, which woke him. He gathered himself for whatever was beyond his eyelids. Nothing had changed. He was still alone. Relief paralleled by anxiety. His energy was up, but he remained lying down, building resolve.

Eventually Boy roused himself out of the bed, finding his footing still unsure. He stood, his cerebellum recalibrated, a modicum of balance returning. He shuffled to the door cautiously. Listening, he heard nothing. He wasn't sure why such a need for caution. Still, he turned the knob slowly, as though he were sneaking out of the room.

With the door cracked Boy could hear voices far down a hallway. He peered through to see a corridor. Not what he'd been expecting.

Simultaneously ancient, yet more modern than any hall he'd ever seen. It looked like a tunnel dug out of the earth, a mineshaft, yet with the detail of a Victorian mansion, or fully restored Egyptian ruins that had been perpetually kept up over the centuries. Softly lit, the lighting was the strangest part of the place. He couldn't tell where the light source was, as though it were emanating from the middle of the space. It was beautiful and haunting.

The voices were moving closer. Boy closed the door. His hand on the knob, he pressed his ear to the door hoping to listen, but door was too thick. The knob turned in his hand. He jumped back, startled. Frantic, he rushed to the bed, the only object large enough to hide behind in the room. His heart pounded, convinced the intruders find him.

There were two sets of steps that entered, and whispers. Boy was unable to make out the words.

Elvis voice spoke. "Boy?"

The voice was benevolent. Boy began to feel embarrassed for hiding.

"Boy?" Elvis asked again, calm, gentle.

"Yeah?" Boy forced out, rising from behind the bed to see Elvis and Johnny T., both smiling, amused, but with kindness in their eyes.

"How ya feeling?" Johnny T. asked.

Fuck. If this is real, and this Elvis really thinks this guy's my dad, does that mean he is? Boy's embarrassment swelled.

"You ok Boy," Elvis said, becoming serious. "Why were you hiding?" His levity returning with this question. "You're looking pretty pale kid, you probably ought to lay yourself back down."

Boy didn't want to be told what to do, though he could tell Elvis's intentions were good. He also knew Elvis was right, but his resentment kept him wanting to stand. After a moment his fatigue won, and he sat on the corner of the bed.

"Why were you hiding?" Johnny T. repeated.

Even though Johnny T. sounded kind, Boy was in a fit of pique. He couldn't help but feel that even this guy, this strange man, was probably part of some grand conspiracy the world, or more precisely, his mom had plotted against him.

"Where the hell are we?" Boy finally surrendered.

"Atlantis," Johnny T. replied.

This brought Boy no further along the path to understanding, save that it corroborated Elvis's story. He wondered how big the club could be. It didn't seem impossible that this was the same place, especially the ostentatious corridor they'd come in through, though the club had been pretty deep under the city. He just couldn't figure out why he would be back at that club, and in a hospital-style bed. He remembered the strange elevator, and how each room seemed to have another hidden room beyond it. Maybe this was just another wing of that underground lair.

"Why am I here?" Boy asked, hoping things would start to fall into place for his befuddled mind.

"You crashed, Boy," offered Johnny T.

So that happened, Boy thought.

"And we could take better care of you here than a New York hospital would have." Johnny T. voice was friendly, yet somehow mechanical, disengaged. "And Prez," he gestured to Elvis, "told you your options, now that you're here."

"Options?" Boy asked.

Elvis joined in, "You don't have to go back to that fame if you don't want to. Boy can be dead so far as the world is concerned, and you can have an anonymous life, if that's what you'd prefer."

"Why would I want that?" Boy wondered aloud.

"You didn't seem happy," Johnny T. offered.

"How could I have been happy?" Boy yelled. "Everything I am, everything I have, everything I've done…it's fake…something created for me by my mother. Even you, Johnny T.. Probably even this place." His voice got quieter as he started to return to familiar despair.

"But your music was going great. Your show was smashing download records. So much of your success was yours. Are you sure it wasn't the pressure?" Johnny T. asked.

Boy remembered having thought Johnny T. could be a convincing actor, but this felt like an act, and didn't feel convincing.

"What the hell are those things, really? I didn't create them, it was all my mom's influence." Boy's jaw clenched.

"You know that's not true. She influenced things, sure, but you wrote the songs, you thought up the show, not her. All she did was support you in your pursuits, she didn't create them for you." Johnny T. reflected.

He was right and Boy hated him for it, for not allowing his anger, for not supporting his collapse into self-righteous anguish. He wished someone would just be there for him, understand him, and not counter his emotions with logic.

"Don't defend her," Boy finally said, under his breath.

Johnny T. kept quiet.

There was a brief silence until Elvis said, "Rest, Boy, and have a look around when you're ready. If you need anything," he motioned to a small button on the wall near the head of the bed. "Or ask anyone. Everyone here will help."

Boy didn't speak. He watched Elvis motion to Johnny T. out of the corner of his eye. The two men left. All the energy Boy had conjured was gone. He was completely exhausted. He closed his eyes, letting his mind race, and fell back onto the bed. It felt so relieving to be lying down, even with his legs off the end of the bed.

He ran down the tunnels, but this time the shadows of the reptiles were coming from Sophie, Johnny T., and his mom, who all called after him. "Leave me alone," he yelled, "just leave me the fuck alone." The shadows stopped. Everything became eerily quiet. The shadows disappeared. He had been listened to, and was now in the dark, under the city, alone. He wept in his solitude, a deep and cathartic cry, until there were no more tears to be had.

56

A new confidence lingered when Boy's awareness returned to the now familiar hospital room. He felt as though he had actually cried the cry he'd been having in his dreams, and the release had shifted his despair into something new. Was this acceptance?

Boy lay in the bed, deciding his next move. Still trying to make sense of his situation he started to imagine it was all a hoax, designed by Johnny T., or maybe his mom. He tried to believe it, that Johnny T. had watched him get totally wasted and pass out in the VIP lounge, and got an Elvis impersonator to come mess with his head, teach him a lesson about not going so hard. Or maybe this was all part of building the rock star persona, another ploy his mother was making to build his career, another unasked for and backwards attempt to nudge him along his seemingly unavoidable path to success. Maybe he really was still in the club, in some super-secret room. In an attempt to convince himself of this possibility he decided to get up try find his way out, hopeful at the prospect.

Boy pushed away the evidence his mind offered to the contrary, that Johnny T. had known about Boy driving off of a cliff, for instance. He continued avoiding thoughts about Elvis telling him Johnny T. was his dad, made even more awkward if it were to have been fabricated by Johnny T., or Boy's mom. He ignored the glaring holes in his plot, hoping to find his way out, hoping to laugh about it all with WJ when he got back out into the street of New York.

Boy left the familiarity of his little hospital room and entered the ornate hall. The walls were covered in similar carvings to the ones he vaguely remembered from the stairwell to the VIP lounge. Humans interacting with large reptiles. They seemed to tell the story of a city being built.

As Boy explored the carvings, curious to decipher the story, his thoughts flashed back to the club, to seeing a huge reptile, to Johnny T. saying he saw it too. His heart started racing. He feared these creatures were real. Or was this just the impact of too many substances still pulsing through his system, and the power of suggestion? He became anxious that this tunnel, this entire place might be where the creatures lived.

Boy's mounting fear quickened his pace until he ran down the hall. Perhaps his anxiety-laden dreams of running down corridors away from the reptiles were prophetic, were finally coming true now. He had no idea which way lead to…anywhere. A part of his mind clung to the ridiculousness of his fear, fighting against the abject terror another part of his mind wouldn't let his focus release.

Noise came from the direction Boy was headed. It sounded like a party. *The VIP lounge?* As he ran, hoping to join the tumult, he noticed the hallway inscriptions, above the door leading to the party, punctuated into a magnificent, gold-leafed, depiction of what could only be some kind of deity. This strange, ominous figure stood in a field somehow familiar to Boy. *Déjà vu*, but not *déjà vu* either. On the figures chest was an eye peering out of a glowing triangle. It was such a familiar, and hackneyed conspiracy-laden image, the eye in the triangle. Boy stopped to take a closer look before his fear propelled him through the doorway.

Boy burst through the door and into a large ballroom. He was relieved that it was full of humans, but couldn't understand how this space couple possible be secret and hidden beneath Manhattan.

It was an extravagant atrium, elegant, and immaculately maintained. The décor held examples of every era, in architecture, interior design, and even furniture. There were elements of ancient Greece, ancient Egypt, what Boy imagined to be ancient India and China. There were other elements he didn't recognize, maybe Nubian, Caspian, Kush, cultures he only vaguely remembered hearing WJ talk about from the ancient past. The size and stately manner of the space was pyramidal in scale, and even more grand. It was simultaneously timeless, antiquated, and futuristic. The People matched, clothing and styles he'd only seen in historic depictions, and the awkward attempts he was familiar with from the avant-garde artist-types that hung around his mom.

Boy was so captivated by what he was seeing that he jumped when the door closed behind him. He was glad to be out of the hall, out of that room, and around people again, but he was also overwhelmed by the amount of people, and the buzz. It sounded like a beehive. And when the door clambered shut, the attention turned to him. Those near gazed with recognition, and he worried he'd become the focus of the room's conversation. But almost everyone that had turned towards him turned away again, unfazed.

Boy started to recognize faces. There was no way this was a hoax coordinated by Johnny T. He slowly recognized Marilyn Monroe smiling at him. She was standing next to Jimmy Hoffa. Hunter S. Thomson was talking with a bearded Jim Morrison. Janis Joplin seemed whispered into George Harrisons ear, nodding towards Boy. Plenty of faces were unrecognizable as well, but there were so many famous people he had known were dead.

Boy returned to the story Elvis had told him. So this has to be a dream. He looked down at his hands. He knew he was awake. *But, how*? He stood in awe of his surroundings. It was as though the conspiracies about the world's upper echelons were true. Had they all been here, under the city, hiding, living, and partying together for time immemorial? WJ would shit himself, or not be surprised in the least, Boy thought.

Boy heard snippets of conversations around him, but was unable make much sense of them. "It's him…He's here…That's Boy…Her son…Has he made the transition…Is he staying…Is that the kid…The one they've been talking about…Do you think he's done it…The high priestess' son…he's perfect…are they done with him…"

Boy's head flooded with words jumbled into incoherence. They must be talking about him, but what were they talking about? Who was 'her'? His mom? What transition? Who were 'they'? Done with what? Or was he still paranoid, hungover, out of it? He looked back down at his hand, still definitely awake.

Boy was awestruck by these people he idealized, and they seemed to be reacting to him the same way. He was discomforted by the strange questions he overheard, his imagination running wild trying to create context for the chatter.

Boy was relieved when Elvis stepped out of the crowd. He considered how ridiculous it was to be relieved to see Elvis, the worlds most notoriously 'not dead' celebrity.

"How are ya', Boy?" came Elvis' smooth, soothing voice as he used Boy to a chair. Noticing Boy's eyes darting around the room Elvis reassured him, "These people are friends."

Boy wished Elvis' words were as soothing as his voice, but this strange reality was hard to believe. Why am I here? Why are all these people here? And why does Elvis want to help?

Boy took a deep breath and looked to Elvis, who was smiling. He tried to relax. Things were going from insane to deeply strange, but somehow more acceptable. He'd always guessed something like this must be going on, but assumed it couldn't be. WJ was sure of it. Boy delighted in imagining how that conversation might go now. Boy looked back at his hands. *Why do I keep doing that?*

As though he could read Boy's mind Elvis offered, "There still there. It's not a dream. It took me a while too when I first got here, so I get it."

Elvis' tone was so understanding that Boy softened. He could tell this wasn't a dream, or a drug fueled hallucination. He could tell it was as real as anything else he'd ever experience. He let go, explored what it was like to accept what he was being presented with.

"So, this is still Atlantis?" Boy finally asked.

"That's right, kid. Always has been, always will be," Elvis assured.

They sat, not speaking, as Boy took it all in. After a moment Elvis asked, "Can I get you anything, kid?"

Boy realized how dehydrated he was, parched. He asked for a glass of water, then laughed at himself realizing he'd just asked Elvis to fetch him a drink.

Boy was astonished by the willingness Elvis had shown. It was as though anything Boy needed, Elvis would do, and no one batted an eyelash. Boy felt like royalty, but didn't understand why. He was famous, but these people were more famous, and yet they had all seemed in awe of him.

Marilyn was first to approach after Elvis had gone for water. She apologized for her boldness. She seemed star-struck. She asked if Boy's mom was there, and the absurdity of the situation stopped being a distraction from his malaise. He concluded the attention was connected to his mother, not him. Discomfort returned to his stomach as he realized even here, in the world's secret society of the glorious and 'dead', his mother reputation changed how everyone saw him. He could tell she had meant no malice, but that only made him more repulsed. Why did Marilyn Monroe care about Boy's mother?

Boy could feel himself shut down. He was watching from a dissociated distance as he returned to an unfortunately familiar routine of bouncing from one conversation to the next. He kept hearing something about 'the high priestess', a nickname he gathered was connected to his mother somehow. Some of the people he stumbled into conversations with tried to explain more to him about how this secret society worked, but Boy was lost in his mind. He was captivated, discouraged by his unavoidable tie to his mother.

Boy caught moments of conversations. He learned passively the ways in which world politics were faked, hoaxes put on by this immortal club; a trick played on the masses to keep them entertained while these wealthy patrons enjoyed any and all the resources they desired. It was suggested that global warming had only become an issue because of the threat of polar ice caps melting, which would eventually expose them, though Boy was unsure how. He was told the world's politicians were mostly robots controlled by a mainframe in Atlantis. The mainframe had been run for millennia by Isis, until she recently passed the baton to Judy Garland. Social manipulation was mostly for fun, and ultimately their intentions were relatively benevolent. He was assured that they loved humanity, and found it rather benign. Someone he took to be a long forgotten empress explained to him that once you can live forever, the meaning of life, the value inherent to living, changes.

The part of Boy that tried to listen believed he ought to have been impressed, bewildered, or worried, but his myopia on everyone's interest in his mom narrowed his focus to such a tight pinhole that he was nearly blind. It drove him crazy to hear the same entitled drivel he had been hearing his entire life. Arrogant, over-privileged people, arguing meritocracy merely because power was in their hands and they wanted to believe they deserved it.

In this sea of hubris and despair Boy suddenly missed Sophie. This pain made him even more upset, Sophie now just another of his mother's henchmen. He fell into the numb comfort of protective apathy. He pretended to listen, saying very little, and these people didn't notice. Why couldn't Sophie, the one thing that had been good, stay good?

It became clear to Boy that he didn't want to pretend to be dead, especially if it meant spending eternity with this insincere crowd. He couldn't imagine he would ever want that. He wanted to leave, but had the distinct sensation the crowd surrounding him was unlikely to let him go. He kept these thoughts to himself, figuring when the time came he would have to find the elevator on his own. Instead he asked for the bathroom, excused himself from an awkward conversation Tutankhamen and Mother Teresa were having at him.

Boy wound through the crowd, gazing up to avoid inquiring eyes, hoping to skirt unnecessary interaction. The atrium was lined by a mezzanine. He scanned it absentmindedly as he meandered. Something caught his eye, and his heart dropped.

Every time Boy had seen the reptiles they'd disappeared around a corner, or vanished into walls. This time the reptile, the size of a large bodybuilding human, in a black suit, stood perfectly still, watching the room. It didn't move. It was so stationary that, if he hadn't seen the others before, he would have thought it a strange and realistic sculpture. He waited for it to abscond itself into the ceiling, but it never did. Sending his gaze around the mezzanine he noticed three more, all still, observing the ebbs and flows of this immortal party.

Boy returned his gaze to the crowd to see if anyone else noticed or was disturbed by the immobile onlookers. If they knew, they didn't seem to care. He wondered if he were the only one who could see these creatures. He remembered Johnny T. had admitted seeing them, though he had been rather nonplussed about it.

Was no one as uneasy with these reptiles as Boy found himself? Searching to understand Boy's mind built a context. This was a group of people he'd thought were dead previously, all of whom were living in a secret underground lair, immortal, secretly running society. He'd just been talking to pharaohs, empresses, and the most notoriously famous people to have ever died. So why would a bunch of reptilian creatures be stranger than anything else?

Despite having a narrative to understand the circumstance through Boy found everything so unnerving that he became frantic. He grasped desperately at calm, hoping to draw as little attention to himself as possible, but he was becoming unhinged and he was sure it would start showing. At the edge of the room he found what appeared to be a main entrance. As nonchalantly and covertly as possible he slipped through the doors and out of the room.

A long hallway, full of windows looking out into a cityscape. Boy was afraid he would be followed, either by one of the throng from inside, or worse, a reptile. He moved to the nearest window and hopped through only to find it didn't lead outside, but into yet another long hallway with elaborate painting of outdoor scenes, so precise he had thought them real, another façade in this elaborate simulacra.

Boy almost felt safer in this corridor, away from the crowds, until he realized the reptiles might use it to get around. He had nowhere else to go, so he picked a direction and started walking with determination. After several minutes, and a labyrinth of intersecting corridors, he stumbled upon an elevator. He had no idea of where it would take him, but looking down the corridor, and seeing he was alone, he pressed the button he guessed meant 'up' on the wall. The doors opened immediately.

Boy moved inside and found a wall of buttons. The top button read, 'surface'. He figured 'surface' must mean back to the street level somewhere in New York. It would be easy to find his way home from anywhere in Manhattan, so he pressed the button repeatedly, as though this would make the doors close faster, expedite his escape.

The doors did close, at what felt a tauntingly slow pace, but then, to Boy's relief, the elevator started moving up. As he ascended the thought of being back in the streets of New York became a new kind of distressing. He didn't really want to go home. He couldn't go to Sophie. He didn't know whom to trust. His mind reeled. The lift stopped.

The doors opened to a foyer. There was another door on the opposite side of the room. A series of signs suggested direction for various destinations: 'airport'; 'front desk'; 'reception'. Boy was disoriented. He didn't see anyone anywhere. He took advantage of the vacancy, and despite not knowing where he'd go once he was out, he moved swiftly to the exit.

Moving through the door Boy squinted against

the glare of a barren, frozen, white landscape. A deep chill hit his face, wind whipping off the ice. This was nowhere he knew in New York, yet at that moment anywhere other than where he was seemed a better choice. He hesitated, feeling the cold, his attire insufficient. Hearing commotion in the room behind him, Boy darted out and into a run.

Boy looked back to see if he was being followed, the entrance he'd just left little more than an implied door in an icy hillside. Everything was ice. He knew if he left this place he would have a hard time finding it again. Though he was barely outside the door, if he hadn't know it was there he might not notice it at all. Though it seemed easy to get lost, he found resolve. He picked a direction and took off, running to avoid shivering, apathetic to the consequence. He moved swiftly across the glacial, frozen ground.

As Boy slowed to a jog his mind tried to put all the pieces together. He was more fatigued than he realized, and inhibited by his recent injuries. He pushed through the strange frostbitten desert. Nothing gave him any sense of where he was. When his exhaustion won and he slowed to a saunter, his chill increased with each step. This had been a hasty and idiotic choice.

Boy started wondered if he was ready to die, which was quickly becoming the most likely outcome of his circumstance. The sudden imminence of his mortality excited him at first, a liberation from the despondency he had been trapped in. Death, solace.

These thoughts passed as the pain of the cold moved into Boy bones, his teeth chatter becoming painfully loud. He realized how much he would actually miss the world; his band mates; his friends, even if they weren't real; Sophie, even if she was hired; and, somehow, even his mom. Tears welled in his eyes freezing on his cheeks. He stopped. His body ached. Exhausted, he curled into a fetal position. The nearness of death, he started begging forgiveness, apologizing his trespasses, telling those he'd loved that he loved them despite their not being there, and losing consciousness.

57

That eerie field, the bright, diffused light, the soft undulating ground, the sense of comfort. Only now, too, the cold. The frost was interrupted by something warm and wet, as though a heated, moist towel was being brushed over his brow. A huge Bernese mountain dog lapping at Boy's face brought him out of the dream.

Boy was still in the frozen desert. Mildly frostbitten, especially where the metal of his medallion lay against his chest. The huge dog peered benevolently down on him. A barrel around the panting beasts neck read 'drink me'. The warm dog was so comforting. Boy was a kind of cold he'd never felt, even in Russia. He unstrapped the vessel from the beast's collar, found a cork in one of its sides. Upon opening the little wooden vessel, delicious steam wafted out. It was full of hot-buttered rum, still almost hot.

The first drink burned, but quickly became the elixir of life, warming Boy's extremities and replenishing mobility. The bearer of this saving grace nuzzled him, generously sharing its body heat. After Boy had drained the little barrel he got the sense he was supposed to climb aboard this horse-sized dog.

To ride atop a dog seemed odd, but in the context, it was much less bizarre than so much else that had been happening. Boy had no idea where he was going. Maybe he wasn't all the way ready to forgive the world its injustices, but he no longer wanted to die. He rode, gazing out towards the monotonous horizon, and he had the vague memory for this place, a hazy distant dream-image.

Starting to feel relief from the intensity of the cold from the heat emanating from the furry friend Boy lay atop, he was reminded of something WJ had told him once, that the last stage before freezing to death was euphoria. *Is this that?* He wondered. *It's nice that I hope not.* The dog's body was so comfortable that Boy started nodding off, catching himself just before slumber only to nod off again as they continued their steady saunter nowhere.

58

Boy's frozen, euphorically dreamless state was broken when he finally fell from his trusty, mild-mannered steed. It hurt to open his eyes. When he did he saw a cabin of sorts. Rugged, yet technologically equipped and advanced. Primarily made of wood so bleached by the sun it was as white as the ice surrounding it. There were icicles and wires tangled together so that the cabin looked like an exposed ice-laden rockslide against the wall of the icebound hill behind it.

A haggard mountain man stood in the doorway, a large beard, hair wild and unkempt, and an permanent squint to his eyes. Slow recognition spread across the man's familiar face. He shouted,

"Boy! My Boy!"

The craggy stranger flailed his arms about frantically, and ran to meet Boy on the ice. He hoisted Boy back onto the dog.

"Get him inside, Bartleby," he commanded the dog, who regained a relaxed pace, despite the man's heightened state, and took Boy into this unexpected the hermit's den.

Panels and computer displays cluttered the walls of the small room, resembling more a space lab than a remote cabin. Yet the décor was of a lost mountaineer's dwelling, exaggerated by the man's Neolithic appearance.

The man helped Boy out of his wet clothes and wrapped him in an inexplicably soft, warm blanket. Boy watched the man as he worked, trying to place the familiarity. Then it struck him. He started to wonder in ernst if he had actually died. There was no logical way for this man to be who he appeared to be.

Seeing Boy's perplexed face the man asked, "You okay, son?"

This only confused Boy further. It was Johnny T.'s voice, and his face behind the beard, but there was no way he could be here, like this. He had just been back at the club, if that even was the club, and he had been clean-shaven, and had looked many years younger.

"Who are you?" Boy finally managed to ask, hoping this would clear things up.

"I'm your…uh…John," said the man, cautiously.

"John? As in Johnny T.?" Boy inquired.

"I haven't heard that name in a long time. They used to call me Johnny T.," he answered, seeming to dissociate into memory.

Boy didn't know what to say. If this was Johnny

T., how long had Boy been out in the cold? But that made even less sense than anything else. This couldn't be the same Johnny T. But then, how would this guy know Boy's name? Perhaps Boy had been out in the freeze a long time. Again, he let go the idea as quick as it came, aware that he would have died in the time it would have taken Johnny T. to grow such a beard.

Again searching for something to make sense Boy asked, "How long has it been since we were back in the club?"

"The club?" The bearded fellow asked.

"Atlantis." Boy clarified, hoping that was the hiccup.

"Son, they haven't let me in there for ages." The man looked forlorn.

"So you're not Johnny T., the actor?" Boy asked.

"Well, I'm the original," said the man, looking down at the ground, his tone diminishing in volume and confidence.

"The original what?" Boy said, lost again.

"The original Johnny T., the actor, but everyone just calls me John now," the man replied.

"What do you mean the original Johnny T.?" Boy couldn't follow.

"You must have met the robot, I take it?" He looked up at Boy now, wincing. "It's so good to see you, Boy. You've become very handsome."

I've become handsome? Boy didn't feel threatened, but the awkward statement didn't help him feel at ease either. He tried to imagine explaining this to anyone; in a tech-cabin, with a lost original Johnny T., escaped from a secret society of the worlds elite 'dead', saved by a humungous dog, in the middle of nowhere, on some sort of ice drift. He wouldn't believe it if he heard it, and he was the one living through it. The man looked at him with concern and tenderness. Boy softened, and decided to just keep asking questions.

"Are you saying that 'the other' Johnny T. is a clone or something?".

"That's right," John said. "Well, something like a clone. Maybe more of a robot replicant. I don't really know, but he isn't me." John looked sad. "There's something else you ought to know." The man struggled. Boy braced himself, even though he had no idea what the man could be so worried to say.

"You see," John began, "The whole reason I am out here, and not down there, with the rest of them, is because of your mom."

"My mom?" Boy asked.

"Yeah, well..." John hesitated. Boy's heart started racing. "Well..."

"Well what, man?" Boy pushed through his teeth.

"Okay," the man said. "You see, Boy, I'm...well... your dad."

Boy almost laughed, but then seeing the man's sincerity he suddenly felt punched in the stomach. Elvis had made the same claim about the other Johnny T. He froze.

"I wrote you a so many letters," said John, who was now rummaging around on a desk until he produced a thick wad of folded papers, "But I couldn't ever send them."

He held the stack of papers out to Boy, who took them cautiously. He unfolded one and started reading a letter that explored sadness at not being in Boy's life, anger and frustration at being sent so far away. Another explained that it was Boy's mom who sent him to this place when things got confusing between them. The letters referred to Boy either as son, or by name, even sometimes calling him sunshine, a nickname only Boy's mom had ever used.

There was too much for Boy to read through. He was touched, but overwhelmed. He'd given up on meeting his father, and never would have guessed a first meeting like this.

Feeling more comfortable he set the pile of letters down.

"I can't read this all, can you just tell me?" Boy asked, a part of him wanting this to be true, another part still struggling to not explain this all as the last thoughts of a dying brain stuck out in a snowdrift.

John shared that he had met Boy's mom back in the early days of his acting career, after becoming a household name. He was surprised Boy's mom paid him any attention, but didn't mind. He'd never met anyone like her before, and was swept off his feet. They became lovers. She carted him around to high society parties. He felt like he was being tested, but he went along with it all.

Things started getting weird. She made John get a peculiar check up from her doctor. It wasn't like any physical he'd ever had, considerably more thorough and in depth. He said it felt more like being tested by aliens wanting to know everything about the human, or rather his human body, which he later found out wasn't far from the truth.

The next thing John knew, Boy's mom was pregnant. He was excited by the prospect. He'd always wanted to be a father, and no other woman was as beautiful or powerful as Boy's mom. But then she told him he couldn't have anything to do with Boy's life. John got angry, wanted to be an active father, and fought Boy's mom, threatening to expose her to the world. He said that he knew, even as he made the threat, that he'd made a horrible mistake. It was at this point that she simply removed him from society, replacing him with the other Johnny T., the one Boy had been interacting with, the robot.

"Wait," Boy pleaded. "What did you threaten to expose?"

There was a long silence. After serious consideration, John said, "I hoped you already knew Boy, but I guess it makes sense that I would be the one to tell you." He was caution, biding.

"Your mom," John continued, "is not human."

Boy laughed out loud. He could tell John wasn't trying to be funny, but he couldn't help himself. That was the most absurd thing he had ever heard. He'd heard people say she was a lot of things, maybe even 'inhuman', but never 'not human'.

"So she hurt you that bad?" Boy offered, trying to take John's story in stride.

"Have you noticed the reptiles?" John asked.

Boy promptly stopped smiling. "What?" he asked, the hairs on the back of his neck rising.

"The reptiles? You've seen them?" John asked, concerned.

"Fuck," was all Boy could say.

"Have you noticed they've been with you everywhere you go?" John looked directly at Boy.

"I fucking knew it," Boy said.

"Did you see them back there in the city?" John asked, steadfast determination in his face.

"The city?" Boy asked.

"Atlantis," John replied. "Wait. Do you know where you are?"

"You mean the club?" Boy said.

"How did you get here?" John asked.

"I got into a car accident and found myself in this small room, like a hospital. But Elvis told me I was back at the club." Boy started to shake.

"That was not a club," John continued. "That was the ancient city of Atlantis. It has been buried for thousands of years, hidden here, beneath the polar ice cap. You're in Antarctica."

There was a clang, like something falling a short distance onto a metal grate, and a box appeared onto a platform in the corner of the room. It simply materialized. John got up and moved it off of the platform absently. Boy also gave it little consideration, focused on hearing where John was going with all of this, so enthralled that a materializing box didn't faze him.

"And my mom?" Boy persisted.

"So…" John continued, "Those reptiles you've been seeing. They're her minions. The true dictators of society. The one's running the whole show."

"Ok, but how are they my mom's minions? They're huge."

"Well, Boy. Your mother is…How to say this…" John paused, "Fuck it…She's The Reptilian High Priestess."

Boy remembered the mass of fame referring to the 'High Priestess', but he hadn't heard any references to reptilian.

"You're telling me my mom is one of those things?" Boy was having a hard time believing this last part. He'd known his mom his whole life, how could he have missed something like this? "And that you're my dad?"

John's gaze moved around the room again, frantic, searching, then realizing something. "Do you still have the pendant I gave you before she sent me away?" John implored.

Boy felt for the amulet against his chest. John pulled something from inside the collar of his shirt. It was the mirror image of Boy's necklace, a half moon on one side, connecting to the outline of a semi-circular serpent. John moved towards Boy, reaching his medallion out. They fit perfectly into each other. Conjoined they made an Ouroboros and a full moon.

"At least she kept that promise," John said, more to himself than to Boy.

Boy's heart sped. He looked up at the inexplicable face of this strange bearded man. Is this really my dad? Part of him wanted this, another part wanted to hate the man, to hate everything. Just because this crazy guy happens to have a matching amulet doesn't mean everything he says is true, Boy reassured himself.

John witnessed Boy's skepticism. He started telling Boy ways he might test the information. He asked if Boy had ever noticed his mom being told she was wrong. Boy couldn't think of a single time. Had Boy noticed how often his mom drank? And, from what kind of cup? Boy immediately pictured the strange ceramic mug. Had he ever noticed his mom aging? Boy was struck by how little, if at all, his mom had aged. Had he ever seen her show any emotion? Boy couldn't ignore how much this man knew, but he still resisted, unsure of what it would mean if true.

John continued, but Boy started only getting more upset. He wanted to escape, but where. He missed his naiveté. Though he'd held disdain for her, it was considerably less disconcerting than the tale this hermit had now planted in his head. He tried to stop listening to John's myriad indicators.

He started scanning the room for anything that might set him free. Wandering listlessly back into the freeze outside was a horrible solution, though the thought of death started to sound relieving again. He knew he couldn't do it, sure that he didn't want to die, so he wouldn't go outside. There was nowhere to go.

Just then another box arrived on the platform. Again John removed it with no explanation. This time Boy didn't ignore it. This time Boy saw a control panel next to where the boxes had materialized. A large red button read 'outgoing'. He watched another box materialize. They were coming from somewhere, so 'outgoing' must go somewhere, and anywhere seemed better than here.

Boy knew he had no real idea about what this machine did, and no idea what the consequence would be, but in that moment he didn't care. The boxes seemed to come through unharmed. It seemed worth the gamble as the bearded Johnny T. just continued rambling details of the reptilian conspiracy. Eventually John turned his back, as he moved the most recent box to go with others in a compartment on the far wall.

Boy ran onto the platform, and slammed the big red 'outgoing' button. His vision spun, as John turned. He heard John's calling out, "NO! BOY, DON'T! YOU'LL GET HURT! PLEASE!"

It was too late. Boy's vision of the strange, pleading old hermit blurred, a smear of colors punctuating in blackness. His body was caught in a tornado, being ripped apart and pushed together at the same time. He lost consciousness.

59

Boy could sense someone sitting next to him as his consciousness returned. He felt sick, pressure on his head from some kind of wrap. One of his legs was in a sling, an IV in his arm, again. He worried he was back in that strange hospital room, back in the club, or the city, which ever Atlantis was. Boy decided to not open his eyes just yet, more comfortable in a moment of not knowing. There was something different, something more familiar about the feel of this place, even with his eye's still shut. The bed felt familiar. Finally his curiosity got the better of him and he peeked as discretely as possible at his surroundings. He couldn't believe it at first, it was too familiar, the view from his bedroom window, looking out over Manhattan.

Boy also discovered that the body next to him was his mother. She was looking over some paperwork, humming quietly. It was hard for him to hear, but it sounded like, 'You Are My Sunshine'. Anger and relief fought inside of him, and the relief won. Tears rolled down his cheeks. In that moment the anger he had been harboring towards his mother couldn't find purchase. He was too happy to not be out in the cold with a bearded old movie star claiming to be his long lost father trapped guarding a secret society of wealthy famous people hidden under the Antarctic ice sheets.

Another voice spoke from a nearby corner of the room. "Boy?" It was Sophie. Boy tried to turn his head, but his neck was in a brace, immobile.

Boy's mom turned towards him. Then, as though she didn't want to skip a beat, she said, "See Sophia. Was all that fretting worth the energy?"

At hearing his mom call her Sophia, or maybe it was merely at the sound of her voice, Boy could feel some part of him cringe, resentment rising back to battle hoping to retake his freshly relieved heart. Yet, as he lay there broken, between these two women he loved, remembering the edge of death before the whiskey barrel and Bartleby's warm rescue, he was reminded of his wish to see Sophie again, and his bargaining to survive.

"Boy?" Sophie's face came into his vision. She was crying. "I'm so glad you're awake. Do you remember…?"

Boy's mom shot Sophie a sharp look.

"He's been in a coma. Give him a break." Boy almost thought his mom meant to protect him. He remembered her ire when he'd been mugged as a child. Sophie didn't seem notice, her attention on Boy.

"You were in a terrible accident." Sophie was happy and sad as she spoke. "We weren't sure you'd make it." She beamed down at him, her words picking up a manic pace. "But you did, Boy. You're alive. And you'll be fine. I knew you would be." She moved in to embrace him, but stopped short. "I would squeeze you, but I don't want to hurt you."

Boy tried to talk, but couldn't get passed the lump in his throat. Instead he sobbed.

"It's okay, Boy," Sophie assured him.

"You'll be fine," offered his mom. "There's no need to cry." She remained emotionless. She got up suddenly, her mug in hand. "What happened, Boy?" she asked, looking out over the city, and away from him. He wished she was just concealing her emotions, wished she was moving away because it was hard for her to see him cry, but he had never seen her emotional. His mind flashed back to John's list of signs. Boy started to feel that something in her question seemed more for her sake than his, like she needed assurance.

His thoughts were interrupted by Sophie, who looked down at him, smiling, tears streaming down her cheeks. "Yeah," she said, "what happened?" She seemed to be genuinely curious.

He cleared his throat, trying to steady himself. He considered a moment, hating that he felt a need to strategize. He opted to frame things as a dream and watch his mom's reaction. A part of him also hoped it might actually be.

"I just had the craziest dream." Boy was still struggling to speak, but as he did he realized how much he wanted what he'd said to be true. What was more, he hoped they'd corroborate. He wanted to tell them everything as though a dream, starting with the reptiles he'd seen over the past year, but imagining saying it all made him afraid. His mother frosty demeanor wasn't helping, nor the ceramic cup in her hand. He realized he didn't know how much could have been a dream, when that dream would have started, or why so many things in the dream were interconnected with what he still considered his actual life. He decided, if any part where likely to be a dream it probably started with the club.

Boy told them slowly, and with a bit of pain, how, in the dream, he'd decided to visit that club he'd been getting invites to. He shared how he had gone through the rooms, how each had it's own atmosphere and esthetic. He shared about ending up in the VIP with Johnny T. He even told them about the drinks and the coke, saying at one point he'd seen Sophie downstairs. He watched Sophie as he shared this part but Sophie didn't change expressions or say anything. He included the part about the reptile he and Johnny T. had seen, watching his mom for subtle tells, but finding none. He remembered to them the part about sneaking out, finding his car, and taking off upstate, despite being inebriated. He recounted how vivid the moment of the crash was, and how his dream stopped just before he'd hit the bottom of the cliff. Something in him told him to stop his telling of the dream, that he needed to keep something untold.

"Then I woke up," Boy looked for reaction from his listeners. Both seemed mildly shocked, but he wasn't sure why.

"You mean when you just woke up now?" Sophie asked, confused. Boy's mom remained conspicuously quiet, or was this her usual quiet?

"No." Boy paused. "That's why I am guessing it was just a dream." He was still unsure of how much more to say. Though he felt the urge to withhold, he wanted more of reaction than he was getting and decided he might as well share everything, as he had nothing to lose.

"I woke up in, still in the dream, but now in a strange room," Boy continued. "Johnny T. was there with Elvis. They said I'd been in an accident, and that I was healing. They were taking care of me. Elvis said Johnny T. was my dad." Boy couldn't believe that even sharing his potential paternal discovery didn't cause his mom the slightest of flinches.

Boy heard Sophie hold back what he figured was a chuckle.

"They told me I was in Atlantis, and at first I figured they meant back at the club. But you know dream logic," Boy was on a roll. "When I left the small room I stumbled down a corridor into an atrium, full of the most star studded people that ever existed. Morrison, Joplin, Monroe…Everyone you can dream of, so long as they were famous and dead. But they weren't dead. They had never died. They live together, in this glorious place, which I later found out was not the club, but the ancient city of Atlantis, hidden in Antarctica, below the ice cap. But I only found that out when I escaped to the surface, and was carried by a big dog to the real Johnny T., who calls himself John, lives in a small cabin in a hillside, and looks a little worse for the ware." Again he carefully looked to see if his mom had any reaction. She remained impassive.

Sophie grinned. "That is the craziest dream I've ever heard," she laughed.

"That's not all," Boy said, still watching his mom. "John, the haggard Johnny T., told me that the one we know and have been interacting with, is a clone, or a robot, or something. The real Johnny T., John, the one from the cabin, explained that the rich and famous lived there, in that city under the Antarctic caps, and from there they control the world, accomplishing this task in two ways: through the media; and through a network of robots who ran the governments of the world, which are controlled remotely. All these elite folks are assisted, or ruled, by a secret group of reptiles, who are the real ones who actually run everything."

Sophie laughed out loud, "The Ananaku? You mean in your dream WJ was right?"

"Something like that." Boy kept his attention on his mom. She simply remained still, looking out the window.

"But it gets even crazier. I had actually seen these reptiles, on a mezzanine in the atrium, watching the crowd. They looked like ones I'd seen before." Still no reaction, neither confirmation nor denial. Boy was starting to hope again that it might actually have been a dream.

"And?" Sophie was excited.

"John, the bearded one, explained he was my actual father, claiming that you, mom, had sent him out to the ice cap of Antarctica to live, because he wanted to be close to me, something you wouldn't allow." Boy both wanted his mom to react, and was almost relieved that she didn't.

"And," Boy continued, "John claimed you were able to send him away like that, and replace him with a clone or whatever, because you are actually the Reptilian High Priestess." He almost thought he saw the most minor of flinches in his mom's shoulders as he said this, but he couldn't be sure.

Sophie sounded uneasy as she asked, "What does that even mean? How'd your brain come up with that?"

Boy could tell Sophie was trying to release the tension by reminding them all it was just a dream.

"John claimed," Boy continued, ignoring the discomfort he knew Sophie was feeling, "That you run the whole show, mom. He said you're in charge of the reptiles, who're in charge of everything else."

Sophie gawked at Boy. His mom didn't move. He forced a little chuckle. "What do you think of that, mom?" He wanted to pull something out of her.

She turned calmly to face him, expressionless, without anger or fear. "What do you think I think, Boy?" she asked, coolly insipid. She looked directly in Boy's eyes, unflinching.

A pregnant pause, a harsh silence, then Boy's mom continued, "It's an amazing, and extremely far fetched dream. I did enjoy hearing it. If you'd like we can have our Jungian analyst unpack it for you sometime." She looked at him with the same, unemotional face she always had. "I'm just glad you're okay."

She left the room saying, "I have to get back to work." She turned to Sophie, "Don't stay too long, Sophie. Boy needs his rest." She turned back to Boy, "I'll check in on you EOD Boy, get some sleep." Then she strolled calmly out of the room, abrupt as ever, like nothing had happened.

Boy wanted to be upset by her callous manner, but even in this fragile state, even after everything he'd just divulged, he would have been more surprised by anything else. He ran it through his internal schema, hoping for clarity, and finding that he was no more sure about it having been a dream or not.

Sophie was less forgiving of his mom's curt departure. "What the fuck" Sophie blurted, then, in what seemed an attempt at comforting him she offers, "She seems like she doesn't care, Boy, but she does. She was here by your side the whole time. I would have been too, but she only allowed me to be here since last night."

Boy wanted to let go of the crazy tale as just a dream, but too many things didn't add up, or rather, too many things did. As he tried to understand what had just happened he remembered that Sophie was merely a hired hand, and he lost the initial excitement of seeing her. A flood of frustration broke the dam happiness had been trying to build. His resentment poured back into his body.

Boy could tell Sophie had noticed the change, and was about to start trying to divert it. "You must be exhausted," She started. But then, as though she knew he would only get angrier if she avoided the truth, she shifted gears.

"You probably still don't trust me," She continued, "but please hear me out. Your mom did hire me to keep an eye on you, report to her occasionally, and make sure you were okay. That's how it started. And I took the job because it was the easiest way for me to get into a good school, and be able to afford it."

Boy wasn't sure where she was hoping to go with this, and so far it wasn't helping him feel any better.

"At first I figured, easy gig, just follow the rich kid around and get a free ride. But as soon as I got to know you, I immediately knew it was the best thing that had ever happened to me. Not only was I being taken care of, but I genuinely liked you, Boy. From the beginning. For who you are, not just for the job. That was never fake."

Boy could tell she was being honest, and it still hurt.

"It didn't stop there, Boy. I started actually having feelings for you. I even got up the courage to talk to your mom about it, and try to stop working for her, because I knew how bad it would hurt if you found out, and I cared about you so much. But she told me I had to keep working or she'd tell you. I didn't know what to do. I tried telling you so many times. I wanted you to know, and I wanted you to not care, to feel the depth of our connection was so real that it didn't matter, or wouldn't matter when you eventually found out, which I knew you would. I maybe even hoped you would, so that you could see you weren't just a job for me." Sophie's eyes were welling up as she spoke. Boy's eyes filled with tears as well.

"I love you, Boy. I have for so long. I know, more than anyone else, how badly all of this must have hurt you. I know how much you hate when your mom imposes herself in your life. I knew, as soon as I got to know you, you would hate me for all of this. But what could I do? I wanted you in my life. I've been so afraid of loosing you."

They wept. Boy wanted to forgive her, to trust her again. He was so tired of the solitude and isolation his animosity was bringing him. And still, he wasn't ready to let it go. He didn't know how to trust anyone yet.

Boy pulled Sophie to him, giving her the best hug he could in his condition before saying, "I can't do this Sophie. I need to be alone. I need to figure myself out a bit. Everything's been so crazy. As much as I can I believe you, and I still can't forgive you. At least not yet. Maybe, some day, that'll change." He had a hard time talking through his tears. Her clutch around him hurt, and began restricting his breath, but he let her stay. "I want to feel better, and I just don't. You were the only person I really trusted."

"I know," was all she said.

Boy knew there was nothing more she could say. He respected that she wasn't push it. He also knew that she knew him well enough that she would be smart about what she did, and in this moment that hurt. Slowly she let him go. She looked him in the eyes before standing up, both their faces red and wet.

"I love you, Boy. Remember that. Know it. I'll be here when you're ready."

"I know," Boy's voice lacked conviction, cracked in sadness, and stopped.

Sophie slowly turned and walked to the door. She left the room without turning back, merely closing the door gently behind her. Then she was gone.

Boy couldn't stop crying. Sophie's explanation and apology had been impactful. He wished it was all he needed to forgive her, but he didn't know how, or knew at least that he couldn't yet. He noticed that his pain around Sophie kept him from having to spend time thinking about his mom. When he started to approach this idea, and started to feel the anger and confusion lingering there, he knew that Sophie and the pain surrounding her was the easier thing to fret over. He let himself. He didn't resist his sobs, and cried until his body stopped, his tears punctuating into a unintentional, but deeply needed sleep.

He bounced along on Bartleby's back, half conscious. John ran behind calling for the dog to stop. They arrived back in the ancient city of Atlantis, Bartleby carrying him through a maze of hallways to the atrium. Everyone turned when he entered, surrounding him. They looked at him quizzical at first, then started laughing inexplicably. Even the reptiles were laughing. WJ was standing among the horde, not laughing, a kind smile spread across his face. The crowd parted as Boy's mom approached. "Why are you back here? You're not one of us, you'll never be." A bifurcated tongue slipped behind her teeth. He clung to the dog. Sophie appeared, pulling him off the dog, and asking him to walk with her. She took him to the undulating field, and then was gone, leaving only an ache in his chest as he realized he was alone again.

60

The next few weeks Boy pretended he was trying to

regain normalcy, what ever that might mean. He spent the first few days alone, recuperating, enjoying the dissociation the pain medicine offered.

He ached for sleep, and slept more than he ever remembered sleeping before. He enjoyed when his dreams were of the undulating field, impressionistic, vague, peaceful. But he also dreamt of tunnels under the city, networks of reptiles working, cogs keeping the machine of society turning. In the worst dreams he was back at the party, shunned, alienated, surrounded by people and more acutely aware of his solitude because of it. As a consequence, despite how much he was sleeping, it was frequently restless, and he wished more and more to be able to return to the undulating field, the only comfortable place his mind would take him.

One dream was particularly recurrent, and felt like a memory. Boy was picked up off a platform by a reptile, surprised by the gentleness with which he was carried. The reptile took him from the platform through a series of tunnels, until he recognized the subway line below his home. They would enter an elevator, like his own, but the entrance was down in the subway. As the elevator ascended, Boy would wake up. This dream was more complex, as he almost felt safe and cared for, but with elements of the dreams he would have otherwise called nightmares.

Thoughts about these creatures, and Atlantis, wouldn't leave his mind. Boy couldn't help but watch his mom for the signs of her reptilian nature any time she came to check on him. Were these indicators merely things he had always subconsciously noticed that had woven themselves into his dreams? She was indomitable, and dominating. She always drank out that strange mug, which was never far from her. She never exhibited emotion. She was stiff, her eyes always distant, her skin too perfect. Still, Boy could explain this all away as hindsight twenty-twenty, things he'd always seen but was now attributing false meaning towards.

Boy restarted therapy, his mom insisting the crash was a cry for help, an attempt at suicide. It was the same therapist Boy had seen off and on his entire life, going back to at least as early as after he was mugged. Boy appreciated that his therapist listened non-judgmentally, never telling Boy any of his thoughts were outlandish or 'crazy'. When Boy shared about his 'dream', his therapist suggested the things Boy had experienced during his coma were mental projections, based off images he'd seen before the crash; all the images on the walls in the hallways leading to, and throughout the club, had become projections of his hopes, fears, and wishes.

Boy explored his story from this perspective, found meaning in the potential projections. He saw how the reptiles could represent his paranoia that he was always being watched. He saw how the image of a reptile, cold-blooded, lacking emotion, would be connected with his mom. He recognized how he was constantly trying to get away from her pervasive manipulation, and how the reptiles 'being the one's who run the show' might be a representation of his mom's covert influence on his life. He could see how, become world famous had taken him into situations he hadn't known to expect, and placed him, like those he'd seen in the atrium, in a position of becoming something that would live on, even after his own death; that his fame made him more than the mere human he was day to day. He explored his struggle with the projection the world placed on him, and could understand how he might dream everything up as a way of trying to understand the pressure he felt.

Boy's therapist pushed him to see if there was anyone Boy might connect with. Boy realized he wanted to see Johnny T., as he had been one of the only people who Boy had felt empathy from. Boy also realized part of his desire to see Johnny T. was to test if the strange actor would admit anything, or at the very least still acknowledge the reptile they'd seen at the club. Boy didn't share with his therapist that he had resolved to go back to the club.

Boy cultivated a fantasy of how things would go as he healed. He imagined the interaction with Johnny T., imagined that he would get verification either way, a dream or not. He kept his plans hidden even from his therapist, who he liked, but also couldn't help but not trust fully, as they were yet another person hired by his mother.

So Boy waited, and when he was well enough he went. He was not surprised at his mounting anxiety when he arrived, apprehensive, and started making his way down to the elevator that would return him to the secret high-society party. He was unnerved as he passed back by the esoteric carvings. Had they been the inspiration for the dream? They must have been. Society wasn't ruled by reptiles, they were merely representations of his anger towards his mom. How could he have ever thought them historical depictions?

Reentering the club Boy's nervous system was on high alert. Despite his attempts to convince himself they were fictional, he noticed considerably more detail, felt he was understanding the carvings better. He noticed how humans depicted appeared subservient to the reptiles, who were shown as a benevolent aristocracy. The club appeared more Masonic, Illuminational even. The three dots making a triangle fueling this idea. He remembered the triangle and eye above the doorway into the atrium, the emblem on the strange luminescent being. Here, again, Boy was confronted by the difficulty of believing all of this had merely primed his mind for the story he created in coma. Something in him didn't believe it, and something else in him wouldn't let him not.

Boy sped directly through the first rooms and up to the VIP lounge. He was somehow surprised to find Johnny T., a pile of coke in front of him, sitting almost exactly where he had been the last time he had seen the man. Johnny T. acted was happy and not surprised to see Boy. Yet, there was something awkward in his welcome, but Boy second-guessed his perception. Could it simply be that Johnny T. felt bad about the role he'd played in Boy's crash? Or was it that he didn't know how much Boy remembered about everything that had happened after?

Pleasantries were shared, then Boy dove straight in. "Do you remember seeing a huge reptile the last time I was here?" He forced a chuckle, affecting light-heartedness, hoping the question wouldn't sound as important, or as crazy, as Boy felt it was. His false tone hadn't been successful. Johnny T.'s face got serious.

"Hmm…" Johnny T. grunted. Was he stalling? "I've seen a lot of shit here, Boy. Especially when I'm as high as we were that night." He pretended to contemplate the question before saying, "But that shit was crazy, so of course I remember." He pointed to the window they had been looking through, "It was over there, right?"

Boy nodded, feeling both excited and righteous, if not stunned at the ease with which Johnny T. was confirming having seen the creature.

"Yeah, sure," Johnny T. continued. "That was hilarious. I wonder where that guy got his costume. It was so realistic, pretty convincing even." Boy's excitement collided with confusion as Johnny T. spoke.

"It must have been Terry, or some buddy of his, using one of the costumes from 'Fear and Loathing'. Or, you know what, it was probably Johnny D., actually. He loves tripping the trippers out, and I think I remember him saying Terry gave him one of the suites."

Boy didn't know what was real, and what was the paranoia induced from self-projection, as his therapist would say. Johnny T.'s answer shut Boy down from asking about anything else. Johnny T. was either telling the truth, or was unwilling to be honest. Either way, there was nothing more for Boy to gain from pursuing the issue. Boy recognized that he was in a bind. He could continue believing everyone was bullshitting him, that they were all part of the conspiracy, and he could find evidence for it where he looked; or he could start believing his nightmare was maybe actually just that, which felt like giving up on himself somehow. He could here his therapist reflecting to him that he was running up against confirmation bias and the fallacy of sunk costs.

After a moment Boy decided he needed to at least bring up his 'dream', if that's what it was, as he had come here to try to connect with Johnny T. Boy didn't feel connected as he shared, Johnny T. too surprised and excited by the absurdity of the story, leaving Boy feeling alone, again.

Boy decided not to mention that Elvis, and the hermit, John, had both told him that Johnny T. was his father. Johnny T. expressed a lack of knowledge concerning the secret society of Atlantis. Boy could tell he didn't trust Johnny T., even though there was no explicit reason not to, and apart from Johnny T. suddenly sharing something to confirm Boy's tale, there was nothing he could imagine Johnny T. saying that was likely to help.

Boy left the club feeling no closer to any answers for the questions nagging at his existentially exhausted brain. He tried to imagine what his therapist would say, how he was probably creating these stories, protection mechanisms so he wouldn't have to deal with the vulnerability of intimate connection. Just words. *Isn't this what conspiratorial overlords would want their subjects to believe?* His intuition told him something was off.

Boy thought again of WJ, a listening and non-judgmental ear. He still hadn't heard from WJ since St. Petersburg. He knew it was likely futile, but he called, only to find the same voicemail as weeks before.

"I'm probably not picking up because they got me. Or maybe I finally joined 'em. Either way, you can leave a message, but I might never call you back." This time WJ didn't seem so sardonic. From Boy's new perspective, the message sounded honest.

Boy decided to leave a message. "Where are you, WJ? I'd love to…I need to talk to you. I know I've been a shitty friend. I haven't even seen you since Russia. Shit has been crazy. It's actually all the crazy shit that's happened since Russia that I'd love your opinion on. Anyways, call when you can my man." Boy couldn't remember ever feeling so desperate.

Despite all the people, or maybe because of the sheer number, the city only felt more isolating. Boy decided to leave. Stopping at an ATM he pulled out enough cash to cover at least a week out of town. He bought a faraday bag and shut his phone down before dropping it in, hoping this would make him less traceable. He headed north, this time sober. He drove through the night, past dawn. Afraid of being tracked by roadside cameras, he took the smaller, more discrete highways and local roads, making his journey longer, but also more interesting. He was in no hurry.

Boy stopped near the remote town of Liberty, somewhere in southern Maine. He checked into a small bed and breakfast, paying in cash so his credit card couldn't be traced. He went to his room and was asleep almost as soon as saw the bed.

Boy walked down the club hallway. The engravings on the wall were moving. The humans were fumbling around, the reptile's stoic, steadier then their primate counterparts. The images depicted the building of a large city. The people and reptiles ran from the city as water overtook it. Then a search; the city dug out of an ice sheet. A fountain still flowing in the city's center. The depictions had an amber glow from the eye in the triangle, it's rays illuminating as it shown down from above.

61

Much of the next week Boy spent alone. He mostly walked around the woods surrounding the nearby town, close enough to have an idea of where he was, and far enough away that he wouldn't see many people. He arrived Tuesday, and got high Saturday.

The first few days Boy barely interacted with anyone. Then, on Friday, as he left he was entering a market to grab some food, a group around his age recognized him and stopped to talk to him. They praised him, and one, hair died, particularly alternative looking, asked him if he needed anything. Boy wasn't sure what the kid meant.

The kid produced a bag of mushrooms, saying, "Here, take these, Boy, I grew 'em myself! They'll give you a good night".

Boy wasn't sure he wanted them, but wanting to seem cool. Boy asked the price. The kid refused money, saying it was his pleasure to 'hook up such an incredible artist'. Boy insisted, and him a twenty nonetheless, thanking him before continuing on his way. Boy noticed how good it felt to receive the praise, struggled to not spin out into self-loathing, trying instead to allow the glow.

The next day, Boy strolled the eerie woods of the northern-most state in the lower forty-eight, with a sack of psychedelics. Part of him thought it probably wasn't a good idea, and he hesitated at first, but then decided that getting high might be exactly what he needed to get some perspective.

As Boy came up, a familiar anxiety surfaced, as though his body was being subtly lifted, a pressure mounting in his chest, like he might gently explode. Half afraid of a psychedelically induced introspective onslaught cresting internally, he also knew this was exactly what he needed, to be blasted open.

Boy's surroundings began a subtle shifting, expressions of the delicate brighter tones, normally hidden, unfolding out of the gray of this northeastern landscape. The dull shades trees becoming vibrant, a gentler spectrum of color than he usually noticed. Things usually fixed moving slightly, alive. He witnessed the teeming of matter, a pulsing, breathing, non-static expression. Being high here, in these woods, was distinct from his experiences in the concrete bound urban-scape of the city. He was a part of his surroundings, as opposed to being apart of his surroundings.

The last time Boy had taken mushrooms, with Sophie, now seemed so long ago. Their conversation on his kitchen floor churned in the fractals of his consciousness. He was sense the mycelia under his feet, the interconnectedness of a mycelial netting, the neuro-network of the forest. He understood, in a way he couldn't explain, as though the mushrooms where communicating with him, that some mushrooms were messengers from alien worlds. Epiphanies blossomed, unfolding, interconnected, lotus pedals in time-lapse. Maybe Sophie had been right, maybe he was the mushroom messiah. He laughed at himself, saying out loud, "Sweet delusions of grandeur!"

Boy mind turned to when he saw the first reptile. The memory was sharp, distinct. The swift way it crossed the room of pretentiously wealthy, the way it disappearing into the wall. He pictured its dark green scales, its awkward grace, its confident movement, no one else noticing its presents. For the first time, rather than fear, he felt awe and curiosity.

Through this new sense of curiosity Boy considered all the reptiles he had seen: the pool in Shanghai; the subway in Tokyo; the carvings of the strange sushi restaurant; the sushi chef's tattoo; on the train in Mongolia; the engravings in the tunnel entrance to the club; on the stairwell to the VIP room; in the strobe flashes on the dance floor; in the ancient artwork on the walls of the Antarctic city; the four stolid sentinels on the mezzanine above the famous swarm in the atrium; riddled throughout his dreams, as though a subconscious invasion.

Could they be here, now, in these woods with me? Boy wondered. A branch snapped under his feet and he jumped. He'd been so caught up in thoughts he'd lost track of his surroundings. He quickly regained bearings, calmed himself. He was still in the woods, in Maine. He glanced at his surroundings and felt safe.

As Boy re-centered his awareness to his current circumstance, he started contemplating the conspiracy surrounding the lost city of Atlantic, the conspiracy he now felt wrapped up in. At first his thoughts had the edge of fear. The conspiracy was against him. He had been left out of the loop maliciously. As his anxiety increased he remembered breathing exercises his therapist had given him. His made sure his exhales were longer than his inhales. He crossed his arms and tapped the opposite sides of his chest as he breathed slowly. He told himself that these feeling, these thoughts, were merely internal expression of insecurity.

Boy considered his therapist, considered his fear of intimacy, reflecting on how this fear dictated his relationship to the world. He saw how this orientation, this framing through fear ended up alienated him from people. He realized he kept people at bay because he assumed everyone just wanted something from him. He realized that thinking the world was against him gave him his excuse to not allow anyone in. He recognized this as the root for his loneliness. *What if everything had been real, but none of had malicious intent? What if this grand conspiracy was benevolent?*

Boy watched his optimism oscillate. He still felt betrayed. He still didn't understand why things had been withheld from him, from anyone. He still felt frustrated that he, and the rest of regular society, had been misled, and he couldn't figure out why. He wondered if this frustration were merely more paranoid expression, another way for him to reinforce his isolation.

In reflecting on his paranoia and isolation Boy's thoughts turned to his mom. He felt how deeply he had always wanted to be closer to her, and he saw how she'd never been emotionally available. He thought of the hermit, John; his kindness, and their matching medallion. He realized he was wishing his mom had been more there for him. He wished he'd had gotten to have a dad at all.

Boy started to feel a sense of clarity. This lack of connection; his mom coldness; the lack of a father; even his isolation from wealth and fame, had resulted in insecurity around deep connection. It wasn't safe to be vulnerable with his mom, and a mother was the first, and perhaps most important person to feel safe and supported in vulnerability with. If he couldn't feel safe with her, how did he expect himself to feel safe with anyone.

This brought Boy's mind to Sophie. He could feel his desire to listen, to forgive her, followed again by the fear of trusting her, trusting anyone. He would have to forgive his mom, and that scared him. He couldn't get past what John had suggested.

What if John was telling the truth? Yet, how could it be true? What would I be if my mom were a reptile? How could I not know if that were the case?

Boy felt human, normal, but he also recognized

that he had no idea what that meant, what it felt like to be human to other humans. Maybe his normal didn't feel human at all. The infinite unfolding of his neuro-synaptic relay burst into patterns pushing him towards the edges of sanity. He craved something grounded, a piece of truth, a semblance of honesty to hold onto, without which he feared his mind would disintegrate into uncontrollable chaotic spiraling. Recognizing the futility of struggling against his high he laid on the dirt and let the patterns run.

After an indefinite period in this ineffable mental tumult, Boy became eager to return home, to something familiar. This was something he'd experienced before with psychedelics; a sudden desire to be with the familiar, to reestablish a foundation in 'reality'. This need was reinforced by what he saw in the beautiful darkness of the forest; reptiles, most of which were probably trees, but not all of which stayed still. It wasn't threatening, just unnerving. It was even kind of beautiful. Likely hallucinations, but *why be alone with them in this unfamiliar environment?*

Boy returned slowly to his hotel, marking the ebbs and flows of comfort and fear. He laughed at the awkward transition from the forest to the town, remembered how this transition always felt awkward on the backside of s trip. When he was back at the room he felt fine to drive, and having already paid for his room, he collected his things and left. He wanted family. He wanted to love and trust. He wanted to return to the world again.

62

It was dark. Boy had no idea of the time. Had he taken his phone out of its faraday case he would have noticed he was again driving through the middle of the night, at the last hours before dawn.

On Boy's way from Maine back to New York he considered the lessons of his trip. He reflected on the cycle of fear and self-loathing that he had been stuck in. He reflected on what he needed to do to shift out of his entitled victimhood, and into a life he felt grateful for and agentic within. As Boy drove back into Manhattan he decided the only way out of his fear was a candid conversation with his mom.

Boy arrived, night suggesting day, sunlight refracting through the sky's nitrogen, soft blue on the horizon, but the sky still star laden. He parked the car on the street, slipping in through the private back entrance, in order to avoid needless exchanges. He didn't want to interact with anyone before his mom, not wanting to loose resolution, and hoping to catch her before she started her day. He hoisted himself up back stairs to avoid anyone in the elevator.

Boy entered the top floor at the end of the hall leading to his bedroom. This was the original entryway, before the elevators had been built. He'd used it as a kid to sneak in and out. He felt like a kid now, sneaking back in before dawn, but this time he wasn't hoping to sneak into the sanctuary of his room, but into an honest talk with his mom.

As Boy entered the familiar hallway of his childhood home he saw his mom's bedroom door directly across from his own. He paused, a wave of anxiety trying to overtake the conviction he'd had on the drive. A familiar insecurity and doubt he had with his mom started to reclaimed him. Then the soft residue of the mushrooms in his bloodstream reminded him how she was the lynchpin of his insecurity. He could see how addressing her, now, would be the fulcrum for shifting everything blocking him from being open to meaningful connection in his life.

With this reestablished conviction Boy burst through his mother's door.

63

Boy nearly screamed.

There, standing in the middle of his mom's room, was a giant reptile.

Anger overtaking fear. Boy moved closer. This particular reptile, gazed back at him with a steely and familiar gaze. It was pulling on some sort of suit.

It was a skin.

It was her skin.

Boy thought he had prepared himself for this possibility, that he had tried on everything the hermit, John, had said. Nevertheless, he fell to the floor in confusion, exhaustion, fear, and disbelief. The creature spoke; his mother's voice.

"Boy," she said.

Boy looked up to see a bifurcating tongue disappear into her scaly green mouth. He turned his head and sobbed.

Boy watched as the last of his hope shattered. The rocks on the bottom caught him as he crashed down. Having not slept, psychedelically physiologically compromised, absolutely vulnerable, he was broken. The delusion of hope he'd held made the fall ever more abrupt, more jolting, and even more painful.

When Boy brought his eyes back towards his mom she was fully in her human suit, approached him. "Boy," she said again.

Boy knew nothing but tears. He was so weak he couldn't resist her as she sat with him, pulling him into her arms. She was so strong, this reptile that was somehow his mother. He felt comfort in her arms, which was confusing.

"My sunshine," she said.

Though the words were emotionless, Boy knew it was an attempt to console. Saline poured from his face, he shook, but he also felt something he only vaguely remembered having as a child. He felt held.

"I'm sorry, my Boy." Was this the first time she'd ever apologized? It simultaneously broke and mended Boy's heart. He cried new tears, warmer, curling into her arms, a small, fragile child. Here, in the vulnerability of a frightening truth, an emptiness in his chest that had been there so long it felt normal, was being filled with a love he'd been unconsciously resisting.

"This is not the end."

Boy didn't know what she meant, but had no energy to worry.

She continued, "Everything you know, everything you've been grappling to understand, it's part of something much larger and more important."

Boy's brain heard the words, but was shutting down, unable to process anything new.

"This whole world is a seed, created by MOL, the Mushroom Over-Lord, who was sent to our planet in order bring life back to the future, which is where they are from. I am the Reptilian High Priestess, and I am your mother. We've been waiting for you for some time. It's you we need. But you had to arrive here in your own time, by your own choice."

Boy was so deeply dissociated that he was nearly passing out from overload, unable to respond.

"Now you are ready."

Nothing was too far fetched for Boy in this moment, though nothing she'd said had really registered.

She pulled a ring from a finger and placed it onto one of Boy's. His vision blurred. "It's time to meet MOL."

Boy started spinning, like when he had jumped onto the platform in the cabin on the ice, like when his car was falling off the cliff. His vision faded. He released.

64

This time, rather than pure darkness, Boy saw a single point of light swiftly approaching. It reminded him of the stories of light at the end of a tunnel when you die. It also reminded him of the lit doorway of the club as he had approached on the elevator. The point of light grew brighter, and opened spherically, until it engulfed him.

The light was warm, and Boy could see movement, like a field of dry grass swaying and undulating as a single entity. He focused. It was the strange place he'd dreamt of so many times. The field that was not a field, the distinct yet diffuse light, the warm glow, and the sense he was not alone.

Boy felt at ease. He heard a soft, round, deep voice. It wasn't exactly hearing. The voice was coming from inside him, yet he knew it was not his mind speaking. Neither was it hearing a voice inside his head, as it was distinctly coming from nearby simultaneously. Even more difficult to explain, the voice didn't speak in words, though everything that was said was intelligible. It was as though the voice spoke in vision-feelings, emotions and images-scapes. Boy was struck by how much more efficient this way of communicating worked. Though Boy had never experienced communication like this before, it's inherent honesty and authenticity set him into a deeper sense of trust than he had previously known.

Despite Boy's vision coming into focus everywhere else, when he tried to look directly at was he knew to be MOL, it was like tracking something always just out of focus. Even when he looked at the epicenter of the 'voice' he was 'listening' to, it was as though he could only make out what was peripheral. Yet, he never felt like he wasn't clearly seeing this luminous something. It was more like the image of MOL was concurrently nondescript while distinct.

Even as he was having it, Boy was sure he would never fully unpack his 'conversation' with MOL, like a hyper compressed file too large for the puny processor of his brain. It felt like all his psychedelic journeys wrapped into one and with considerably higher fidelity. He might approach the overarching feelings he left with, might remember moments when they returned, but never the details in any absolute, concrete way. He knew that trying to pin any aspect down with words, the words would no longer describe the experience he was hoping to express. Poetry grasping at the ineffable at best, and even that seemed generous. The description was never the described.

The sound-emotion-vision-scape that came from MOL to Boy was so inexplicably genuine that Boy understood why the use of words for communication could never be wholly honest. With words, it is easy to misinterpret the meaning of what someone is trying to express. With MOL's communication, understanding was effortless, clear, and shared.

MOL took Boy on a cognitive journey, showing him how life had begun on the Earth.

MOL showed Boy how they had been sent from the future Pleiades as spores. In relation to Boy's time-line, the Pleiadians had not yet come into being.

When the Pleiadians had become intelligent enough to research the origins of life on their planet, they found evidence it had come from another planet. As they started isolating possible planets in the Universe, they discovered some of the key signatures on Earth, and a planet they called Dogon, from the Sirius system. As researched continued, however, they discovered a residue of matter imprint that almost seemed to have originated from their own planet.

There was something strange about the imprint that might have been Pleiadian. It took them decades to understand that what they were seeing was a near-future expression of their own DNA encoded into what looked like DNA from Earth and Dogon. In other words, Pleiadian material from the future was sent back in time to seed life on Earth and Dogon, which would later (but still in Pleiadian past) resend spores to start life in the Pleiades. An Ouroboros.

Though they could identify the DNA that had seeded life in the Pleiades, there was some kind of temporal bio-lock that made every attempt they made at sending it directly back to their own system not work. This was beyond their science, and made little sense to them, despite their best computer analysis and models. The one thing that seemed necessary was for the DNA to develop in the past on these separate planets. The Pleiadians decided it was easier to send spores back in time to these two planets than it was to break the code on how to simply directly reseed their own star systems. They concluded that not everything in the cosmos makes sense.

MOL was created as spores that could travel back through time without damage. MOL had been created to regrow itself indefinitely, able to watch over the development of life on the two planets. MOL was a seed, and a caretaker, there to watch over, and support the direction of life on Earth and Dogon in order to recreate the correct bio-signature coming into being, and actuated DNA sequence that could travel back through space, for the purpose of reseeding life in the Pleiades.

MOL had a set of DNA instructions from the future Pleiadians. Life in the Pleiades required a combination of mammalian life from Dogon, and reptilian DNA that originated on Earth. MOL was to stimulate life's beginning and monitor it's evolutionary curve, with the specific charge of finding supporting the development of the particular mammalian and reptilian DNA.

The correct reptilian DNA had come into being much faster. Once the reptiles were ready and advanced enough they were sent from Earth to help monitor the mammalian development on Dogon. However, on their first attempt to return to earth with mammalian DNA they accidentally crashed into what is now the Gulf of Mexico, causing a mass die off of most of the original reptilian life on Earth.

MOL, being nearly immortal, was patient and worked with the surviving retiles to rebuild civilization on Earth. During this time mammals continued to develop on Dogon with the help of the reptiles that had stayed behind. MOL taught the reptiles how to help form social networks to support mammals in developing larger neocortex neural networks, a requirement for the actuation of the future Pleiadian DNA.

The first reptilian return to Earth had resulted in similar mammals growing on Earth, and civilization was reconstructing itself. MOL identified the potential in one particular mammalian species to develop into actuators of DNA through conscious interaction. This was the species with the fastest growing neocortexes in relation to their body size. MOL believed that for these homo sapiens to complete their actuation potential they had to believe they were in control, so they and the reptiles and MOL started working covertly.

MOL also sent reptiles who had been living in the Sirius system back to Earth with homo sapiens from Dogon to cross breed with the homo sapiens of Earth. This was around 13,000 years ago, resulting in another crash landing, this time in the North American ice sheet of the Younger Dryas period. This crash caused the subsequent worldwide floods that resulted in much of modern mythologies flood myths. This was also the perfect opportunity for the reptilian aristocracy to become even more covert, as MOL saw human DNA moving towards their goal.

MOL had recognized Boy's mom when she was

born, identifying her as having the specific DNA for the reptilian aspect of this future seed. She became the Reptilian High Priestess. Since then they'd been waiting for the mammalian expression.

Mol put Boy's mom in charge of shaping the social landscape of the promising humans in order to increase the likelihood for the particular DNA to express. She created different roles for herself throughout history. She was always watching, always influencing social perceptions of fitness. in order to influence what DNA expressions became more dominant at any given time. She did all this manipulating in order to create this last element for the genetic life-seed. She'd shaped beauty throughout the ages to make sure certain genes were favored. She'd done this most recently through the modeling and entertainment industries.

Then Johnny T. had been born. The most promising DNA thus far. There had been similar genes in recent times, and Boy's mom would mate with all the potentials, but none of the offspring had resulted in the life-seed DNA. When Boy was born he was the most promising they'd seen yet.

A crucial element was that the DNA had to withstand time/space bending. With every other attempt there'd been complications. None of the others had been able to survive time/space bending, this tele-transporting. The reptilian DNA had always tele-transported fine, making tele-transportation the preferred means of reptilian transport. The mammalian DNA always disintegrated during transportation.

Boy's mom had become particularly attached to him, and insisted that he, Boy, not be forced or coerced into going into the transport. MOL was infinitely patient, and was in no hurry, so they granted Boy's mom her request. They recognized that choice effected DNA. They had been very excited to see what would happen when Boy's DNA tele-transported, but it needed to be his whole living body, and he needed to choose it.

They had planned to explain everything to him once he arrived in the city of Atlantis, but they saw the value of not rushing Boy. Then they watched with anticipation as Boy ran out into the tundra and eventually arrived at the hermit John's cabin. They weren't sure Boy would send himself through the transporter without knowing what it was, which would have been the preferred method. John also knew the details of they all were hoping would happened, and had planned on sharing it with Boy had he stayed longer. They were also concerned that John's human emotions, his paternal attachment to Boy, might inspire him to stop Boy from transporting, for fear Boy mammalian DNA would disintegrate as all the other's had before him. So they watched.

To their delight, Boy had jumped into the transporter without prompting, and had put himself through the very test they needed him to complete. Even better was Boy's survival. He had transported through time/space successfully, body and consciousness intact. He was in fact the one they had been waiting for, something that seemed obvious once it was established. Everything having its time and place.

Boy was the life-seed of the Pleiadians. He was also, therefore the reason life would start again, so many billions of years ago, on Earth. Boy's DNA was the culminative zenith of the entire drama. Boy's DNA fulfilled the original intention that started life on Earth. And the key, suggested MOL through thought-feeling communication, was the process Boy had gone through, and a change from the attachment both his parents had had to him and the volition he had taking in choosing to teletransport un-coerced. MOL saw now that the quantum expression of the molecules in Boy's DNA had needed the projection of his parents and Boy's conscious participation in order to actuate. MOL showed Boy a shift in his DNA that occurred, from quantum entanglement, when the pride from his mother was met by the pride from his father and combined into Boy's own agency. Not everything in cosmos makes sense.

Through MOL's communication Boy felt released. He understood that there was nothing more he had to do. All that was required of him was to have come into existence and choose, and he had done that. MOL showed how ultimately this was all that is required of anyone. It was because of everyone and everything surrounding Boy that he existed, that his DNA came into being and was able to actuate. And now that he existed, there was nothing else necessary for life on Earth to do. Everything else was icing on the amazingly multilayered cake.

MOL shared with Boy that the intentional deception was no longer necessary, as the personal agency necessary to actuate the DNA had been accomplished through Boy. Accordingly, the story was now Boy's to tell, and could tell it in any way he wanted, though MOL did offer perspective to consider. MOL shared images of what had happened at times when they had shared too much information too quickly with the developing mammalians and it had resulted in unforeseen negative consequences. MOL images left Boy with the impression that the best way to share the information would be in a way that people could choose to explore it, but not make a truth everyone had to swallow.

MOL's last images showed how they would now build spores out of Boy's actuated DNA to send back to reseed Pleiadian life. The Ouroboros was complete. Boy was invited to join in the journey, or he could remain on Earth, free to explore what else he might discover about existing. All that was needed of him was his interstellarly stalwart DNA. He had as long as wanted to consider. He chose to sleep on it.

65

Boy awoke in his bed, as though MOL had been a dream. His interaction with MOL could have been another thing to doubt, but because of the clarity of MOL's communication, its vivid depth, Boy knew it had in fact happened. It had left an imprinting into the fiber of his being. The non-verbal expression this luminous something used to tell their story set Boy's heart at rest. It was the first time Boy felt at peace since before he'd been mugged as a child. He'd heard Buddha walked the Earth after his enlightenment with a subtle smile barely showing in the corner of his mouth. He wondered if his smirk shared a similar, nearly imperceptible uptick.

Boy had always struggled with all the secrecy surrounding how society was formed, how society was run, and how life on this planet had organized. MOL explained it all in a way that helped Boy understand its purpose. Boy wonder in his half asleep state how he would share what he'd experience in a way that would offer the option of believing, but allow for people to maintain their comfort in their status quo if need be.

Boy knew the experience he'd had, the understanding he'd been given, would likely be too much for most people. The difficulty he'd had in trying to understand everything he'd gone through made it easy for him to see how others might not believe it. And, it didn't ultimately matter if people knew, or believed. He understood that for most, life might seem more exciting when there appeared to be more purpose than to simply be. The only real purpose for his life, for all life, was fulfilled through the actuation of his DNA. He understood that everyone had completed everything they were supposed to by simply being a part of the process. He understood that any other purpose is up to us to create, and is only as real as we make it. Boy knew, when people were ready, when they wanted to understand, they would. Boy finally fully comprehended that the grand conspiracy was never against him, but with him, for him, for everyone.

66

Boy's mom was at his bedside when he awoke. He looked at her, completely comfortable with her for the first time he could remember. He felt full of appreciation and understanding he had always wished to have. He smiled up at her, noticing she was humming you are my sunshine under her breath.

Noticing Boy awaken she asked, "Get up, there's somewhere we gotta go."

Before MOL his mom's command would have

worried him, but in his settled state he merely asked, "Is it true?"

Boy's mom considered him before asking back, "Would you like it to be true?"

Boy looked past the round circles of him mom's pupils and felt like he could see her true eyes behind. Trusting her eyes felt soothing. He replied, "Sure. Where're we headed?"

"Get dressed, you'll see when we get there." She got up and moved towards the door, her same cold demeanor, but now Boy saw it differently, as who she was, not as an attack on him. She turned before leaving and said, "Dress warm."

Well bundled, they walked through the office. Here too, for the first time, Boy was amused by all the models, remembering that their 'beauty' was manipulated to shape DNA for space/time travel, remembering that even the idea of beauty was merely a way to shape DNA. He laughed aloud, a glimmer of understanding in his mom's eye as she turned to see why he'd laughed.

They entered the elevator, and she pressed a hidden button Boy had never noticed. A small triangle of lights, made of three dots, appeared where she'd touched the panel. They descended down past the ground floor, and into the subway line. He recognized this entrance from one of his dreams.

They alighted, wandering along the tracks in a hidden passageway to an antechamber with a guard. The sentinel barely moved, giving a small nod as they walked into the big room from the same dream. This must have been where Boy had arrived from John's cabin. The room had a platform and control panel identical to the one he'd used to escape Antarctica. He followed his mom through the room, recognizing the reptile at the controls. Boy was completely at ease now, even comforted by the creatures.

On the platform his mom nodded silently to the reptile at the controls, who pushed some buttons. She held Boy's hand for the first time since he was a child. She checked that he was still wearing the ring she'd put on him before visiting MOL. He was.

The room spun, his vision went black, and he realized the ring was an Ouroboros. Again light started as a point and opened into an ever-broadening sphere, filling his vision. This time, however, it wasn't into the warm, undulating field, but back into the John's technophilic cabin.

Boy didn't know how to react. He'd wished for this when he was kid. He'd always wanted to know his father, yearned to be with his mom and dad at the same time, and now it was happening.

John looked stunned as well. He said, "Oh...Hi," a tear pealing down his bearded cheek. He walked cautiously up, scooping them both into a big embrace.

Boy was the happiest he'd ever been. His heart opened in a new way. Not only his mind, but his body was forgiving. He forgave his mom for never being honest or emotionally available. He forgave his dad for never having been there. His parents had done what they thought they had to do.

After briefly catching up, Boy's mom said, "Let's get the hell out of here. This weather might be alright for you warm-blooded, but it's killing me." Boy and John shared a laugh.

They climbed onto a dogsled and rode to an airport concealed near the entrance to the city of Atlantis, the same one through which Boy had escaped. There was a plane waiting. As they approached, a figure appeared at the boarding dock. WJ.

"What are you doing here?" Boy asked.

WJ smiled. "Hey, Boy."

John and Boy's mom directed someone where to put the luggage, and WJ asked, "Is that the real Johnny T.?"

Boy was impressed. "Yeah. He goes by John. How did you know he was the real one? More importantly, did you already know that the other Johnny T. was a replicant?" Boy was delighted by this silly, out of place interaction.

"Yeah. I kind of put everything together on the train after a particularly psychedelic night. I always thought something was up with the other Johnny T., and then one night I saw him freaking out near an electrical outlet and realized he was at least partially cybernetic. I went to tell your mom and accidentally caught her partially out of her skin. Lucky thing, I'd been checking in with her for so long that she trusted me."

"Wait, what?" Boy watched a rush of residual angst threaten to surface. He turned to look at his mom and John who were boarding the plane and hadn't seemed to notice WJ.

"You still haven't gotten the whole story?" WJ was so disarming that Boy was calmed.

"What's the whole story, WJ?" Boy realized that things must be going better, because he wasn't as afraid of what WJ was going to say as he would have been days earlier.

"Well, I know you know Sophie was on the payroll, so I figured you knew we all were." WJ spoke so matter-of-fact that Boy couldn't image a time he would've been hurt by anything WJ was saying.

"You all were? Who all?" Boy saw his old triggers, but witnessed they no longer held strength over him.

"Everyone except your mom." WJ's voice was gentle, and Boy stayed silent. "But it's not really that big of a deal. The silly thing is, we all would have been in a band with you anyways, and we definitely would have been your friends. Your mom was overprotective, and who do you know that would say no to being paid for something they'd be doing anyways?"

Boy thought about how Sophie had said nearly the same thing to him. Hearing WJ say it now, it made sense. He knew that Sophie was telling the truth.

"We all love you, Boy, and you are kind of significant, as your DNA is the whole reason we were grown in the first place. I told you the Pleiadians were behind it all, and that the reptiles were real, didn't I?" This was the kindest 'I told you so' Boy had ever received. He smiled knowing it was true, and he could tell that WJ was watching him reach understanding. Boy appreciated that he didn't need to say anything back to the kind man standing in front of him.

"How did you end up here though?" Boy asked, not minding changing the subject.

"Well, when I caught your mom out of her human skin on the train she gave me the option of disappearing on my own, or joining Atlantis. So, obviously, I agreed to keep my mouth shut until the end of the trip, and now I'm here." He smiled big at Boy. "And I love it." They were quiet for a moment before WJ continued. "Look, Boy, I just wanted to make sure that you know, we were always in it for you, with you. Especially Sophie. It'd be silly not to forgive her."

The plane engines started.

"Boarding time." WJ grabbed Boy into a big bear hug. "I'll be here. Come back and visit, okay?"

"Sure. Yeah. Of course," Boy yelled over the engine roar.

"It's so fun and relieving to not be hiding anything from you anymore Boy, I never wanted that part. I love you, Boy. We all do, and we always have," WJ yelled back before letting go.

"Thanks, WJ, I love you too. And everyone." Boy was happy to see his long lost friend.

"Get out of here," WJ hollered. "And call me when you're ready to record the rock opera."

"The rock opera?" Boy asked, unsure if he should already know what WJ was talking about.

"What else are you doing to do with this crazy story?" WJ asked, pushing Boy towards the waiting plane.

Boy smiled. What a great idea. "You got WJ. I'll see you soon." He responded as he walked backwards away from his enigmatic friend.

"All time is soon, compared to eternity." WJ waved, backing away. Boy appreciated WJ's quirky way of expressing deep things playfully.

Boy's mom, and dad, were sitting comfortably at two of four chairs surrounding a small in-flight table. They motioned for him to sit. For the first time they sat together, a family, flying the long distance back to New York.

They spoke, sharing details of their past, getting to know each other. Boy was not surprised when his mom excused herself from the conversation to start typing away on her phone. After a couple of hours, his fatigue caught up with him and he fell asleep.

Sitting quietly in the undulating field, Boy

noticed the nondescript being of MOL, like an implied eye floating in a pyramid, emanating, vague, and golden. He realized the eye was content, completely without judgment. MOL became brighter, as space folding in spherically around the eye as it returned home, to the future, to the Pleiades.

67

Landing at LaGuardia woke Boy. He stumbled from the plane to the limo. The door closed behind him. Neither his mom nor John had entered. It was too dark to see clearly, no lights. He started to feel nervous as the car began moving. He watched his mind search for the evidence that all the recent revelations were just more layers of deception and façade.

"Wait," Boy called out. "What the hell?" He hollered towards the driver, but the cab privacy window stayed closed. His panic started to rise to a frenzy. *No fucking more, please,* he pleaded internally.

A tender voice spoke from the darkness, "It's me Boy."

Dim lights came on. It was Sophie.

Boy's relief was monumental. He took a deep breath. Seeing Sophie's face in this moment was a kind of relieving he had maybe only ever felt on MDMA. It was not just a relief that he wasn't being taken into some new nefarious world, it was that he had missed her, longed for the safety he knew through her. He knew it was because he loved her, was in love with her. He was ready to see her in a new light, through forgiveness and understanding.

He knew now that he got to choose his focus, and, if he wanted to, he could focus on the beauty in the world, instead of the despair and distress. He also knew that to shift this focus would take practice and effort. He could feel how quickly paranoia could resurface, fear, anger, distrust. But he also knew he was ready, hungry even, to start the practice of building trust, understanding, and an orientation towards the revelry he felt seeing Sophie's face.

"Sophie," Boy said, an invitation, a commitment, knowing he meant 'I love you'.

Sophie dove across the seats to embrace Boy. They held each other for a long time, saying nothing.

Nearly back to his building they released enough to look at each other, face to smiling face.

"I'm sorry," she pleaded, a beseeching smile spreading across her face.

"I know," Boy replied. "Me too."

After a long moment Sophie pulled Boy's face slowly towards hers, kissing him gently.

"What the hell happened, Boy? Your mom made me come to the airport, had the driver pick me up, said it was urgent."

Boy laughed. So that's what mom was doing on the phone last night, he thought.

"There's so much to tell you, Sophie." He didn't know where to start, and he knew it didn't matter.

The car stopped under his building. They got out, holding hands. They arrived up to his room just in time to see the early morning sun peeking between the buildings. Boy's happiness felt stronger this time, deeper, less shakable. In that happiness he remembered the last sentiment MOL had offered him:

"The Ouroboros' tail is content to give its head

something to eat, its head content to eat in order to feed the tail something to grow. This is not a conspiracy *against* you, but *with* you, *for* you. The sun seeing it's imagine in the sun flower."

An Atlas of Atlantis,
Based off, "Atlantis! a conspiracy theory rock opera" (2007)
By Kai Lelion.
Book started in 2010, first draft completed in 2011.
This edit started 8.2.24, and completed July 24th, 2025.

ATLANTIS!
a conspiracy theory rock opera

(Music starts with the Guitar
Slow picking:
Fiddle, Bass, Keys and Drums come in after 1st phrase,
narration begins after 2 or three phrases at the
beginning of the second Bm)

(Bm, F#, F#, Bm, G, D)

The story im about to tell you may sound far fetched
but I swear that every word of it is truth
I know its true,
because it happened to me...
This is my story...

(Transition: end on the D,
Fiddle 'blues walk down' from D to C
Guitar starts,
Bass, Drums, and Keys [some 'picsicado' fiddle, and
touches of horn], come in after first Phrase,
Then narration restarts)

(C, F,)

I grew up in new york city.
And I had one hell of a strange childhood.
It was just me and my mom
This was not the strange part of my upbringing.
The strange part
was that my mother
was not your typical
single-mom-from-the-suburbs sort-of-a-lady..

To put it lightly...
...my moms fucking loaded!
I mean filthy ... **filthy**-fuckin-rich!

An independently wealthy woman;
who seemingly conquered **her own way** to the top!
An Empress,
A Queen,
A... uh...
a really, really rich lady
is the point I'm trying to get at here.

And yet,
in some ways,
she was a single mom like any other
Taking care of her son!
Just her...
and, uh,

several hundred stunningly gorgeous women.
professional models!
You see my moms business,
her stock and trade,
her empire,
was...
The Modeling Industry!
Yes, The Modeling Industry ladies & gentlemen!
the buy, sell trade of the chosen ones:
the fit & the beautiful

and yet even amongst the madness
of running a multinational modeling firm
she still took the time to be around me,
to be my mom!
she even somehow found the time
to sing me lullabies in bed.
we always sang my favorite song:

(transitions on F into
'You are my sunshine Chord progression')

(C, C,
F, C,
F, C,
C, G, C)

"you are my sunshine, my only sunshine, you make me
happy, when skies are gray. you'll never know dear,
how much i love you. please don't take my sunshine
away."

(Final C is first C back into
C, F,
progression)

And as a child my mother gave
me
two of my most treasured things
the first is this beautiful
necklace,
the second is this curious ring.

But after the years in this same
old game
Anything I would try to do my
mom always found a way
to help along with her riches and
fame
so that nothing I did ever felt like

I did it
I began to see that when you are given privilege
and a mind to question it
you realize that privilege doesn't hold water,
but it sure is full of shit

**(music rocks out for two phrases,
calming abruptly at 'I Quit.')**

you see the game
and who seems to be running it,
and you want to shout,
"ya know what, thanks anyways but, I QUIT."

i wanted to do something genuine,
something authentic,
something true,
i wanted to be something worthwhile
something new.
so i started a band,

**(transition on the F,
music interlude
Fiddle Starts the Melody)**

"I wanna play that funky that funky dixie land,
pretty mama wont you take me by the hand,
by the hand [hand]
take me by the hand [pretty mama],
wanna dance with your daddy all night long"

**(All Interments back into C, F,
right at the end of the first time through)**

the music was decent,
my enthusiasm high,
and we blew up in the scene with out even trying

i found fame
but I found fame just the same,
another fake face game,
people lost in pain
and displacing the blame,
another song, another check,
some more drugs, what the heck,
a trip to jail, to top the charts,
no honesty, nothing from the heart,
another money making machine,
honed, toned, lean and mean,
ruthless and for one purpose alone,
to steel your money
and strip your soul right off your bones.
And so i cried in my solitude,
the only thing that kept coming up
amongst all the chatter, talk of some mysterious club,
one of those clandestine high society joints,
invite only, some sacred place
for rock stars and royalty
big time actors and of course big time money
a night club, infamous beyond reputation or public list...
a place, where the truly elite rub shoulders and kiss
this club called... Atlantis.
Atlantis. **All Hail Atlantis!**

**(Transitions
At the end of the final F,
on the one Drum rolls [dugada da]
Then all instruments and Singing)**

(C, D, F, C, G)

"Way Down Bellow the Ocean,
That's where I want to be,
She may be." (X2)

(Volume of instruments and

energy comes down)

This type of place you'll never hear of unless
you're cursed, or blessed, to be one of the proud,
one of the beautiful, the fit, top 1% of the top 1%,
so all the fame came with a touch of pain ,
and an invitation was sent.
so I went,
I don't really know why,
hoping to find answers of how to feel alive
underneath the public eye.
hoping for a real life inside this dream!

When I got to the club it was just as i thought,
it was the same lecherous crowd and i felt caught
unable to breath, disgusted at the lies, mistrusting all these people, unsure of why - anyone even tries,
to pretend that they are happy,
and so into a bottle i dove,
and after i had too many
i hopped in my car and drove,
off the railing, off a cliff,
out of my mind with no will to live,
I crashed...

(narration ends on the G, Drums [dugada da], all instruments and singing, no break in time)

"down bellow the ocean,
that's where I want to be,
she may be" (X2)

(Volume and Energy comes way down)

...and when i awoke a soft voice spoke,
familiar, and yet i cannot give a recollection of what was said,
as though merely a dream inside my head,
and then i heard a tv announcer say,
"the poster boy for rock and roll died today"

**(Transition on 'died today', which rolls into next chord progression.
one phrase with just Guitar and Bass
C, F, G, fm)**

he was talking about me and i thought,
"could this be heaven?",
but that feeling quickly passed,
as john travlota came over
to offer me water in a glass
and to ask me how i was feeling,
a distant smile on his face,
and all i could muster to mutter was,
"who are you, and what is this place?..."

"this is atlantis," came a gentle voice,
as john turned and walked away,
and i saw elvis presley,
looking as though he hadn't aged a day,
now i know this sounds fantastic,
in fact i wouldn't believe it if i were you,
but this is the way it happened,
and its just the beginning of all that's true.

(Instruments end on a lingering Fm)

Just the beginning!

**(Transition
Keys Solo, plays melody for 1st Phrase,**

Bass Comes in 2nd Phrase,
Guitar 3rd Phrase,
Picsicado Fiddle 4th Phrase,
Narration starts 5th Phrase,
Am, C, G, F)

Dazed and shaken, I swore this a dream...
This man a fraud, "Atlantis??"
"heha... You look just like Elvis man..."
I spoke... still confused and drugged.
"That can't be right! I mean... right ?!?
Atlantis was just that freaky club that I went to last night..."

(Fiddle, Horns and Drums all come in on the one
Music is low volume and energy and slowly pics up)

"that's not quite true," said the man all elvis clad,
then he said, "did you know that man who just left is your dad?"
"fuck you," I said, before I knew what i'd said.
"don't feel bad kid, just get up and look instead."
and then he left, and I was shaken, but I got up even so,
and I started walking around this place
all these faces, half human
ageless smiles
famous
and I heard them all talking something about lizards

it was like an entire city was built underground,
with ancient relics intermixed with the most incredible technology i'd ever seen.
Everyone around me seemed pretty happy,
but it also felt like we were being watched,
and I could have sworn I saw what looked like alligators,
but they were standing on their hind legs
lurking in the corners.

then hunter s. walked by muttering,
"who are all these reptiles something terrible is happening all around us.."

and every time i tried to get a better look,
someone would jump in front of me,

Like Marilyn Monroe
as she spoke to Jimmy Hoffa, saying:
"oh, that's the child of the reptilian high priestess!
it must be amazing to be her child.
do you think i should go meet him?"

soon I was cornered by a group of famous
people I thought were dead,
all trying to tell me things I couldn't fit in my head

like: I was told that they control us all
the government robots;
the irrelevance of the average Joe;
Isis used to run the computer that ran the world
but she got bored,
passed the job to Judy Garland,
so she could control the vicious hordes
controlled by the robots
controlling the world
unconsciously controlling every boy, every girl
every cognizant creature and many who aren't
from the daftest of life forms, to

the incredibly smart

I watched and I saw, all these
things
big scaly backs and fat diamond
rings,
I was struck by the arrogance of
these people that "ruled
the world" like a toy, the rest of
us merely fooled

I thought:

**(Cuts to just Guitar, Bass, and
simple Drums
for two phrases,
[singing in the style of 'part of
this world'
from 'the little mermaid']
Then everyone Loud for two
phrases of,
'they want more, they want
more')**

look at this place
look at this stuff
these people all fake
this reality's fuct
lookin around
yeah you'd think, hey, they've
got everything

they've got gizmos and gadgets a
plenty
they've got hoozits and whatsit
galore
you want thingamabobs they've
got 20
but who cares
no big deal
they want more
they want more!

**(all interments stop,
everyone does a cappella 'aah',
Narration starts after two
phrases)**

I wanted to run, but didn't know
how to start
consumed by fear and the
beating of my heart
so I ducked into a room, then ran
down a hall
then jumped through a window
only to fall
finding only an elevator which to
my surprise
took me out of this place, to grey
colored skies

**(Guitar comes back in quietly
playing the melody the Keys
started with
slowly the rest of the
instruments come back in
subtly)**

it was a landscape
all covered in snow,
the type of place
where no one would go.
barren, freezing,
and somehow desert like,
but i was so afraid of what i had
just seen
that i started to hike
through the dry desert snow
until i fell to the ground.
i must have laid there for hours
before i was found
by a huge bernese mountain dog
with a barrel around it neck.
it gave me the whiskey
and took me on deck
and pull me for miles
through this great barren land
until we came to a cabin
housing a strange bearded man.
i didn't recognize him at first
because his beard was so thick,
and when i finally figured it out
i figured it must be a trick,
because i had just seen this man
back in that place
accept back then
he had no hair on his face.
it was john travolta,
but looking haggard and strange
much different then in the
hospital room,
but how had he change?

that was only a matter of hours
ago,
something was wrong.
nevertheless, he took me inside

**(Ends on with everyone holding the F
and the Fiddle completing the Phrase)**

and he sang me this song.

**(Just Guitar for the first Phrase,
then Guitar, Bass, and Simple Drums
through the first Chorus,
Then everyone playing simple folk-rock style)**

(verse: C, E, Am, F
chorus: Dm, G, F)

(verse: C, E, Am, F)
my boy, my boy, it's been so long
i've been waiting here and i
wrote you this song
in case i ever met you, which i hoped i would
so that you could see that i'm not no good

i could have tried a whole lot harder to be your dad
i hope in hearing this you are not mad
i have always loved you as any father would
i hope you can see that i'm not no good

(chorus: Dm, G, F)
i am your dad
i am not bad

(verse: C, E, Am, F)
i was seduced by your mom so long ago
then when things went wrong
she put me out to this snow
far away though i gave it all i could

and i hope you can see that i'm not no good

(chorus: Dm, G, F)
i am your dad
and i sure am glad
to be seeing you

(verse: C, E, Am, F)
i wish i could show you all the love and all the care,
i've had this whole time even though i wasn't there
believe me when i say i did all i could
i hope you can see that i'm not no good

(Slowing)
i am so sorry i could never say
i love you my sunshine i hope you had a nice day

(Just the Guitar outro
chorus: Dm, G, F)
i am your dad
i am not bad
i sure am glad
to be seeing you
today

**(Transition
Bass starts on the one following 'today',
Narration starts on 2nd bar,
Bass Trombone and Violin follow,
Then vocal 'woe, ohh')**

(D, F#, G, A)

i felt scared and confused,
just come in from the snow,
and now john travolta with a beard
is telling me things as though he thinks he's my dad,
could that actually be true?
after his song he looked like he could guess, or he knew,
all the things in my head,

as he took a chain from his neck
with a medallion which looked
familiar, so i took mine out to
check,
and sure enough they matched
perfectly,
like two parts of one coin.
a gift my mother had given me
when i was just a small boy.

**(Keys, Drums, and Guitar come
in on the one)**

then john smiled a sad smile,
a tear rolling down to his chin
and he said, "sorry for the
terseness son,
we haven't got much time, so i'll
just begin."
then he told me a story even
stranger
then what i had just seen.
that place was atlantis
not just some scary dream.
and all those famous people
were real and still alive,
controlled like worker bee's
inside a hive.
with my mom as the queen,
though she wasn't a bee,
she was the high reptile
priestess,
she controlled the whole thing,
with her minions of reptiles as
second in command,
they were the true underground
leaders
ruling almost everything that
happened on land.
atlantis, he told me, was the
same
lost city from the history tales,
hidden under the antarctic polar
ice caps
like a resort, in a jail,
for the worlds elite
who kept the whole show going,
controlling all through the media
though none of them knowing
why they do what they do,
but they just keeping doing it

because
they liked all the lime light,
all the big media buzz.

**(Stayin Alive chorus,
one time through.**
"maybe their your brothers,
or maybe it's your mother,
but they're stayin' alive, stayin'
alive.
feel the city breakin' and
everybody shakin'
and they're stayin' alive, stayin'
alive.
ah ah ah ah, stayin' alive, stayin'
alive.
ah ah ah ah, stayin' alive, stayin'
alive.
stayin' ali-i-i-ive.")

then without me asking John
told me
the man i had seen back in that
place
that looked just like him
but without the big beard on his
face,
was a clone my mom had made,
long ago when she sent him
away,
to this small, remote cabin,
on this big chunk of ice.

(but ohh, those summer nights)

**(Transition,
Guitar start,
picking the melody [notes not
chords]
all instruments come in on 3rd
phrase)**

**(G-A#-C-C#-D-F-G [X3]
G-F-D-C#-C-A# [X1]
[repeat])**

i didn't want to believe him,
this strange bearded man,
making claims that any other
point

i wouldn't even remotely understand.
but after all the crazy things that i'd seen
i almost believed him,
though i still thought this might all just be a dream.

he could see my uncertainty,
he could tell i was distressed,
so he gave me some signs to look for
beginning with how my mother dressed,
and the food that she ate,
and the way that she walked,
and the amount of water she drank,
subtle tones as she talked.
by the time he was done
i had a huge list i could check,
but i felt so damn tired,
felt like my life was a wreck.
i told him to eat all his words,
saw a button on his desk marked "don't touch".
i thought, 'fuck this shit',
and slammed the button a whole bunch,

i faintly heard as he yelled,
'no. my boy. don't go yet',
but the button was pressed,
my destination set.
i felt like i was spinning through space
as though i was staying still but moving fast
and all at the same time everything passed.

('spinny' musical interlude, maybe:
[notes not chords]

(G-G-F-G, D-C#-C, G-A#-G [X2]
chords while singing:
G, A#, F, [X3]
G, C, A#, C)

"I've been waiting so long,

to be where i'm goin',
in the sunshine of your love."

(G-G-F-G, D-C#-C, G-A#-G [X2]?)

(Transition out of melody into Trombone and Fiddle, Narration after two phrases, with the Guitar [finger picking] simple Bass, Drums and Keys following.)

(Am, G, C, F6
Am, G, C)

and i found myself awaking
to familiar sounds,
to a familiar place,
as though i'd just suddenly come down
from the craziest trip i'd ever been on,
and i looked out my window
to a clear distant dawn,
felt a sharp pain in my head,
found my mom by my bed,
my head all in stitches,
and my mom she cried as she said,
'oh my god, my boy,
my sweet sunshine,
your still alive, i knew it,
i knew everything would be fine."

she told me i had nearly died,
drove myself off a cliff,
that she had taken me home from the hospital, unsure if i'd live

reassuringly she sang:

(Ending on the second C, then, on the one All instruments)

(Bb, F, Gm7 [x2]
Db, Ab7, Bbm7 [x2])

"oo child, things are going to get

easier
oo child, things will get brighter
(x2)
someday, we'll get it together
and we'll get it undone
someday, when the world is much brighter
someday, boy, we'll walk in the way of a beautiful sun
someday, when the world is much brighter"

i quickly decided it all was a dream,
that while i was out, the whole time i was gone
there must have been a movie staring john travlota on,
and that everything i thought i had just gone through
might not be any more real for me
than it all must have sounded to you

(but oh those summer nights)

so i gave a little chuckle
and told my mom my crazy dream
and i noticed she laughed,
but behind her laugh was something that seemed
as though she wasn't quite comfortable
with the things i was saying,
so i asked he if she though it was 'bull',
and i felt like she was delaying,
before she said, 'what do you think i think,
it sounds pretty far fetched.'
and as i took out my necklace,
it seemed like she almost retched.
but for only a moment
i couldn't be sure really was there,
so i asked her about the necklace,
for a moment she stared,
then she told me the same story i'd heard a million times,
she gave me that necklace
and it's the only one i'd ever find,
that looked anything like it
and i didn't want to sound crazy,
so i dropped it all then,
hoped it would all become hazy.
a distant thought from my past,
but the more i ignored it,
i started to notice the signs,
even though i abhorred 'em.

**(Transition,
Ending on the Gm7
and moving through F#m
then to the one.
starting with Guitars and Keys
playing chords and melody together.
creeping build up)**

(Bm, F#m, A, E)

just like john had told me,
my mom controlled all whom she knew,
she slept very little,
drank lots of water and kept few whom were close to her,
always seemed ahead of the game
never made a mistake,
never took any blame,

i started to think i was going crazy
so i took a trip on my own,
i didn't tell anyone i was leaving,
i just needed a short time alone.

but when I got back to new york,
where this whole journey began
I found something more menacing
and much more scary at hand.
i found my mom WAS a reptile,
her human suite only half on.
where once were her legs
now all humaness gone.

no soft pink skin,
only dark green scales,
a bifurcated tongue,
and a huge slithering tail.
she turned towards me
and I screamed and I yelled
and I fell to the ground,
and on the ground I dwelled,
in my misery and fear,
in my shame and my guilt,
on all the false truth
upon which my meaningless life had been built.
I was Blinded by an anger
so deep i felt i couldn't see a thing,
not knowing what to do
i tore off the necklace and through off the ring.
but my mom saw me there in my rage,
and she knelt down where I lay,
and told me the craziest things
I'd ever heard anyone say.
and I am sure you stopped believing me
a long time ago,
but I wrote a lullaby of what she said,
just in case you wanted to know.

(Ends on a drawn out E)

She sang:

**(Organ Solo,
Everyone sings,
through the first chorus,
Then all instruments enter.)**

*(verse: C, E, Am, F
chorus: Dm, G, F,)*

(verse: C, E, Am, F)
Boy don't cry
it's gunna pass you by
everything that scares you
it's all only a lie

it's all part of a larger
more important thing

every plant and animal,
every human being

(chorus: Dm, G, F)
this is all a seed,
and i may be queen,

(verse: C, E, Am, F)
for the mushroom overlord
the great fungal god-king
who was sent to our planet
so that he could help bring

life back to the future
which is where he is from
far after the light of this sun
will be gone

(chorus: Dm, G, F)
and i may be queen,
but it's you we need
and i sure am glad
to be seeing you today

(verse: C, E, Am, F)
come with me to meet MOL
be ready to live,
by loosing control
you're life a gift to give

so that those that created us can come into being
here my darling, just put on this ring
Come meet the great fungal god-king

**(End on a drawn out F,
Guitar Starts by picking,
Fiddle, Bass and Horn 2nd Phrase,
Keys 3rd Phrase,
Drums 4th Phrase,
Then narration starts)**

(Bm, F#7)

and even though I was confused and scared
I did what she said, and now I am surprised that I dared

and when I put on that ring I was taken
to a strange beautiful place
and met a being with no look on it's face,
neither man, nor woman,
neither animal or plant,
so it was not hard to believe it'd been sent
from a strange distant future, as a seed for all life
and he spoke to me strangely, as I will now try
to portray for you, so that you can now know
why we were planted here, and why we must grow
here's what he said:

(only Fiddle, Horn, and Keys play)

you are the future we need,
the one who was born of a reptile
by a mammalian seed,
able to withstand the journey
to our beloved pleaides,
as an encrypted spore
with your dna at the core
But don't be afraid,
we just need to know,
if you would survive
and if you would grow,
and you did and that's great,
so now you can just sit back and contemplate
the beauty that is life, the love, loss and strife
the joy and the fun, the excitement of living
under this beautiful sun,

(All instruments return)

mol said all of this,
with an nondescript face.
then the fungal god-king
turned to gaze into the emptiness of space,
the being was saying these words
but conveying much more
that i've tried to portray,
but my translation is poor,
though i do recall
the last thing that was said,
as though the soft but strong words
still ring in my head.
mol told me to tell you,
"if you want to live,
and wonder where to begin,
you must simply and sweetly
let the sun shine in.
just let the sun shine..."

(on the one everyone transitions into 'let the sun shine)

(Bm, F#7, F#7, Bm, G, D)

let the sun shine, let the sun shine, the sun shine in! (X4)

(instruments cut, a capella)

let the sun shine, let the sun shine, the sun shine in!(X2)

**(interments come back in with the finger-picking, gypsy-style
from the very beginning,
everyone except the narrator sings quietly,
narration starts immediately)**

and as the mushroom overlord left me,
my mom took me on one last crazy trip,
back to the polar ice caps,
right back to the tip,
to a small wooden cabin,
where a bearded john Travolta dwelled,
and we both went inside,
and my heart almost burst as i was held

by my mom and my dad,
in a big warm embrace,
like a bright ray of sunshine,
falling on my big smiling face.
and i just...

Bm   F#7
you are my sun shine,

F#7   Bm
my only sun shine,

G   D
you make me happy,

Bm   F#7
when skies are grey,

F#7   Bm
you'll never know dear,

G   D
how much I love you

(back into original lyrics (X6) and end with: a capella "let the sun shine" with one person singing "you are my sunshine over the top" walking off stage with audience singing along)

Original Band:
narrator: Dusty
guitar/conductor: Kai
accordion/piano/harp: Jesse
bass: Dabu
drums: Skinny DW
fiddle: JJ
bass trombone: Gyorkos
story board: MIMO

Atlantis! (A Conspiracy Theory Rock Opera)
Written By Kai Lelion (2007)

Made in the USA
Coppell, TX
19 January 2026

68491426R00182